ZERO PROOF

ZERO Proof

A CULTY DETECTIVE NOIR

BENJAMIN LYON

ISBN: 979-8-9931920-1-7

First Edition

Published by Ilgamish Ink LLC

www.benjaminlyonauthor.com

Printed in the United States of America

10 9 8 7 6 5 4 3 2 1

"Anything uttered after midnight in a bar can be dismissed as rubbish. Especially if said rubbish is prefaced with the ol' *This is a true story.*" Trucker Holmes took a sip from a tumbler splashed with the remnants of a watered-down Negroni. A dried half orange slice clung to his lips as the clock struck midnight. "That said, this is a true story."

1

WALK-INS UNWELCOME

It was nine in the morning, early July, with the sun trying to break through brittle newspapers pasted across the floor-to-ceiling windows of a large, empty retail space known as Suite 1402B. A snoring mass of humanity was hunched over a ramshackle countertop that, in a past life, had been a key feature of commerce. Cashiers on one side asking the paying customers questions, "Care to join our premier plus perks program? Or are you already a premium partner?" Now it was no more than an uncomfortable makeshift bed, and the questions had been replaced by empty airplane bottles of Campari, and Sweet Vermouth, and a hacked-up clementine skewered by a dull Swiss Army knife.

The hulking, snoring mass had a name, several names actually. Some were nicknames, some were impromptu insults, some he would need to invent on the fly as part of his work. But his birth certificate on file somewhere in the electronic bowels of Hollywood Presbyterian Medical Center, formerly known as Queen of Angels Hospital, read:

CERTIFICATE OF LIVE BIRTH
DOB: 5 – 25 – 1983
Name: Trucker S. Holmes
Sex: Male
Mother: Elisabeth P. Holmes
Father: —
Location: Queen of Angels Hospital, Los Angeles, California

Trucker was safe. The sunlight could not break through the window-papered periodicals to interrupt his snoring. The failed sunshine merely blanketed him and the entirety of the empty retail space in a warm aged-paper glow.

He was safe. Safe from the sunshine, but not the outside world filled with people going about their important people business. One of these people going about their business did what the sunshine could not; they woke Trucker Holmes from his slumber with a knock on the door of Suite 1402B.

Trucker attempted to ignore the disruption to his very much needed yet uncomfortable rest, but the knocking continued. He visualized the knuckles as they wrapped against the papered glass door in a faint yet steady and polite cadence. A woman, middle-aged, petite. He deduced the mindset connected to these feminine knuckles tapping against a clearly closed storefront with no signage. Lost? Confused? The knocks politely continued and became a touch stern. Too determined. They're not lost. "Did I lock the door?" Trucker mumbled to himself. "I hope I locked that door."

The door slowly opened.

"Damnit," Trucker mumbled again. "I gotta remember to lock that door. This is not a great neighborhood."

In walked a woman with an exceptional blonde dye job, wearing an athleisure style, flamingo-pink tennis dress. A thin white scarf draped over her shoulders and a Row Margeaux tote bag held loosely in her hands. She stood before the resting Trucker and said, "Hello . . ."

Trucker raised his head. He slid off the countertop, knocked the airplane bottles and skewered orange to the floor, grabbed an old cashier stool, propped it upright, and slumped upon it. "We're closed," Trucker coughed. "Regardless, don't take walk-ins."

The woman paced back and forth in front of Trucker. She examined the countertop, shoddy shelving, and leftover artifacts of the former retail space. "Nice place you have here."

"Ya know, it's rude to lie to strangers. Or anyone for that matter. Let alone as a conversation starter," Trucker quickly reached underneath the countertop, which startled the woman and made her fingers clutch tightly around her designer tote. Trucker dug out a plastic costume helmet wrapped in broken Christmas lights and tossed it to the woman, who made no attempt to catch it as it bounced around her pristine pink running shoes.

"I lease the place out to a Halloween shop for a month in the fall. A holiday décor company in the winter. Some tax guys set up shop in the spring. And if I remember to contact them, some ladies sell pencils, notebooks, and binders toward the end of summer," Trucker said. "But, you're not here for the space. So, who are you? And what do you want?"

"My name is Heather Young, and I need your help," she said.

"You're not here with bone cancer and an insurance policy, are you?" Trucker asked dryly.

"Excuse me?" Heather asked.

"Nothin'," Trucker said. "How'd you find me? How'd you know to come here? Like I said, I don't do walk-ins."

"That's what they said," Heather responded. "No walk-ins."

"Who are they?" Trucker asked, then guessed. "Some group of organized gossipers?"

"Mompowered," Heather answered. "It's online. They said you are the best."

"Did they tell you about my app?" Trucker held up his cellphone and shook it back and forth. "Cuts down on conversations that start with lies. Also makes sure I get paid."

"They did," Heather said and fumbled her phone from her tote. "But I am a bit of a klutz with technology."

"I am surprised they knew where to find me," Trucker said. "Quite informed, these online moms."

"They also said you were sober," Heather pointedly said.

"I quit drinking ten years ago," Trucker responded.

"I can smell the liquor from here," Heather said. "And . . . those cute little bottles."

"I've been sober for ten years," Trucker said. "Last night was a hiccup. A statistical anomaly. Much like a bunch of online moms being accurate." Trucker stood up. He clawed through his thick salt and pepper hair and straightened out his six-foot one frame that was carrying an extra twenty-five pounds, give or take. He shifted in his clothes, smelled his shoulder and guesstimated they could make it another day, maybe two, without needing a wash.

Trucker rubbed his watery bloodshot eyes with the palms of his hands and began to size up the Mompowered member Heather Young in as fast of a fashion as he could manage. She was either coming from or going to Pilates or yoga or shopping. Or all three. There is most likely a black or silver new-model luxury electric SUV with vanity plates parked outside. Several plastic surgery procedures, but all remarkably well done. Probably doctor Stevens or Yameen. She was clinging to youth. But in this world, who wasn't? A semi-colon tattoo had been lasered off her left wrist. The removal was also well done, but it was there. Her handbag alone could cover the lease of this place for half the year. No wedding ring. But a silver band on her right hand, fancy but not incredibly expensive. Hard to make out. Green glint from a gem turned inwards. Trucker squinted. Opposite the gem were three engraved letters: CTR. Chose the right. She was or is a member of the Latter-day Saints. Which might explain her willingness to drive to a crappy neighborhood based solely on the advice of online strangers. Faith was funny like that.

All of this could be helpful, or not. In any specific moment, it was notoriously difficult to see what could be useful.

"What can I do for you, Heather?" Trucker asked.

"My baby is missing," Heather said.

Trucker leaned on the countertop, "Baby baby? As in crying without a rattle and binkie? Or baby, as in your Jack Russell terrier . . . or boyfriend . . . or car . . . or —"

"— my son. My baby, Edward. He is missing."

"How long?"

"It has been two days."

"I assume you went to the police before plunging headfirst online?"

"I did. I went to the police immediately. An hour after I realized he hadn't called. He always calls."

"And what did the police say?"

"They said nothing! They had me file a report," Heather stammered. "That was it. And I was persistent."

"I have no doubt," Trucker said. "Let's back up a sec. How old is Edward?"

"Eddie is twenty-two."

"Well, I think I may understand the initial law enforcement reaction," Trucker kindly explained. "A twenty-two-year-old son did not call his mother within the hour she expected her phone to ring. Please take no offense, because none is intended, but that does not reach an emergency response level in Los Angeles. Probably not even in Wichita."

"But it has been two days now! And nothing."

"Okay," Trucker said. "Let's keep our wits about us and go over some questions."

Heather calmed herself and said, "Okay."

Trucker thumbed through his phone, "By the way, all these questions are available on my app when applying to be a client. Just a heads-up. Also, don't report back to the empowered moms that I take walk-ins now. Walk-ins are always unwelcome. But, since you are here," Trucker propped himself up on the countertop and went through a preliminary checklist, "Okay, let's knock some of these out. Name is Edward Young. Age, twenty-two. Sex, male. Current whereabouts are unknown, missing. Where is his place of residence?"

"Home," Heather said. "Home with me. He lives at the house."

"Okay, has he done this before? Disappeared or gone off on his own without contacting you?"

"No. Never."

"Does he have any friends he might be with? Do you know where they may live?"

"He doesn't have any friends. But not because he isn't likable. He is just very busy."

"Were there signs of disturbance at the house? Things out of order? Broken? Any signs of trouble?"

"No. It was perfect. Nothing out of place."

"Is there any known person of concern? Anyone giving him grief? An estranged . . . parent? Any recent conflict with anyone of any kind?"

"No."

"When was the last time Edward was seen?"

"Almost exactly forty-four hours ago, at our home."

"Okay. And how certain are you that he is missing and not just late, or that there was some kind of miscommunication? On a scale —"

"— There is no other explanation. None. He is missing. Something terrible has happened, I can feel it. I am not wrong."

Trucker slid off the countertop and put his phone away. This is why he stood by his rule of walk-ins being unwelcome. He didn't enjoy telling people *no* to their face. Or saying *no* in general. On the app he could scan the information, realize that it was not a situation he wanted anything to do with. That it was a wild goose chase at best or a Kobayashi Maru at worst. If the rules were followed, all he would have to do is click a button declining his service and try to go back to sleep. But here stood walk-in Heather Young.

"Heather," Trucker said. "I sympathize. I really do. But —"

"— I'll give you ten thousand dollars, right now." Heather pulled a stack of crisp, banded hundred dollar bills out of her designer tote bag. She waved the bundle of cash back and forth and tossed it toward Trucker, who made no attempt to catch it. "Ten grand to find my baby, today."

2

TEN GRAND WORTH OF EFFORT

Out in the parking lot of the sometimes seasonal shop, Trucker watched Heather climb into a matte black electric Mercedes-Benz SUV. The license plate read 4EVA YNG.

Trucker flicked through the crisp, banded stack of hundred-dollar bills. He waved goodbye to Heather and blew a soft long raspberry through his lips, imitating a cartoon car commanded by George Jetson, as her Mercedes silently whisked her away. He was not poking fun at Heather's mode of travel. He would gladly pick one up himself if it weren't for his current economic condition. A condition that made accepting ten thousand dollars to track down a maybe missing twenty-two-year-old man all the easier. Even if his gut told him to say *no*.

The truth of the matter was that Trucker had been getting plenty of client submissions through his introvert-approved app. Enough business for a real office and real assistants and maybe a real life. But he had started clicking the "no" button far more often than he ever selected "yes." He wasn't sure why but could guess it was because something in him was missing and he didn't believe he had the effort inside himself to track down that missing piece. Regardless, that piece would have to remain lost for a little while longer. Because today he clicked "yes" and would somehow have to pull together ten grand worth of effort and locate Heather's baby, Ed.

Heather wasn't lying when she said she was a klutz with technology. She seemed to have a complete lack of understanding of the world she was living in and how things truly work. Want to halt the march of time and natural deterioration? Pay a hairstylist and surgeon. They may as well be witches and wizards in her mind. Want to travel in complete luxury and feel like you are saving Mother Earth? Go down to the dealership warlocks on Figueroa, and give them your gold. Your son is missing? Find a sorcerer scout who is adept at tracking, and hand him a stack of hundreds. To Heather, money equaled access to magic. Maybe that was a reach. Maybe Trucker had that wrong. But over the course of his life, he had witnessed an uptick in that kind of thinking. People that seemed to be ignorant of reality, while they reaped the benefits of those that created it. Once again, maybe that was a reach and maybe Trucker was just being cynical, but then again maybe he was a sorcerer scout.

One thing was certain. Heather did not know how to use all the features on her phone, aside from apparently the log-in screen for her Mompowered group. If she had delved a little deeper into her portable magical device, she would have found the family-locating service.

It took Trucker two minutes with Heather's phone to find that she, or more likely a young mage at the cellular store, linked up her and her baby's phone locations.

Ed's phone was no longer turned on, but luckily its last known ping was not too ridiculously far from Trucker's sometimes seasonal shop. It was but a couple hops, skips, and bus rides away, and there Trucker would be able to narrow his search.

ELBOWS, AURAS, AND ICE CREAM

It was a quarter past eleven by the time Trucker stepped off the Metro bus near Highland Park and the last known ping from Edward Young's cellphone. The sidewalk was already radiating that low invisible shimmer like it was exhaling heat that it didn't want. Cars baked in place. Even palm trees, framed against the bleached sky, looked as if their patience had evaporated, and pigeons were on phones with their lawyers to complain about intolerable working conditions.

Trucker shuffled down the sidewalk through the wafting aroma of coffee, cannabis, car exhaust, and something slightly electrical. He patted the banded ten grand tucked into his left front pocket and took out his cellphone to look over a series of screenshots he had pulled from Heather's phone. A shot of the family-locating service map and a few pics of Ed, all of which featured the faithful Heather Young hugging, kissing, and doting on her baby.

Trucker stopped his shuffle. Here was the spot. The spot where Ed's phone took its last batteried breath.

There were a few options within eyesight that offered opportunities to gather information. Some, Trucker's gut told him, would be more open to an honest back-and-forth with the least amount of pain. There was a lounge called The Velvet Elbow that was pretending to be a dive bar. A psychic advisor storefront a few doors down named The Aura Authority. And an ice cream shack across the street with a cardboard sign that read *Our Sundae Best.*

THE VELVET ELBOW

The average inattentive comer and goer may think that The Velvet Elbow had been here forever, as if it grew from the cracks in the hot sidewalks sometime in the seventies and had never left. It wanted you to think that. There was a flickering and buzzing neon sign above the faux-relic'd door with the L in velvet burnt out. But the L wasn't connected, and the flicker and buzz were too rhythmic to be anything but artificial.

Caged light bulbs were strung under an amber awning over a tiny narrow patio lined with rust-stained metal stools. It wanted you to believe it had always been this way and always would be, but in truth, Trucker knew it was most likely commissioned by a design firm last summer in Echo Park at the behest of a hospitality group called Grit, Brass, and Ledger. Or something similar. Trucker didn't know all of this for sure. But he felt like he knew it for sure.

The inside was no different. Exposed brick, retro and relic'd movie posters, a scratched-up jukebox programed and curated with playlists by some vinyl-obsessed intern back at the home office, a vintage pinball machine collecting dust by the door. The patrons looked the part: waxed jackets on a ninety-plus-degree day, packets of cigarettes that probably hadn't been opened in two years. Everyone trying a little too hard to look like they were not trying at all. Trucker imagined that if he had to pee, he would find the men's room tagged with sharpied quotes that seemed spontaneous but were regurgitations from social media posts dated two weeks ago. But Trucker didn't have to pee and would never know. He also was open to the idea that he was wrong about all of this. That The Velvet Elbow was indeed authentic. It really didn't matter one way or another at this moment; it was just an observation. What mattered was information leading to the location of one missing Edward Young.

Trucker ponied up to a barstool upholstered with ruby-red faux leather and stitched with a logo of a whiskey bottle and took a seat.

The bartender was prompt and had a light spring in her step. Her shaved head made the scripted tattoo above her left eyebrow all the more prominent. Trucker thought it said *Poised* or maybe *Poison* but didn't want to stare to confirm one or the other.

"What can I getcha?" the bartender said with a bubble.

Trucker inconspicuously pulled a hundred from the bundle in his front pocket and put it on the bar. "Glass of water."

The baldy bartender quickly filled a pint glass with ice, hit the H_2O from the bargun, and slid the refreshment on a coaster in front of Trucker.

"That it? Nothing else to get ya going?" the bartender asked.

"Nah," Trucker took a sip, then pulled another hundred from his pocket and put it on top of the other. "Quit drinkin' about ten years ago. Here because I am lookin' for someone. Maybe you have seen 'em?"

The bartender tilted her head and added a friendly smirk, "Ya know, it is bad manners to start a conversation with a lie."

"Excuse me?" Trucker asked.

"You were here a few months ago. Completely blotted," the bartender said. "Kinda hard to forget. You proposed marriage. To me. And a few others. Had to throw you out because you wouldn't stop preachin' about rainbows to the regulars."

Trucker looked around the place, at the décor that he previously meticulously judged. He did not remember being here before. At all. "Apologies," Trucker said. "Must have been a hiccup. A statistical anomaly. Haven't been a drinker for ten years."

"Well, you were that night. But it's all good. You left without a fuss. Happens sometimes," the bartender said as she took one of the hundreds and pushed the other back. "Who are you looking for, rainbow man?"

Trucker held up his phone and showed the bartender a pic of Edward Young with his mother.

"Which one are we looking for?" the bartender asked.

"The kid. Her son," Trucker answered.

"They look like a couple. Harold and a Barbie Maude," the bartender said.

Trucker turned his phone around and took a look. "I guess I could see that."

"When was this Harold supposed to have been here?" the bartender asked.

"Would have been two days ago, Thursday."

"Hmm," the bartender wrinkled her nose then scrunched her eyebrows. The tattoo definitely read *Poised*.

"Remember anyone like him at all?" Trucker asked.

"Yeah. I think so," the bartender said. "He met a girl who was waiting for him at the bar. She was nothing like Barbie Maude."

"You sure?" Trucker asked.

"I mean. Kinda," the bartender answered. "It is not like they were throwing around engagement rings and causing a ruckus. But I am pretty sure they were here."

"Do you remember anything about them? What they were talking about? Anything?" Trucker asked.

"They were . . . normal. I wasn't eavesdropping," the bartender racked her poised brain to remember as much as she could about a fleeting moment. "They knew each other and seemed friendly. Almost annoyingly so. Hmm. She was brunette. Pretty. Prettier than him. But they kinda had the same vibe. She got a little tipsy but nothing truly stupid."

"Anything else?" Trucker asked.

"You're lucky I remember that much," the bartender answered.

"True," Trucker said. "Did they leave together?"

"I don't know," the bartender said. "I think so. But who knows?"

Trucker stood up and slid the declined hundred back to her. "Thanks a bunch. And again, apologies for before."

"Not a thing. Don't worry about it," the bartender said. "Good luck with finding Harold, rainbow man."

THE AURA AUTHORITY

From a near distance, the place looked innocent enough. The brick façade and scalloped awning had been painted periwinkle blue with cream trim. An antique brass bell dangled above the door, and "The Aura Authority" was spelled out on the windowed door in a loopy, harmless script. It could pass as a hobby shop run by a fairy godmother selling lavender soaps on ropes along with scarf and vest crochet patterns designed for wayward cats.

But on closer inspection, Trucker could see the well-worn psychic shop staples. Poorly sculpted glass skulls propping up an array of books in the display window behind sun-faded, suction-cupped dreamcatchers. Some of the books featured were *Talking to the Dead for Beginners*, *Reincarnation: You Were Somebody*, and *The Lemurian Diet: What the Ancient Aliens Ate*. Chunks of different colored minerals were piled around the books and skulls. Handwritten labels on torn paper were strewn across the rocks that read *Protection. Healing. Faith.* And three sealed Mason jars were set to the side, all with the word *captured* scrawled on their lids, followed by random dates and times.

Trucker reached for The Aura Authority's door handle and noticed a small chalkboard hung by a piece of frayed hemp rope that let the public know: **walk-ins welcome**. That was good because he was about to become one.

The antique brass bell jingled twice with dull enthusiasm as Trucker stepped inside.

The air was immobile with the scent of mint and incense trying desperately to mask time and mildew in the overstuffed room. The lighting was uneven with a scattering of half-charged Himalayan salt lamps, contrasted by the hot sunlight coming in from the window display.

The wooden, planked floor creaked and squeaked under Trucker's feet.

Near the entrance was a narrow display case filled with "divine" jewelry and trinkets. Tangled chains with astrological symbols, necklaces strung with simple raw stones, and bracelets of coiled snakes. It was all severely overpriced, apart from a box of mood rings that were marked two for seven dollars.

Behind the case stood a woman with the frame of a tall, wilted weed. She was easily two inches taller than Trucker, plus a decade older, and draped in a long plum smock that looked homemade. She leaned forward with her elbows on the glass and greeted Trucker with a knowing nod, as if she were indeed an authority on his aura. But he assumed that the only truly supernatural possibility was that she could smell the ninety-eight hundred dollars in his front pocket. This wasn't a problem. He would use her cash-focused bloodhound nose to his advantage. Anything could be used as an advantage, Trucker believed. Anything at all.

"Hi!" Trucker greeted the woman. "My name is Jack Dawson, and I'm looking for a friend who may have happened by here a couple days ago."

"That's strange," the plum-smocked woman said with a rasp. "Isn't your name Trucker S. Holmes?"

Trucker kept his composure, "No. No. I think I would know my name."

"So, it is not Trucker S. Holmes?" she asked.

"Nope. Jack. Dawson."

"Jack Dawson? Isn't that the name of that actor in Titanic?" the plum-smocked woman asked.

"That's Leonardo DiCaprio," Trucker said. "Jack Dawson is the character's name. Same as mine. Very common name. Old English."

The room was suffocating — jammed with books, bottles, herbs, stones, statues, and shelves overflowing with nonsense — so much so that Trucker did not notice the thick black curtain at the back, embroidered with sigils and circles.

And then that curtain moved.

From behind it emerged a short, portly, elderly woman with a slow crooked waddle. Her hair was long, silver, and pinned into a loop with what looked like a rod carved from some mythical animal horn. She wore a pitch-black floral caftan that blended with the fabric of the curtain, giving her the appearance of a floating head.

She looked through Trucker and said, "Dear Mister Holmes, I am Madame LaBu. Come this way."

Behind the curtain was a fabric'd claustrophobic cave, suffocating and disorienting. A psychic tomb that may have seemed welcome to some desperate seekers looking for insight from an experienced clairvoyant, but all Trucker saw was a trap designed to separate those longing for clarity, comfort, or connection from their hard-earned cash.

The smell was intense, mint and mildew replaced with sandalwood and patchouli that certainly was not emanating from the candles that weren't candles but plastic shells with flickering LEDs meant to mimic wax and flame. There was also a hint of corned beef and sauerkraut, the probable leftovers of a mystic Reuben takeout lunch basket.

A small octagonal table was centered in the dark chamber with a tufted and sauerkraut-stained parlor chair on one side. Madam LaBu took a seat and pointed across the room to a stack of folding chairs leaning against a wall. Trucker pulled one out, opened it up, and joined LaBu at her table.

"Okay —" Trucker tried to start.

"— Shhhh . . ." LaBu hushed. "Just listen. Listening is important."

On the center of the table was a simple quartz crystal lying upon a brass plate.

Madam LaBu jerked her head backward and shuddered her shoulders. Trucker cocked an eyebrow.

LaBu whipped her head forward and said in a hushed tone, "Oh my goodness. This is quite special . . . we have an archangel joining us."

The table began to rock, and the crystal moved slowly around the brass plate. "Is it you, Archangel Michael?" LaBu asked.

The table jerked and the crystal popped upward.

"Archangel Michael, are you here to talk to the man known as Trucker S. Holmes?" LaBu asked.

Once again the table jerked and the crystal jumped.

"Speak through me, Archangel Michael," LaBu said and then continued slowly. Pausing slightly between each word and phrase, "Man. Piece. Of. Man. Missing. Given task from unexpected visitor. Fulfill task. Missing piece. Will return. When complete task."

"Umm," Trucker tried to interrupt. "Can I ask some questions?"

The table rocked violently, and the crystal spun around the brass plate. "Resistance," Madam LaBu said with a scowl. "Resistance. Man. Child. Man is child."

"I just wanted to —" Trucker tried to interrupt again.

"Cold," LaBu kept going. "Closed-minded. Man. Not Ready. Man not ready to embrace truth."

Trucker coughed, "Done?"

Madame LaBu shook her head as if she accidentally swallowed a bug. Which was entirely possible. She spoke plainly and normally and claimed, "It is not me. You have clearly upset the Archangel Michael."

"All apologies, Mike," Trucker said.

The table shook again. The crystal danced.

Madame LaBu began her staccato speech again, "Respect. Language. Language matters. Respect matters."

"Of course," Trucker said. "Almighty Archangel Michael, may I humbly ask a question?"

Madame LaBu nodded in affirmation.

"Archangel Michael, has this lady been doing this for so long that she has started to believe the bit?"

Madame LaBu was not amused but remained calm. Trucker was not the first nor would he be the last to question her gifts.

"I mean, Angel Michael, has she been doing this for so long that she doesn't realize she isn't a spring chicken anymore, and it is obvious she is knocking the table around with her wonky foot, makin' that discount crystal seem possessed? Does she even know she is doing this? Subconscious or a con, Mike? What do we think? A bit of both? Could always be both."

The table stopped rocking, and the crystal came to a halt on the brass plate.

"Archangel Michael has left," Madame LaBu announced.

"That's too bad, was about to tell him I was ready to embrace the truth," Trucker said. "The truth that a few months ago I obviously wandered in here after getting blind drunk at The Velvet Elbow, and I don't remember any of it, but you guys do."

Madame LaBu's entire face shifted as if another personality had taken over entirely. She appeared to lose her color, her cheeks became gaunt, and the irises of her eyes darkened to nearly black. It was as if she suddenly became the antagonist in a black and white horror movie with a shrunken field of view. Aside from LaBu's partner-in-crime's bloodhound nose set to detect cash, this was the only other nearly unexplainable supernatural thing that Trucker had witnessed since he walked into the shop. But he knew it was still explainable and purely psychological.

"You thought we were a public men's room," LaBu said.

"Yeesh, sorry," Trucker apologized.

"You peed in our enchanter's cauldron," she said.

"Oh my god, really sorry," Trucker said, and meant it.

"You wouldn't stop talking about rainbows," LaBu continued.

Trucker put his head in his hands.

"We were going to call the police, but you left on your own," LaBu explained. "We nearly changed our walk-in policy, but foot traffic is sixty-four percent of our business"

Trucker reached into his front pocket, peeled off a hundred from the strap of cash, careful not to expose the full bundle, and placed it on the brass plate, covering the crystal.

Madame LaBu looked at Trucker, looked at the hundred, and then looked back to Trucker.

Trucker reached into his pocket, peeled off another hundred, placed it on top of the other, and said, "One for the performance. One for cauldron cleanup."

Trucker flipped through his phone, showed Madame LaBu one of the photos of Ed, and asked, "Have you seen this man?"

LaBu repeated the routine of glancing at Trucker, the cash, and back to Trucker.

"Last one," Trucker said as he placed a third hundred on the brass plate and showed the photo of Ed again. The color returned to LaBu's face, and her eyes brightened. She looked closely at the phone as Trucker swiped through multiple shots of Ed, all of which featured his doting mother, Heather. "Have you seen him?" Trucker asked again.

"Is he cheating on this woman?" LaBu asked.

"That's his mom."

"Hmm. Very close. Too close."

Trucker asked again, "Was he here?"

Madame LaBu jerked her head backward, and the table began to tremble.

"Whoa, whoa, whoa," Trucker interrupted and put his hands on the table to stabilize it. "No fake angels necessary. This can just be between me and you, LaBu."

Madame LaBu slowly brought her head back down, and the table stopped trembling.

"He was here," LaBu said.

"And?" Trucker asked.

LaBu glanced at the three hundred dollars.

"No more hundos," Trucker said. "Can you tell me anything at all that is useful? Go against your usual judgment if that is possible. See how it feels."

Madame LaBu exhaled and recalled, "He was a good boy. Very polite. Very put-together in appearance, yet naïve. Very open to the spiritual process. Intrigued by my divine gifts. He was with a woman. Not mother. She was also polite, but not naïve. She seemed to barely tolerate him and the sanctity of my spirit realm. I do not believe she truly liked him, yet there was something between them. They were bonded beyond this world."

Trucker incredulously raised his eyebrow but let LaBu continue.

"It is true. Not hogwash. They were clearly connected," LaBu insisted. "We have many third-date couples. Was not unusual. I gave them the standard. They were famous in their past lives. Now destined for more great things. Will overcome obstacles. Yada, yada, yada. The standard. Harmless. He paid and added an extremely generous tip. They thanked me and left."

"Harmless," Trucker agreed. "But you're still a professional liar."

"Likewise, Mister Jack Dawson."

Trucker emerged from behind the curtain and returned to the mint and mildew of the main room.

"How was your session?" the plum-smocked woman asked.

"Enlightening," Trucker said, eyeing the divine jewelry case, where neat rows of mood rings shimmered under the glass. Tiny bands wrapped in shifting spectrums of color.

When he'd first launched his fledgling investigative operation, he'd gotten in the habit of giving clients a small token at the end of each case. Nothing extravagant, just a modest keepsake to mark a job well done. People liked it. And he liked giving gifts.

He didn't love the idea of handing over another nickel to LaBu. But if he ever did find Edward Young, he figured the mood rings felt like the proper memento. They kinda spoke to him.

"How about boxing up a couple of those mood rings?" Trucker asked.

Madame LaBu waddled out from behind the curtain, eyes narrowed. "Free of charge, Pam," she instructed.

The plum-smocked Pam selected two rings from the case and placed them gently into a simple cardboard jewelry box with a soft tuft of cotton and *The Aura Authority* stamped on the lid in silver foil.

She handed the box to Trucker with the ceremony of a spiritual transaction.

He slid the boxed rings into his pocket, and the antique brass bell above the door jangled twice as he made his leave of the psychic shop.

"How much did we get?" Pam asked.

"A hundred dollars," LaBu answered.

OUR SUNDAE BEST

The ice cream shack sat across the street, wedged between a laundromat and a tiny parking lot made of cracked pavement and filled with hot car hoods. It was no bigger than a box truck, and the sun-faded orange paint job was chipped and peeling.

A sidewalk chalkboard stood out front, its frame warped from decades of summers. Today's selections were printed in thick block letters above a list of flavors. Pistachio Nana, Bob's Blackberry Swirl, Apple Cinnamon Oatmeal, Choco Chip Cookie Dough, with a note at the bottom that read . . . *and as always Straw/Vanilla/Chocolate.*

The service window had a cardboard sign taped on the corner, letting customers know, in smudged cursive, that they'd be back in about five minutes. But "they" were already back and serving cold treats to a trio of middle-schoolers.

Trucker stepped in line and waited his turn, which came quickly.

"What are ya havin'?" the teen silhouette in the service window asked.

"Were you workin' a couple days ago?" Trucker asked.

"Yeah, mom and dad are on vacation, and sisters are at camp," the teen silhouette answered.

"Have you seen me before? I didn't happen to propose or pee on anything around here, did I?" Trucker asked.

"No to all three," the teen silhouette answered, not remotely fazed by the questions.

"Good. I will take a scoop of cookie dough on a sugar cone," Trucker said.

The solo silhouette operator of Our Sundae Best moved so quickly that the cone was ready in the same amount of time that it took Trucker to pull out his phone and present the teen with an image of Ed.

"Seen this guy before?" Trucker asked.

"You a cop?"

"No."

"Really? Let me see your shoes."

Trucker stepped back from the window and showed the silhouette his shoes.

"Nope, not a cop," the teen silhouette confirmed. "Too bad. Cone woulda been free."

Trucker held up his phone again and swiped through the photos of Ed, "Seen him?"

"No. Cute couple though."

"Aren't they?"

"Cone's gonna be a buck fifty."

Trucker carefully peeled off a hundred in the pocketed bundle of money. Once again, he made sure not to display it to the world, but also made sure it didn't look like he was hiding ninety-five hundred dollars on his person.

He handed the hundred to the teen silhouette.

"Can't break a hundred."

"Just keep it."

"Thanks, dude."

Trucker moved far off to the side and made room for the family in line behind him. He stood near the tiny parking lot and tried to enjoy his cone before the heat could demolish it. Sweat dripped down his temples, and his fingers became sticky. "Should always lock my door," he said to himself. "Should always lock my door, and I should always insist clients use the app." He was losing his race against the blistering sun, and a chunk of cookie dough dove kamikaze-style onto the scorching sidewalk. "Use the app and there are defined rules and terms. Clear pricing. Timeframes. Nonrefundable," Trucker had gotten down to the cone part of the ice cream cone. "I didn't have that lady Heather sign anything. She gives me ten grand and says find her son today? And I say okie dokie? App or not, I should have said *no* and went back to sleep. I am not finding that kid in a handful of hours even on my best day. Barring an act of God."

Trucker took the last bite of his cone and licked his fingers. He looked over the neighborhood; everything seemed to move in slow motion from the heat. "Four hundred square miles of city, and yet months ago I just happened to be in the exact same spot as this missing kid? That's . . . odd," he said to himself.

"Is it odd, or is it God?" a woman's voice said.

Trucker looked over to his right, toward the voice. An apparently unhoused woman in her twenties was there sitting on a forest green bus bench. Trucker guessed that the bench had to feel like a hot griddle. He was also guessing about her being unhoused. But truthfully, she did not look all that more destitute than Trucker. She said again, "Is it odd or is it God?"

"Just odd," Trucker said. "Want a cone?"

"No. Got any spare change?" she asked.

"Who ever has change?" he asked back.

Trucker dug into his front pocket, thought *Why not?* and handed the woman a hundred from the bundle.

"Oh my God, thank you. This helps so much. You are a kind soul," the woman said and then ran into the street, dodged a car, and jangled the brass doorbell of The Aura Authority.

Trucker shook his head and leaned down to sit on the now-vacant bench, which happened to allow him to come "eye to eye" with a giant golden eye. Specifically, a giant stylized eye radiating squiggly lines in the center of a long vinyl advertisement stretched across the bus bench's backrest.

The advertisement was for *Ascend-A-Palooza: The Convergence Conference at the LAX Rosewood Hotel and Convention Center from July 9th through the 12th*.

13 STAGES. 7 DIMENSIONS. 1 TRANSCENDED YOU!

It proclaimed with certainty that attendance would manifest a divine reality. And underneath, in a dizzying array of different fonts, it added: *Featured events include energy healing, astral projection lessons, group quantum breathwork meditations, galactic heritage genealogy panels, and the legendary Doug Martino channeling Khalood!*

If that didn't seal the deal, the ad also claimed attendees would witness and participate in the transformation of the world with hundreds of exhibits, speakers, surprise events, and much more. All sponsored by the HERA Network.

Trucker did not sit down on the bus bench griddle. "Hmm . . . could have gone there, I suppose," he said to himself while he read the advertisement for Ascend-A-Palooza, again. He turned to survey the neighborhood, crossed his arms, and harrumphed. He looked at The Velvet Elbow and said, "Ed breaks free from his mom's enmeshment to meet a pretty girl at a bar. This is not the first time they've met. They have some drinks. They're tipsy, not wrecked," Trucker shifted his vision to The Aura Authority. "They continue their date and wander into the psychic shop. Ed is into it. A true believer. Her not so much. If I were to trust LaBu, mystery girl does not care for Ed but has been tolerating him across multiple dates. Why does anyone tolerate someone they don't like? Hmm. Ed has money. Or the Young family, in general, has money," Trucker contemplated getting another cone while piecing things together.

"Ed and mystery girl leave the psychic shop," Trucker turns to look at the bus bench advertisement. "Ed is already emotionally primed for nonsense after LaBu's performance, and the first thing he sees is the big golden eye of Ascend-A-Palooza. Which is why it is plastered here in the first place. Perfect targeted ad placement for potential customers. Smart."

Trucker wiped the sweat from his temples and forehead, "Okay. Time to go to Ascend-A-Palooza."

4

ACT OF KINDNESS

"How much!?!" Trucker accidentally barked at the Ascend-A-Palooza ticket-booth attendant just outside the LAX Rosewood Hotel and Convention Center. The involuntary outburst startled a few nearby staff members and prospective attendees. He didn't want to draw any more attention to himself and turn his mini ruckus into a full-blown scene. So, he took a breath and calmly said, "Give me a minute," and stepped out of the ticket line.

Although only a couple hours earlier he had tipped a bartender two hundred dollars for a glass of water, three hundred dollars to be yelled at by an angel, a hundred dollars for a melty ice cream cone, and another hundred to support the maybe unhoused Los Angeles community that technically went to Madame LaBu and Pam — bringing the charlatans' haul to four hundred dollars, covering their sage supply for the year — Trucker was having a very hard time forking over sixty dollars to the organizers of the mass collective delusional event called Ascend-A-Palooza: The Convergence Conference.

Trucker considered the previous expenditures as a necessity to find the kid. There was actual evidence that Ed had been in that neighborhood. Totally reasonable. But this? This was a bus bench advertisement long-shot leading him to navigate what he assumed would be a gauntlet of madness. Looking for a needle in a stack of needles, and the needle he was looking for may not even be in the stack. Entirely unreasonable.

Dozens of would-be ascenders flowed around him as he stood motionless in front of the entrance atrium of the LAX Rosewood.

Trucker felt that something wasn't quite right. And it had nothing to do with the young woman who walked by wearing a full-dress World War One officer's uniform along with a half-roll of aluminum foil smushed to her head as a hat. Nor the three bald men who followed behind her wearing matching teal Buddhist robes with pink plastic triangle pins on their chests. Nope. It wasn't external. It was internal. Something wasn't quite right inside himself, and he knew it hadn't been right for some time now. He couldn't put his finger on it. But it was as if his intuition was on the fritz and wasn't firing properly. His instincts would kick in, lead him down a path, and then those instincts would vanish and leave him stranded. Like when a word is on the tip of the tongue. The word is known. It is right there. It just can't be found and spat out. But instead of a simple word, this was Trucker's entire ability to do anything with any confidence at all.

"Okay," Trucker said quietly to himself. "You're here. Your gut brought you this far. Your gut is telling ya that Ed is somewhere in this soup of woo. Whether it is right or wrong . . . go in . . . look for the kid."

Trucker haphazardly headed toward the ticket window, reached into his pocket, and instead of carefully pulling out a single hundred, the entire bundle of cash popped free and became undone.

Ninety-five starched hundred-dollar bills floated and scattered around him. "Oh, no," Trucker dropped to the hot cement and scrambled to pick up the loose bills. "Gawd damnit . . ."

Panic set in as he hurriedly tried to collect the remainder of Ed's bounty. Some of the bills began to wander with the help of a small gust of wind. He slapped and clawed at the crisp cash and hard pavement. He slid to trap one hundred under his right-knee, then another under his left foot. He was doing his best in what looked like a desperate public game of cash grab twister. But the hundreds began to dance just outside his reach. He attempted to smash his palm onto a stray hundred when a small white designer sneaker beat him to it and trapped the Franklin.

He looked up and there was a woman who seemed entirely out of place. She was tall, athletic and wore a light blue sundress that belonged at a high-priced brunch — trying to avoid spills from mimosas and bellinis — not a convergence of unconventional beliefs and channeled aliens. The sneakers looked fresh from the box — chic, pristine, and too good for a city sidewalk. Her hair was cropped close, a sharp brunette pixie cut that made her eyes seem focused and surgical. And there was a glow about her that made strangers stare a second too long and forget what they were doing. Which is exactly what happened to Trucker.

The woman bent down and helped him wrangle the rest of his runaway hundreds. She scooped up the bottom of her dress, used it as a fabric basket and together they corralled all ninety-five hundred dollars.

"Thank you so much," Trucker said to the kind woman as he started organizing the bills she had collected in her improvised dress basket. He pulled out the loose cash, stacked them all neatly back together, and put the ninety-five hundred back in his pocket. "Was in a bad spot for a minute. Ya saved me."

"No biggie," the kind woman said. "That's a lot of . . ."

". . . yeah, it is a long story," Trucker said, then looked at the convention center entrance. "You really going in there? No offense, but you don't really seem the type."

"Oh, absolutely," she said. "Are you not going in?"

"I am," Trucker said. "But not exactly by choice. I am an investigator. Looking for someone." He pulled out his phone and showed the kind woman the photos of Ed and Heather. "Don't suppose you have seen this guy?"

"Hmm," she said. "Can't say that I have. But that is a darling mother and son."

Trucker paused for a moment, "Yeah . . . she is very concerned for his safety."

"Well, I hope you find him," she said as she turned toward the entrance. "It is not all crazy in there, ya know. Just mostly. A gem here or there. You should play it by ear and see what happens."

The kind woman began to walk toward the entrance.

"Hey, what's your name?" Trucker yelled out.

She stopped, turned around, and said with a smile, "Jennifer. Yours?"

"Trucker."

"It is nice to meet you, Trucker," and Jennifer disappeared into the crowd.

5

AURALITE TWENTY-THREE

Trucker felt a flash of rejuvenation as he walked back to the Ascend-A-Palooza ticket booth, "One ticket please."

"Great, it'll be sixty dollars for a day pass —" the teen attendant said while he visibly chewed on a piece of neon yellow gum. He had a *Hello, my name is* . . . tag on his right chest pocket with TIM scrawled upon it in glitter pen.

"— okay —" Trucker started to dig back into his front pocket. Carefully this time. But Tim was not finished.

"Sixty for the basic Day Pass. That gets you into some exhibit halls and all the free events.

One hundred ninety-nine for the four-day Moonstone Pass. Same thing as the Day Pass, but, ya know . . . for four days.

Eight hundred forty for the upgraded Moonstone Plus Pass. That adds access to *some* special events and priority seating. Still four days.

One thousand, one hundred eight for the Auralite Twenty-Three Pass. That's full access to all halls, all events, all special events, priority seating, and the Lapis Lazuli VIP Lounge . . . for four days.

And finally, the Celestite Package. Seventeen hundred. Gives you everything in the Auralite Twenty-Three Pass plus hotel accommodations here at the Rosewood.

Oh, and of course tickets to see Doug Martino channel *Khalood!* are sold separately. First come, first served."

"Tim," Trucker rubbed his left eye and sighed, "nothing against you personally. But . . . what in the hell, Tim?"

Tim started again, "It is sixty for —"

"— no, no, I got it," Trucker said. "Here's the deal. I am actually on the clock. Not here for recreation, reincarnation, or ascending or whatever it is that goes on here. I am an investigator looking for a missing person. And they could be anywhere in there."

Tim got up on his tippy toes to get an angle on Trucker's shoes, "You're not a cop."

"No," Trucker said. "Hired by the mom of a missing kid. I got a lead from the LA County Metro Transportation Authority that he might be here."

"You want to talk to my manager?" Tim asked.

"Not really, would they let me in for free?"

"Probably not."

"How about I walk in there and look anyway?"

"Security would stop you without a pass."

"They're thorough?"

"Yeah," Tim said. "You wouldn't get very far."

"Hmm," Trucker mentally ran through options. "Can you make an announcement to the conference from here? An *Edward Young, please meet your mother at the entrance* kind of thing?"

"No."

"How about your manager?"

"No."

"Why not?"

"It's their policy, just how they have it set up," Tim explained. "It's intrusive. Might interrupt ascension."

Trucker ran through some more options, "How about I give you — you personally, Tim — two hundred cash to knock me out a pass."

"Would," Tim said. "But they track all transactions and passes." He glanced at a security camera above them, "Even cash."

"Hmm," Trucker was running out of options, other than pay for a whatchamacallit pass that granted full access. "How much is the full access pass, again?"

"The Auralite Twenty-Three Pass is one thousand, one hundred and eight dollars, which will get you everywhere for four days, except to see Doug Martino channeling *Khalood!* That's a separate ticket with no priority seating. Seventeen hundred for the celestite package if you want a hotel room."

"Once again, nothing against you personally," Trucker said, "but it's the third day of this thing already."

"Yeah," Tim said. "It's just how they have it set up. Their policy."

"It's criminal," Trucker said.

"It is," Tim agreed. "Too bad you're not a cop; you could do something about it."

"And I would have gotten a free cone," Trucker said.

"Huh?"

"Nothing," Trucker said while digging out twelve hundred dollars from his front pocket stash while he groaned. "Give me the Auralite Twenty-Three Pass."

Tim took out his neon yellow gum with his index finger, chucked it in the trash, and then started punching options on a touchscreen, "Name and email address?"

"Wait," Trucker held onto the twelve hundred dollars. "You take everyone's name and email address?"

"Only for moonstone guests and upwards," Tim answered.

"Can you check for the name Edward Young?" Trucker asked. "Hundred bucks?"

"It is against their policy," Tim glanced up at the camera. "Invasion of ascender's privacy."

"Yeah," Trucker said, slightly defeated. "Worth a shot."

"Yeah," Tim said and went back to his touchscreen. "Name and email address?"

"I.J. Fletcher, fletcher@hushmail.com" Trucker said.

"I.J. Fletcher?" Tim looked up from the touchscreen.

"Irwin Jessica Fletcher," Trucker confirmed. "It's Scotch Romanian. Mom wanted to name me after her great uncle. Dad wanted to name me after his great aunt. They compromised."

"Cool," Tim said and continued to punch on his screen, "ID?"

"Huh?" Trucker asked.

"Identification to confirm who you are," Tim said. "It's how they have it set up. Their policy."

Trucker dug into his back pocket, pulled out a Los Angeles County Library eCard and handed it to Tim who flipped it front to back. "This is a library card," Tim said.

"All I got."

"The name's been worn off?"

"I read a lot."

Tim shrugged and continued to punch options on the touchscreen. A printer came to life behind him, he swiveled around, ripped a printed piece of purple plastic out of the machine, strapped a lanyard on it, and handed it to Trucker. "Welcome to Ascend-A-Palooza, sponsored by the HERA Network, Mister Irwin Jessica Fletcher! Become ascended."

6

ASCEND-A-PALOOZA

The entrance lobby atrium of the LAX Rosewood Hotel and Convention Center was an overwhelming assault on the senses and an affront to every shred of rational thought that has ever existed, since roughly two million years ago. Two thousand millennia ago, a lone *Homo-erectus* critically examined a pile of rocks, intentionally selected the right kind of stones, planned which ones could strike and shape the others for a specific purpose, and developed a method to give them form using an intuitive yet accurate grasp of angles. Then, he took that stone — which was now an effective, useful axe — and taught another fellow *Homo-erectus* how to accurately repeat the process. The world stopped happening to them. It was now possible to bend nature to their will. Not just to survive, but to negotiate with it, using logical reasoning.

Ascend-A-Palooza: The Convergence Conference — emblazoned across a massive lilac purple banner hanging from the third-floor mezzanine in the lobby atrium — took that concept born with *Homo-erectus*, that reasoning, that reality, and said, "Nah."

Only six steps in and Trucker regretted being born with eyes. He was also having a hard time even remembering that this was an actual hotel. Not only that, but a hotel he had stayed at before, multiple times. It had been completely transformed into something other-worldly tacky. To his left should have been a gourmet coffee shop, but now it was remade and rebranded into the Third Eye Celestial Café. Staff adorned in teal jumpers and pink aprons bustled about, serving rebranded coffee and tea along with starseed seaweed snaps, transcendental toast, flat-earth flax thins with activated almonds, and the fan favorite, organic astral funnel cakes.

He could see the beverages and snacks being served, but the normal aroma of coffee beans and crisp tarts was overpowered by the mix of sage, incense, sandalwood, patchouli, and dozens of essential oil diffusers pumping lavender or lemongrass throughout the lobby — all comingling with the body odor of ascenders. The smell wasn't totally intolerable, thanks to Trucker going through the intensive aromatic desensitization bootcamp Madame LaBu unintentionally put him through back in her psychic chamber in The Aura Authority.

To Trucker's right, he remembered there was once an elegant sitting area with leather couches and loveseats. It used to be a comfy and refined respite for travelers of all types, a place to relax before check-in or to wait for a car to take them about their people business. Now, the posh furniture had been removed and the relaxation replaced with a disturbed intensity. A small selection of vendors and exhibitors had set up shop in what was now named the Pre-Ascension Prep Portal, according to the banner slung above the booths.

A little further into the lobby, Trucker remembered an inviting, tranquil open area, with a grand rosewood staircase on the far end. Now, there was no open space and zero tranquility. It had been replaced by a large stage, bunted in rainbow rope lights and flanked by flags for countries, or worlds, or dimensions that Trucker knew did not exist.

And the banners. Banners and flags were everywhere in all shapes, sizes, and shades of teal, purple, and orange. The banner directly above Trucker, scrawled in yet another shade of purple, heralded:

WELCOME ASCENDERS! You are in the right timeline!

If the lobby was only the first small experience of this baloney factory, then Trucker doubted he could handle the whole enchilada of inanity. It was already too much, but he had no choice. He took the money. He took the job. He made a promise. He clicked "yes."

And Tim, the teen ticket attendant, was spot on. Trucker only ventured another four steps before a burly security officer, wearing all black and sporting a HERA Network wristband, approached. The security officer asked in a stern tone, "Sir, do you have a pass?"

Trucker had been nonchalantly fiddling with his overpriced piece of purple plastic by his side. He held it up to the security officer.

The security officer's stern tone shifted to cheerful enthusiasm. He gently took the pass and lanyard from his hand and delicately put it around Trucker's neck as if he were awarding an Olympic gold medal. "Mister Irwin Jessica Fletcher, we are grateful for you. As we are for all Auralite Twenty-Three guests."

"Well, ya know," Trucker returned the enthusiasm, "seemed like the only choice."

"It was an excellent decision. Is there anything I can do for you?" the security officer asked.

"Yeah, I'm a first timer. There are a few things you could help me with," Trucker said. "Most importantly," he pulled out his phone and showed the photo of Edward to the security officer, "have you seen my son? His name is Eddie."

"No, afraid I haven't," the security officer said. "But the convention is even bigger this year, and there are several thousand attendees. What else can I help you with?"

"Any way we could do a little announcement?" Trucker asked nicely. "Have him meet me at the Third Eye Celestial Café for some of those astral funnel cakes?"

"I do apologize, but it is against HERA Network policy to interrupt the natural quantum frequency and overall energy harmonics of the conference with unnecessary announcements. Could alter ascension practices and disrupt consciousness lattices of the attendees. Anything else?"

Trucker was extremely impressed with the security officer's ability to rattle off such nonsense. He imagined the training that went into stringing so many words together, words that had actual meaning, and not using any of them in an accurate way. But then he imagined that it wasn't simple training; it was belief. And as much as he wanted to point out the lunacy of it all, getting thrown out in the first four minutes would not be productive. And he also imagined that Auralite Twenty-Three Passes were nonrefundable.

"That makes sense," Trucker said. "Don't suppose you have a map of the festivities?"

"Sure do," the security officer pulled out a stack of colorful postcard-sized conference maps and handed one to Trucker. "Here you go, Mister Fletcher."

"You've been a big help," Trucker said. "Thanks." And the security officer went back to his stern façade to greet another new attendee.

Trucker checked out the map. It resembled something you'd find at the entrance to a theme park like Disneyland. But if the kingdom of the mouse was the happiest place on earth, then Ascend-A-Palooza was the most paranoid. It claimed to offer spiritual transformation, inner clarity, pathways to abundance, and true healing. But all Trucker saw was polished nonsense wrapped in hopeful marketing that smelled like a con. And it all covered a lobby, a ballroom, and three floors of halls and meeting rooms of the massive LAX Rosewood Hotel and Convention Center.

The task of finding Edward Young in this mess was going to be exhausting and possibly impossible. Trucker knew he had to get moving.

THIRD EYE CELESTIAL CAFÉ

With a quick scan from the front doors, Trucker could see that Ed was not currently a customer of the Third Eye Celestial Café. This glance also revealed a slight advantage to searching for Ed Young in a place like this versus a gathering of realtors or tax accountants. Ed was clean-cut and well put together; that much was clear from the multiple photos with his mom and confirmed by the charlatan LaBu. Here so-called normal stood out like an advanced mathematics textbook in a comic book shop. Trucker wasn't making a judgment on the so-called normalcy of anyone. Everyone was a unique snowflake from his point of view. Maybe the man washing down starseed seaweed snaps with sips of temporal shift tea worked as an insurance adjuster out in the real world. But here at the Convergence Conference, he — and most of the men — dressed like they'd either bought their wardrobes at places called *Soul Flower* or *The Silk Seer Shop* or hand-stitched them at home. Ed? Heather definitely bought Ed's outfits at the GAP. Ed's so-called normalness would stick out.

Trucker headed to the . . .

PRE-ASCENSION PREP PORTAL

There was only a dozen or so booths and vendors and a smattering of attendees in the Prep Portal, an amuse-bouche of fringe belief whackness. Trucker thought he would have no problem knocking this out quickly. He walked up to the first booth, not even paying attention to what they were saying or selling or proclaiming on their clipboard sign-up sheet. He smiled politely, held up his phone, and asked, "Have you seen my son? We got separated."

The booth exhibitors shook their heads "no." Trucker thanked them and moved on. So far so good. One down, too many to go.

Trucker moved to the next booth, and before he could raise his phone, a woman in a wide-brimmed sun straw hat and yellow flowing dress excitedly said, "You have such a strong aura. Striking, really."

Trucker held up his phone and asked, "Have you seen my son? We seem to have gotten separated."

The straw-hatted woman dug into a wicker display basket and pulled out a handful of different colored stickers in the shape of stars. "I started using these little energy patches. They're like modern acupuncture, but no needles. Don't feel a thing."

"Uhm hmm," Trucker nodded and still sported his smile.

"I was struggling with chronic migraines, brain fog, and a touch of fibromyalgia. Nothing helped," the straw-hatted woman continued and waved the stickers. "Until I tried these. Total game changer. Within twenty-four hours — poof — the lights came back on. New woman."

Trucker held up his phone again, "Have you —"

"— I had tried everything. Everything. So many doctor's visits," she continued. "When I first heard of these patches, I thought . . . total B.S. But I figured why not? And they actually worked!"

Trucker was still holding up his phone.

"Here, I've got an extra one," the straw-hatted woman peeled the back from a gold-tinted star sticker and gently placed it on the back of Trucker's hand that was holding up his phone. "Try it out. Stick it and forget it."

Trucker's smile was fading.

"Honestly, I wasn't even looking for anything other than relief from my conditions," the straw-hatted woman continued. "But people kept asking me, *what worked? What has made such a drastic change?* And so — I thought — it would be so wrong of me not to share. Ethically evil to keep them to myself," the straw-hatted woman tilted the wicker basket full of stickers toward Trucker. "Honestly, this is just part of who I am now. What I do. Covers half of my rent some months."

Trucker dropped his star-stickied hand and phone by his side, and the smile was gone.

"There's actually a referral program, nothing pushy. Just . . . if people like it . . . and they totally will . . . *and* they want more . . . you get a cut. It kind of just keeps building upon itself," the straw-hatted woman made a triangle shape with stickers in each hand.

Trucker wasn't quite sure why he was still listening.

"One of my friends started two months before me; now she is full time. And a friend of hers?" the straw-hatted woman fake-whispered, "Bought a cute little Porsche."

Trucker's left eye involuntarily twitched. He raised his phone again, "Have you —"

"— I'm not trying to sell you anything. I just think this could be big." The straw-hatted woman shook the wicker basket, "I am going to be giving a quick little info sesh around three-thirty in the Etheric Energy Restoration room on the third floor. No pressure. Would love to see you there."

Trucker paused, making sure no more words were going to pour out of the straw-hatted woman's face. None did. He held up his phone and asked, "Have you seen . . . umm . . . my son? We . . . uh . . . seemed to have gotten separated."

The straw-hatted woman cheerily studied the photo, "She would make a great representative."

"The guy — not the woman — the man," Trucker asked again. "Have you seen him?"

"Hmm," the straw-hatted woman thought. "I don't believe so."

"Thanks," and Trucker moved on to the next booth.

The next few booths and vendors went smoothly. In and out. "Have you seen my son?" Followed by a series of no's. And then a booth with a pair of exhibitors slowed him down. Not by a sales pitch or insistence on a soul realignment or anything of the sort. Trucker slowed himself down, only slightly, when he saw the pair of unlikely comrades.

In the booth, under a banner that read *Off-Grid Freedom*, sat a youngish crunchy-granola girl whose blonde dreadlocks were soaked with strawberry oil and who had a smile ear-to-ear that looked like it could coerce joy out of a town's entire population. Next to her was a scowly stone-faced man with a fifties-style banker's haircut who looked like he might snap at any moment.

"Looking for advice?" the stone-faced man asked in an academic, teacherly tone that belied the scowl.

"I don't think so," Trucker said as he looked back and forth between the two.

"You really should," the granola girl said with a hint of condescension. "It is important to be prepared."

"Unless you are already on the path," the stone-faced man said.

"Path?" Trucker asked. "Like . . . of ascension? Enlightenment?"

"No," the granola girl quickly snapped back.

"The off-grid path of preparation," the stone-faced man kindly said. "The path of freedom."

"Oh," Trucker said. "You two are off the grid?"

"We are," the granola girl confirmed. "It is important to be off-grid and prepared. Truly self-sufficient and reliant on no one but yourself. Free."

Trucker looked around the LAX Rosewood's massive lobby atrium. "Isn't this building on the grid?"

"Listen —" the granola girl barked, but the stone-faced man put his hand on her shoulder.

"We are here to help free other like-minded individuals who are still stuck in the machine," the stone-faced man said.

"Don't talk to this guy," the granola girl said to the stone-faced man. "He's a cop. Maybe a fed."

The stone-faced man leaned forward and looked at Trucker's shoes. "This man isn't an agent."

"You two on the run?" Trucker tried to ask delicately.

"Would be pretty dumb to sit here on display if we were on the run, wouldn't it?" the granola girl pointed out. "It is dumb anyway. These weirdo sheep are all helpless." She made a noise like a thirsty lamb toward the attendees.

"We couldn't possibly be on the run from the law," the stone-faced man added. "We are citizens of the Earth. There is no human being who has sole jurisdiction over the Earth or us. Although we do — on occasion — respect the county sheriff."

"Unless he starts being a giant a-hole," the granola girl tacked on.

"Very interesting," Trucker said. "I should have tried that approach with security here. Citizen of the Earth. Can go where I want. Do what I want."

"Exactly," the stone-faced man said. "But it isn't simple. You have to use precise special language."

"We are giving a lecture during the Free Man Forum in the reception area on the second floor at three-thirty. Lessons on self-sufficiency and how to be free," the granola girl said. "That is, if you really aren't a fed and care about freedom."

"Rats," Trucker said. "I might be tied up with energy-healing stickers. But I will see if I can't work something out."

"Ditch the sticker nonsense," the stone-faced man said. "Here's a little taste. A freedom freebie. Never sign any documents unless you've created and hand-drafted those documents yourself. If you have to — and I mean *have* to write something, use red ink and go all capitalization."

"Good to know," Trucker said.

"Also," the granola girl added snobbily, "Galatians five one."

"Galatians five one?" Trucker asked.

"Galatians: chapter five, verse one," the stone-faced man said. "*Stand fast therefore in the liberty wherewith Christ hath made us free, and be not entangled again with the yoke of bondage.* King James Bible. Who has authority over God himself? Nobody. God doesn't care what kind of shoes you're wearing. Drop that verse on 'em the next time *they* try to infringe on your sovereignty. Judges. Police. The tax man."

"And that works?" Trucker asked.

"Are you questioning God?" the granola girl asked back.

"Have you tried it?" the stone-faced man added another question for Trucker.

"Have I quoted Galatians from the Bible to get out of paying a parking ticket or taxes?" Trucker said. "Nope, can't say that I have."

"Well, there ya go," the stone-faced man said. "Give it a shot next time."

"Hmm," Trucker thought for a moment, then asked with a purpose. "Wonder if that would work for a speeding ticket in China?"

"I don't see why it wouldn't," the stone-faced man said.

Trucker thought for another moment then said, "I don't know. We'd have to get to China to even get the speeding ticket. And getting to China on our own, without *any* help . . . that's gonna be difficult," Trucker paused briefly. "I'm assuming our self-sustained off-grid freedom spot is not on the beach, so boating to China is out of the question. That leaves air travel. So, first things first — we are gonna need an airplane capable of international flight. That's a tough one. Those don't grow like potatoes. And we can't buy one because we are self-sufficient and off the grid."

Trucker went on, "I'm also assuming we don't have fifteen million lying around to buy a Gulfstream — so regardless, we gotta build it from scratch. No parts ordered from China, funnily enough. Which means we gotta smelt our own metal for the airplane parts from raw materials. I am taking it for granted that our land is on a large mineral deposit full of the appropriate ores needed for aluminum and titanium."

"After all that grueling mining and smelting, we have to get to work machining every screw, bolt, piece of fuselage . . . oh my goodness, the jet engines? Those are going to be extra tricky to build. But that's okay because we need time for the rubber trees to grow so we can do the whole vulcanization thing and make the tires to assemble the landing gear," Trucker paused. "After stripping all the copper from our homemade ham radios for the wiring, we got ourselves an airplane. Throw in a couple cows for leather seats."

Trucker thought for a split second and didn't even care if the off-grid self-sufficient preppers were listening or not.

"An airplane capable of international flight is useless without an airport. We are going to hafta clear, level, and pave a half mile of land at the minimum. I am gonna assume we have the heavy equipment for runway construction because building those, also from scratch, will put us back a bit. The jet fuel will be easy — I am confident we have access to multiple alcohol stills and chemical labs on —"

"— I have no desire to go to China," the stone-faced man interrupted.

"Fair enough, but I haven't even got to the part where we dodge Canadian, Russian, and Chinese radar without clearance or a flight plan and land this flying contraption." Trucker smiled and held up his phone to the off-grid sovereign citizen preppers. "Seen this kid?"

"No," they said in unison.

"Thanks," Trucker began to move to the next set of booths and vendors before turning back for a second with sincere excitement, "Oh! Better idea! Hot-air balloon!"

He was still wondering about the impossibility of total true self-sufficiency with no other assistance from society as he quickly knocked out the next few booths and vendors with his phone held up, "Seen this man?"

"No."

"Notice this kid anywhere around here?"

"No."

"Looking for my son, seen him?"

"No."

Trucker was moving right along in his search for Ed and had reached the last booth on the edge of the Pre-Ascension Prep Portal, the last exhibitor before entering the open area of the atrium.

A man stood on a folding chair in front of that final booth, gripping a microphone wired to a child's portable mini-karaoke machine, which had clearly been collecting dust in his garage for years. The man was passionate. Very passionate.

"Berenstein or *Berenstain*! Oscar Mayer or *Oscar Meyer*! Is the Mona Lisa smiling or not? Where is New Zealand, do you know? Did Nelson Mandela die?" The microphone man did not stop. "The movie *Shazaam* existed! And it starred the comic legend Sinbad! Our reality is shifting, people!" He went on and on.

The man was preaching about the Mandela Effect — a known form of collective false memory where large groups of people remember the same event, detail or fact incorrectly. Memory is a funny and faulty thing. When someone recalls a moment, they are not playing an exact replica of that instance. They are not rewinding a mental movie and replaying it exactly intact. They are rebuilding the whole thing from scratch. Every time. And on a planet with over seven billion people, there are bound to be plenty of wonky rebuilt recollections that line up. Misremembering wasn't supernatural. It was psychological. And the Mandela Effect was this process on a large, sometimes worldwide, scale.

Trucker thought briefly, while the microphone man continued his tirade, that of all the things Nelson Mandela ought to be remembered for, humans misremembering the logo of an underwear brand should be pretty low on that list. And maybe a little higher up should be his profound ability to move forward in life with forgiveness and unity instead of retribution and paranoia. That is the real Mandela Effect that should be shouted from microphones. Or so Trucker thought.

And in the spirit of Mandela, Trucker decided to forgive microphone man's completely misguided passion. But he still needed his attention because he had an idea.

"Hey!" Trucker yelled, but the microphone man was oblivious.

Trucker leaned over to the karaoke machine and flipped the switch from "Public Announcing" to "Barney the Dinosaur Backing Track."

The jingle stopped the microphone man's monologuing cold.

"Hey, man, what's the deal?" the microphone man asked.

"I'm really sorry," Trucker said. "But I need a favor, and you might be able to help me out."

"What, man?"

"My son is missing, could you yell out his name for me?" Trucker asked. "I'd really appreciate it."

"Would love to — but no can do."

"Why not?"

"Because we are all missing, man. The reality has shifted. It might have shifted again just now."

"Well, can you shift to a reality where you yell for a kid named Ed Young?"

"I don't have that power. I wish I did. I can't shift it on my own," the man explained. "*They* have the control. We're just along for the ride."

With every second, one of Mark Twain's quotes echoed in Trucker's mind:

Never argue with stupid people. They will drag you down to their level and beat you with experience.

So, with Twain and Mandela on Trucker's mind, he waved goodbye to microphone man and the Pre-Ascension Prep Portal and said, "Thanks a bunch. See ya around."

THE SPIRIT RESONANCE STAGE

It had been half an hour since Trucker became an Auralite Twenty-Three Pass holder, or was it only five minutes? Trucker truly couldn't tell. The overload of stimulation at Ascend-A-Palooza was starting to play tricks on his mind. The exhibitors, vendors, and attendees were all swimming in an ocean of fringe false beliefs that ran the gamut from simple homeopathic healing to alien overlords ruling atop ancient Antarctic pyramids. And Trucker had jumped headfirst into the waters with them, hoping to track down Edward Young.

None of the nonsense on display was real, of course — or was it? It all certainly wanted to *sound* real, with words of scientific meaning jammed into grand gibberish. And it was definitely real to most of the audience in front of The Spirit Resonance Stage, who were enjoying a performance by a woman dancing poorly with a long red ribbon attached to the end of a silver baton. She had a three-piece band backing her: three young men jamming on a tongue drum, a synthesizer, and a ukulele. Trucker suspected the ribbon-twirling woman may have been hearing-impaired, as she was not in rhythm with the odd instrumental trio in any discernible way.

Also out of sync were two bald monks whose robes defied any monastic order Trucker had ever seen. The monks performed standing squats behind a young, athletic, shirtless man giving a yoga demonstration to no one in particular.

Trucker couldn't spot the clean-cut Ed among the revelers. He would have to go deeper into the ocean of what he considered pure collective madness.

He walked through the lobby, past the stage and eclectic performers, through the attendees, and across the normally polished marble floor, which now was covered in flyers and pamphlets that had been trampled into a glossy pulp. The mass of papers advertised a variety of workshops and services, all similar in tone: spiritual healing, flow-state hypnosis, channeling higher selves, and the occasional ghost encounter opportunity. Nearly all appeared to be made with a free seven-day trial of Photoshop, featuring stock images of men and women meditating in the lotus position.

"These people really love the color teal," Trucker mumbled to himself.

By the time he reached the escalator leading to the second floor, rebranded the Elysium Level, Trucker knew he was being followed. He'd noticed the man eyeing him earlier during his search through the Pre-Ascension Prep Portal. The guy was hard to miss. He resembled a hard-boiled egg propped up by a couple of toothpicks, with a neck that looked like it had blown a bubble to form a head, topped with tufts of greasy, long hair. He was wearing a camouflage-patterned military vest with neon-orange crossing-guard trim.

There was no judgment from Trucker, only observation. The man was noticeable. Very easy to spot.

Trucker wasn't sure if the paranoia of this place was contagious and he was just catching the infection. Or if the military-vested, hard-boiled egg man was indeed tracking him. Regardless, Trucker pressed on, stepped onto the escalator, and ascended to the . . .

7

ELYSIUM LEVEL

A HERA Network security officer stood at the top of the escalator, wearing their trademark black uniform and stern expression.

"Pass?" the officer asked, running on autopilot until he caught a glimpse of the purple iridescent Auralite Twenty-Three Pass hanging around Trucker's neck.

"My apologies," the officer said quickly, inspecting the pass. "Welcome to Elysium, Mister Irwin Jessica Fletcher. We appreciate our Auralite Twenty-Three guests. If you hurry, you'll be able to catch Robert Thompson giving a talk in the Divination Chamber."

"Robert Thompson?" Trucker asked.

"A highly respected and renowned psychologist," the security officer said with enthusiasm. "Most people don't know he is *the* Ezra from *Revelations of Splendor.*"

"Ya know," Trucker said with actual sincerity because he had no clue what this officer was talking about, "I did not know that."

"You'll have a chance to purchase a copy of the book, *Revelations of Splendor*, after the presentation," the security officer said.

"Great," Trucker said. "Can never have too many copies."

"No, you cannot," the security officer confirmed and added, "They also make excellent gifts."

"Well, I'll be sure to catch Bob giving his speech and pick up another copy of his book," Trucker said and then held up his phone to the security officer. "I've gotten separated from my son. I was too enthralled with energy healing patches," Trucker flipped around his hand to show off the faded gold star sticker, "and Ed just wandered off on me."

"No, I have not seen him," the security officer said. "But I will keep an eye out. Let your son know you're looking for him."

"Appreciate it," Trucker said, then started down the second-floor concourse. He spun back around to the security officer. "Which way to that . . . what did you call it? . . . Divination Chamber?"

"Yes," the security officer said, pointing in the opposite direction Trucker had been walking. He loud-whispered, "Near Hall C, right before you get to the second-floor reception area. And don't forget you have priority seating."

Trucker gave the security officer a thumbs-up and headed toward the . . .

DIVINATION CHAMBER

A moderate but dense crowd had congregated around the chamber doors. There was immense excitement, yet no rowdiness or chaos. Everyone wanted to get inside as quickly as possible, but barely a sound was made, creating an eerie calmness that hung in the air. A few of the shorter attendees rose up on their toes, trying to catch a glimpse of what lie ahead in the room.

The air was much cleaner than in the lobby, no patchouli or sage or lingering mixture of Convergence Conference funk. If anything, there was only a hint of laundry detergent and maybe lavender oil.

As Trucker patiently waited behind the orderly crowd, he realized the one advantage that he had previously leaned on was gone. The majority of attendees shuffling into the Divination Chamber appeared clean-cut and, for lack of a better word, normal. Or would at least appear normal to the world outside of Ascend-A-Palooza. And Trucker could safely assume that all of the men around Ed's age had received GAP gift cards on their last birthdays.

Sprinkled among the crowd entering the Divination Chamber were copies of Robert Thompson's book, *Revelations of Splendor*. The book's cover was rather conspicuous. The title had been embossed in reflective gold above an image of Earth with a bright sun rising over it, welcoming a new day. Some of the copies in hand were unblemished and brand new, but most were tattered and jammed with colorful thin bookmarks and small cords of hymnal string as if they had been studied and flipped through hundreds of times.

As the last of the overly ordinary and mild-mannered attendees made their way inside the chamber, Trucker caught sight of an easel propping up a dry-erase board just outside the door. It read:

NDE Robert Thompson LCP ABPP

Revelations of Splendor

By Josh Pilate

Trucker knew the letters behind Bob's name meant he was a licensed psychologist, but for the life of him, he couldn't place the "NDE" that came before it. And he was surprised to learn that *Revelations of Splendor*, the book Bob was clearly pitching and selling, hadn't been written by Bob at all — but by some guy named Josh Pilate.

Trucker went back to the acronym "NDE" and ran through possibilities in his head:

North Dakota Earthquake . . . Notre Dame Equestrians . . . Non-Descript Envelope . . . No Denying Entropy . . .

His brainstorming was interrupted as a HERA Network doorman for the Divination Chamber approached and asked, "Would you like to join the event? Priority seating is still available."

The Divination Chamber wasn't exactly a chamber, and it was definitely not divine. Trucker was confident that just a few days earlier it had probably been filled with business executives from some obscure company that shipped widgets worldwide. He could still make out the tracks in the carpet where the Rosewood Hotel staff had wheeled in a portable buffet and private bar.

It may not have lived up to the "Divination Chamber" moniker, but it wasn't a closet of a room either. It could easily fit two hundred people. And as the HERA doorman-usher kept leading him toward the front, Trucker began having second thoughts about entering the event. He tapped the usher on the shoulder and said, "Hey, I can just stand in the back. It's fine."

"I'm sorry, sir," the usher replied. "The room is at capacity. Standing room only. All remaining priority seating is in the front row."

"Okie-dokie," Trucker said as he scanned the attendees for Ed. "Front row it is."

Trucker really wanted to get in and out of this meeting room. Staying low profile and out of sight was a key rule he normally followed in situations like this. *Don't draw attention* ranked right up there with *make sure clients use the app* and the all-important *no walk-ins welcome*. He was breaking that rule, as he had the others, when the usher placed him in the only open seat available: front row, dead center. He might as well have been on the stage himself, which sat only three feet in front of him, complete with a fake fireplace and two wingback chairs angled toward the audience.

He looked over his right shoulder at the eagerly anticipating crowd. He could still get in and out, he thought.

He scanned the room. There were a dozen possible Eds and even a few potential Heathers, which did him no good. He kept up his search until an elderly couple — seated directly behind him with their copies of *Revelations of Splendor* gripped tightly — started staring straight at him.

"Hello," the elderly woman said cheerfully. Her voice and demeanor were welcoming and pleasant, but there was a strange quality to her eyes — an intense anger and judgment bubbling just under the surface.

"Hi," Trucker said, then quickly turned back toward the stage.

The elderly couple began whispering between themselves, though they were clearly out of practice or possibly in need of new hearing aids. Trucker couldn't tell if they were talking to each other or trying to talk to him.

"An apostle has confirmed all of this, you know," the elderly woman said, "and they have made him a bishop."

"Yes, made him a bishop of his ward. And it wasn't just one apostle. His account has been confirmed by seven of the twelve. That is what I've heard," the elderly man replied. "They just haven't made an official announcement . . . yet."

"They will," she said.

"And we'll be ready," he confirmed.

The eavesdropping ended when everyone in attendance suddenly rose to their feet and began applauding. Trucker, a bit confused, was delayed but eventually joined in.

An unremarkable, string bean of a man in his late fifties, wearing a forgettable light-grey three-piece J.C. Penney suit, entered stage right. He adjusted the silver strands of a comb-over as he was followed by a HERA Network representative dressed in the standard head-to-toe black uniform.

The two made their way to the chairs without acknowledging the audience.

The crowd settled back into that eerie calmness that seemed to be practiced to perfection.

"Welcome, everyone," the HERA Network representative said. "We're glad to have you here. And even more excited to have Doctor Robert Thompson with us to share his experience . . . his vision."

Trucker still didn't know what "NDE" stood for, but he was certain there wasn't an MD, DO, or PhD anywhere behind Mister Thompson's name. It could have been an oversight. Or Bob here could be a "doctor" in the same way as Seuss or Feelgood.

"What do you say, doctor?" the HERA Network representative asked. "Want to get right into it?"

Robert Thompson sat there, expressionless for what felt like a lifetime but was probably only fifteen seconds. Then he said in a slow, soft-spoken, almost droning tone and manner that made the audience lean in to listen, "When I died the first time . . ."

Ohhhh, Trucker thought. *NDE. Near death experience.*

Trucker was dumbfounded and a little disappointed in himself for not immediately deciphering the meaning of the N, the D, and the E. Was the Convergence Conference dulling his senses? His intuition had been misfiring lately, on the fritz. But usually only about bigger things. Not three little letters that most could have guessed in the context of Ascend-A-Palooza.

This place was doing something to him. He was breaking more rules, mocking people like the off-grid preppers, and drifting in and out of focus from the one goal that mattered: finding Ed Young.

While Robert Thompson half-hypnotized the audience with his methodical and gentle cadence, Trucker occasionally glanced over his left and right shoulders, scanning the rapt crowd for any sign of Ed. He faked a stretch here, another there. If he accidentally caught someone's eyeline, he played it off with an eager nod, as if to say, "Isn't this guy amazing?"

The amazing Doctor Robert Thompson meanwhile regaled his congregation with tales of near-death. Or deaths, plural. The good doctor claimed to have popped through the barrier between life and death six times. Once while snorkeling off the coast of a Caribbean island. Another when he tripped on his porch and bonked his noggin on a ceramic gnome. Trucker's favorite, though, was the story of Bob dying during a colonoscopy.

According to Bob, during the routine procedure, his blood pressure dropped to zero, and he began to hover above his own body. While in this spirit form, he heard one of the nurses shout, as if she were in a soap opera, "We're losing him! We're losing him!" During this tense moment, Bob watched them miraculously save his life with a doodad up his bottom.

One would think, as Trucker certainly did, that almost dying six times might mess someone up. Might leave them physically or mentally a little worse for wear. The human body, after all, is a fragile thing and can only take so much abuse.

But not Bob's.

Bob not only survived death six times and lived to tell the tale, but he gained power from each experience. With every brush with the beyond, he said he could see farther beyond the veil of this mortal life. He knew things others did not. He could tell whether someone had a good spirit or a demon inside of them. He could commune with the trees that made the chair he was sitting upon. He knew the true past and the inevitable future.

And the future wasn't cheery. In fact, it was decidedly uncheery. Floods, earthquakes. Nuclear war. Armageddon.

Naturally, all of this was confirmed and verified by the angelic visitors who dropped by to see him, which they did often. Bob and the angels were besties. Thick as thieves. Ride or not die, as it were. The open-door angelic policy applied to Bob at all times and all places: barbecues, bowling nights, shoe shopping, even during therapy sessions with clients. Didn't matter. They could, and did, pop by to tell Bob this or that. Sometimes just to hang out and see how he was doing.

During one of these otherworldly visitations, an angel said to Bob, "Hey, Bob, you need to tell people all about this. This is important information we're giving you."

Well, Doctor Robert Thompson couldn't just ignore angelic instructions. The problem was — Bob wasn't much of a writer.

He needed a scribe.

Enter author Josh Pilate.

Mister Pilate listened carefully to everything Doctor Robert Thompson told him. The not dying, the porch gnome, the colonoscopy, the spirits, the demons, the end times, and the supernatural power Bob now carried.

And Mister Pilate said, "This is amazing stuff, Bob! We have to tell everyone immediately."

And so, *Revelations of Splendor* was born.

Sadly, author Josh Pilate would pass away shortly after crafting and publishing this powerful tale. Josh didn't get the *near* part of the NDE. He got the DE. The real deal.

Trucker had had enough of Doctor Bob and his tale of becoming some kind of sanctified superhero with end-times knowledge. He was almost certain that Ed wasn't in the room, but he had to be sure. And sure in a speedy way, so he wouldn't be subjected to any more of Bob's droning twaddle.

He broke out a tried-and-true sonic locating method that had worked in the past.

Trucker coughed while mumbling, "Ed," then glanced around the room.

The congregation remained half-hypnotized, still laser-focused on Bob.

Trucker coughed again, louder this time, and said, "Ed," with more clarity.

Still nothing. No movement. No reaction.

Trucker gave it one more try, coughing even louder, and this time clearly saying, "Ed."

A few attendees turned and stared at him. None were Ed. But one other person did take notice: the HERA Network usher who was now making his way down the aisle. He knelt next to Trucker's seat.

"Sir, is there a problem?" the usher asked politely.

Trucker looked around the room once more, then turned to the kneeling usher and said, "I'm sorry, I have chronic quantum fatigue syndrome. CQFS." He rubbed the side of his cheek. "Also, a tiny bit of pineal gland dysphasia. And my vestibular sync is all out of whack." He punctuated his conditions with a light, sympathy-inducing cough.

"Oh," the usher said, genuinely concerned. "Is there anything I can do?"

"I just need some fresh air," Trucker replied, rising from his seat and heading toward the door, the usher guiding his way.

As he walked up the aisle, Trucker kept coughing, each cough less "coughy" than the last, the words growing clearer and louder with each step and gaining more attention from the attendees.

Cough, "Ed!"

Cough, "Young!"

Cough, "Edward Young!"

Cough, "Mom's looking for you!"

The door to the Divination Chamber closed behind Trucker with a soft slam, somehow polite, but firm and final.

Trucker was confident that Ed wasn't in the audience listening to Doctor Robert Thompson. Just as confident that Bob didn't have a direct line to the hereafter. And as confident as he was that Bob was possibly psychotic, suffering from some kind of mental disorder, or maybe just a straight-up lying con man. Or all of the above.

He briefly contemplated all of that outside the Divination Chamber.

He thought about the poor patients of Doctor Bob. Real people with real problems, going to see a licensed and credentialed therapist who looked overly ordinary on the outside but was clearly disturbed underneath. Trucker wanted to tackle this somehow. Report it. Call the appropriate licensing board. Get someone to look into it. But that would have to wait; he'd have to put it in his back pocket for now.

Then he saw a small sign of decent, rational humanity. It was a literal small sign on the wall opposite the Divination Chamber entrance. It didn't look official and had no sponsorship from the HERA Network. It was a normal letter-sized piece of paper that was duct-taped to the wall. It had a simple message written passionately in red thick sharpie marker. The message was this:

Warning to Women: Don't fall prey to predatory gurus. Be vigilant.

It made Trucker feel a bit more hopeful that somewhere in this building, somewhere in this Ascend-A-Palooza: Convergence Conference, there was at least one person operating with sanity and real empathy and looking out for others while asking nothing in return. If he had a nail gun on him, he would make sure it stayed up in this hotel hallway forever. Maybe do some fine-tuning with his own sharpie and change *gurus* to *people* in general.

Below the hope-inducing warning was another sign. This one official. It had a large purple arrow and read: *Second-Floor Reception Area and Luminal Nexus Stage this way.*

Trucker looked down the concourse in the direction of the arrow — and there he was again, the man Trucker had earlier thought was following him: the hardboiled-egg-shaped man in the military vest trimmed with neon orange. When the egg man noticed Trucker looking at him, he quickly scurried out of sight, heading straight toward the second-floor reception area.

"Yeah," Trucker muttered to himself. "That guy is definitely up to something."

LUMINAL NEXUS STAGE

The hard-boiled egg man was nowhere to be seen by the time Trucker reached the second-floor reception area. But that didn't matter, he needed to pull focus. He needed to find Ed.

Earlier, Trucker had regretted being born with eyes. That still held true. But now he was also beginning to lament his ownership of ears, as a hard-rock glam-metal band performed on a stage branded Luminal Nexus.

This wasn't the name of the band, as far as Trucker could tell, just the name of the stage, rebranded like everything else around here and sponsored, naturally, by the HERA Network.

The band was apparently called IronSpirit, according to the faded metallic gothic banner strung from a small lighting rig. Trucker had never heard of IronSpirit. He doubted he was alone in that, though a few attendees seemed to be devoted, die-hard fans. A small few.

The dance floor was mostly filled with middle-aged women who looked like they'd purchased Ascend-A-Palooza tickets specifically to see this show. A few elderly gentlemen danced among them — men who, if they'd ever had rhythm, had left it somewhere in the 1980s.

And just off the dance floor stood what might have been the band's most devoted fan: a man in his early thirties wearing a sleeveless T-shirt, cargo shorts, gas-station aviator sunglasses, and flip flops. He was mouthing every single lyric, which was impressive, considering the portable sound system was crackling under the weight of the leather-pants-clad lead singer's vocals.

Ed did not appear to be a fan and in attendance for the small show. But maybe these IronSpirit enthusiasts had seen him.

Trucker approached the sleeveless man, held up his phone, and asked, "Seen this guy?"

"IronSpirit is the best band on Earth," the sleeveless man replied.

Trucker watched the band for a moment, then said, "Earth? Is that where I am?" He glanced at the stage, then back at the sleeveless man. "Never heard of 'em."

"They're Hungarian. Very popular in Korea," the sleeveless man added.

"North or South?" Trucker asked, already shifting a step toward the dance floor. He held up his phone to a middle-aged woman dancing with an elderly man old enough to be her father. "Seen this guy?"

Trucker didn't think she was purposefully ignoring him, just zoned-out with IronSpirit mania — but ignoring was also possible. She and her dance partner let out a series of off-kilter *woo-hoos* as the speakers crackled through a guitar solo.

With a little bit of help from a lot of electronic audio feedback and a shorted-out speaker, Trucker finally got the attention of all three: the sleeveless man, the middle-aged woman, and the elderly dance partner.

"Any of you seen this man?" he asked, holding up his phone again.

"No," said the sleeveless man.

"No," echoed the middle-aged woman.

"That's a classy lady, right there," the elderly man said as he leaned close and stared at the phone. "Easy on the eyes."

"And her son?" Trucker asked quickly, holding the phone closer to the elderly man.

"Um, no. No, I don't believe so."

"Great. You three have been very helpful. Have a nice ascension," Trucker said, turning to leave.

"Ascension?" the middle-aged woman asked.

"Life, ascension, whatever the future may hold," Trucker said as he walked away from the Luminal Nexus Stage sponsored by the HERA Network.

The rest of the area beyond the stage performance wasn't all that different than the booths, vendors, and exhibitors Trucker had already encountered in the lobby — just slightly louder, slightly more spread out, and, overall, slightly *more*.

Before Trucker could even make it to the first booth to continue his search, a young woman intercepted him. She wore four too many scarves draped around her neck, and both of her wrists were weighted down by oversized beaded bracelets. She approached him with a little wiggle of her hips and the casual familiarity of an old friend.

"Do you believe in past lives?" she asked.

"Right now, I barely believe in this one," he answered.

She moved her hands fluidly around the top and sides of Trucker's head.

"A little Reiki never hurt," she said.

"I suppose not," Trucker replied, then held up his phone. "Ever Reiki'd this guy? Seen him around?"

She stared intently at Trucker, completely ignoring the phone and photo.

"I feel we may have been partners in a past life," she said.

"Me and you? Partners?" Trucker asked. "Like . . . married?"

"No, silly," she smiled and continued. "Business partners."

"Really?" Trucker said, not at all surprised.

"And since —" she began, but Trucker finished her pitch for her.

"— since we were in business in a past life, why not carry on in this one."

"Exactly," she said, lighting up.

"What are we selling?" Trucker asked.

"Opportunity," she said, smiling.

"We're selling an abstract concept?" Trucker asked.

"No, silly . . ." she said again, but this time with a slightly more serious tone. "We're selling coins."

"Do these coins have the word *opportunity* engraved on them?" Trucker asked.

"No, they're Quantum Past-Life Reintegration Coins," she explained.

Trucker said nothing.

"Say you were Napoleon in a past life," she explained. "We implant those qualities — Napoleon's essence — into the coin through proprietary tech. Then, whenever you need the power of Napoleon, just rub the coin and place it under your tongue."

Trucker paused, then said, "Didn't Napoleon devastate most of Europe, reject freedom of speech and the press, bring back slavery, and say women weren't allowed to handle money?"

The woman said nothing.

"So, if we went into business, and I used the Quantum Past-Life Napoleon Nickel . . . this business we are starting would technically belong entirely to me?"

She remained silent.

"Seen this guy?" Trucker asked again, holding up the photo on his phone.

"No."

"Thanks," Trucker said and moved on to the first booth in the second-floor reception area.

There was only a collection of about twenty or so booths to check out on the perimeter of the second-floor reception area, but it might as well have been two thousand. Trucker was growing incredibly weary of the nonsense. It was eating away at his rational mind. He looked across the banners. There was so much codwaffle on display he didn't know if he could take it.

Sacred Spiral Systems™ — Customizable sacred geometry wall decals for "vibrational alignment."

Crystal-Fi™ — Wi-Fi extenders made from geodes and Himalayan salt.

Sound Bath Baptism Booth — Lay back in a dry tub while gongs, singing bowls, and a dolphin audio track shift you into a new spiritual dimension.

GalactiWear™ — EMF-resistant bodysuits woven with "Pleiadian memory silk."

. . . and more. And more. And more.

Trucker shook his head and went to work. He kept an eye on the wandering attendees while moving from booth to booth. There would be no idle chatter, no arguing or sarcastic retorts, no more listening to prattling sales pitches. He wasn't going to let this place get to him any longer. He wasn't going to slip into their pseudo-scientific-spiritual song and dance. And he was not going to stop for any reason whatsoever. One goal, achieved with one simple question: "Have you seen this man named Ed?" Ask it. Wait for a response. Then quickly move on.

The answers were all the same.

"No."

"No."

"No."

"She looks familiar."

"No."

"No."

"No."

A chorus of no's.

And then Trucker came upon the last exhibitor at the far end of the second-floor reception area, right before the hallway leading to a ballroom.

There was something noticeably different about this exhibitor. Well, maybe not drastically different, but different enough. He was a tall, lanky, bald man in his early thirties, with a scruff of brownish-greying hair ringed around the back of his head. His wrinkled, short-sleeved linen shirt was unbuttoned, exposing his chest and small belly. Trucker could detect a sadness inside of the man as he sat on the table in front of his booth, which had no banner or signage of any kind. He held a pair of dowsing rods that swayed slowly and erratically from side to side.

Trucker knew about dowsing rods. People had been using the L-shaped sticks for what seemed like time immemorial — sometimes they were made of metal or wood or anything really, as long as they could be held in both hands and swing outward or cross inward. Originally, he believed they were used to find things in the ground, like precious metals, ore, water, or treasure. But somewhere along the way people started to also call them *divining* rods and used them to talk to ghosts, spirits, anyone really. Anyone who didn't actually exist.

Trucker guessed that if he went back to The Aura Authority, toward the beginning of his search for Ed, he'd most likely find a pair tucked away in one of Madame LaBu's dusty drawers. He also guessed they were being sold in bulk somewhere here at the Convergence Conference. And like everything else on display, they didn't do what was advertised on the box.

They couldn't find special rocks. Couldn't find water. And they certainly were not capable of communicating with spirits or angels from the great beyond.

It was all a psychological trick for those that truly believed. The dowser, with rods in hand, would ask a question to a deity or dead uncle. Innocuous things like: "Should I buy a new sweater at the shop on the corner?" And then a well-documented process, understood by psychology and science, would take place. The process was called the ideomotor effect. If the dowser subconsciously wanted a new sweater, guess what? The rods would cross and indicate, "Go get that sweater, sweetie. You deserve it."

The true believer wouldn't realize they were subtly adjusting the rods with tiny micro-movements; essentially talking to themselves and reinforcing whatever they already wanted. And that subconscious movement would then trigger another psychological response — induced euphoria. Because the dowser truly believed they were communicating with their dead uncle Pauly. Or the Aztec god of sweaters. Or whomever. And who wouldn't break down into tears if they *truly* believed they were chatting it up with a god, and that god really wanted them to have that sweater?

A self-reinforcing cycle built on belief, not reality.

All fine and good if all the dowser wanted was a new knit sweater.

But not if the questions stopped being innocent. Not if they became: "Should I jump off this cliff?" or "Should I remove my son from school and teach him using nothing but cookbooks from the fifties?"

Then the rods stopped being a fun, self-fulfilling sweater selector and became something else. Something possibly dangerous.

Also not fine and good when the L-shaped sticks were in the hands of people who didn't believe in their mystical power, but did believe in the real power of money. People without an internal moral compass to stop them from getting that real and powerful money in any way they could.

They'd use the rods to artfully separate the hopeful or gullible from their cash and coins.

"Uncle Pauly says you should give me a twenty spot." Rods cross.

"The Aztec god of realty says you should sign over your house to me." Rods cross.

"This is the only way to true freedom and happiness. Look, the rods are crossing."

Trucker approached the nameless booth and the man with the sad dowsing rods. He could see that in the back of the exhibit space was a hammock strung end-to-end near an open cooler filled with water, quickly melting ice, and spoiled sandwiches. A few cans of SpaghettiOs mingled with red plastic Ziploc bags, and a worn, beaten-up suitcase with a skull painted across the top leaned against the back wall. This man was living here, Trucker could clearly see, or at the very least, camping.

"The name's AK," the man said as he dropped the dowsing rods, brushed a pile of multi-colored rocks and quartz crystals off the table, and slapped the spot next to him, "Want to pop a squat?"

Trucker looked around and broke yet another rule. One he had just made in that very room.

He hopped up on the table and sat next to AK.

AK looked at the Auralite Twenty-Three Pass hanging around Trucker's neck and said, "Big spender."

"Seemed like the only real choice at the time," Trucker said.

AK closely examined the pass and said, "That's not your real name."

"No, it is not," Trucker confessed.

"Here undercover?" AK asked.

"Not really. Just on the job and don't like giving my name," Trucker said.

AK glanced at Trucker's shoes. "You're not a cop. What kind of job are you on? You one of *them*?"

"*Them?*" Trucker asked.

AK strained his eyes upward. "You know," he nodded toward the ceiling repeatedly. "One of *them*."

"I'm not sure what that means," Trucker said.

"One of **them**," AK started to get agitated. "Are you here for me?"

Trucker looked at the man kindly, "I'm not one of *them*. But that is exactly what one of *them* would say. So you're just going to have to trust me."

"Okay," AK began to relax again. "*They* haven't visited me in a long time. I was actually hoping you were one of *them*. Or with *them*. Give me some direction."

Trucker looked over AK's camping spot and briefly tried to put things together. "Were you in the military by any chance?"

"You could tell?" AK pulled out a worn military ID. "Deployed six years."

Trucker and AK sat in silence for a moment, with the whirl of Ascend-A-Palooza circling around them.

Then AK broke the silence. "A while ago," he started, then paused, then started again. "A while ago I was standing in my kitchen late at night, around one in the morning. Made myself a snack. Then went to feed Barkie, my pup. Came back to the kitchen, and the clock on the microwave said it was way past four a.m." AK paused and looked hard at Trucker. "Now, it didn't take me no three hours to feed that dog."

Trucker didn't say anything.

"I didn't think much of it at the time. I mean, it was weird. But whatever," AK said. "Went about my business."

AK dug into his pocket but came up empty. He continued, and Trucker quietly listened.

"Months go by. I'm just doin' my thing. Just normal stuff, watchin' videos online. Random stuff you'd normally see. Cats playin' the xylophone. Kid's screamin' while playin' video games."

"But then, up pops this lady," AK said excitedly. "She looks so peaceful and serene with a good energy, ya know? And she explains the exact thing that happened to me in the kitchen with the clock on the microwave — lost time, they call it."

Trucker was about to speak but decided not to make a peep.

AK continued, "I start watchin' this lady, day and night. She had lots of videos, and I couldn't get enough. She showed me exercises in gratitude, how to be my authentic self, that sort of thing."

"Good things. Makes sense," Trucker said.

"Took me a while, but I had gotten myself into a place of pure enlightenment and bliss. I tell you; I had never felt better in my life. And it was exactly as she described. Livin' in the now. Bein' present with oneself and the universe around you," AK explained. "And then she breaks out a new thing." He grabbed the dowsing rods.

AK stared intensely at Trucker and asked, "Did you know — and this is gonna sound crazy — but did you know that you can talk to spirits with these things?"

"I have heard that, yes," Trucker said politely.

"So, this online lady shows ya how to use 'em," AK said, "and I followed her instructions to the letter. But they didn't quite work."

Trucker just listened.

"Then one night, I break 'em out again. And I am focused. As focused as one could be," AK said, smiling. "And they worked. I didn't know who I was talkin' to at first. But I watched more videos, studied and learned . . . and I got good. Really good," AK nodded to himself. "I was eventually able to talk to Feefers — she was my pup before Barkie. And she said she was good, and she loved and missed me. And I was so happy. I was so so happy that Feefers was okay up in heaven."

Trucker was almost about to break another rule he had. The rule about crying in public, but he pulled it together.

"So, I'm enlightened. Feefers is okay in heaven," AK said. "I decided to really get goin'. I started to talk to others through the rods. Higher selves of people that were still livin', but that I was on the outs with," he said. "Ex-girlfriends. Baby mamma. My sister. Even my a-hole of a dad."

AK added with a light nod, "It gave me real insight into how to interact and get along with everyone."

"All good things," Trucker said.

"Right?" AK asked rhetorically. "So, I figure, let's cut to the chase. Why not? Let's ring up the big man himself. I ask to talk to God."

"And what did he say?" Trucker asked carefully.

"Oh, he didn't answer," AK said. "But guess who did?"

"Who?" Trucker asked.

"His son," AK smiled widely. "Yup, sure as Shinola, Jesus answered," he said with a faithful grin, waving the metal sticks. "These rods right here gave me direct access. I know it wasn't God himself — I mean, arguably they are the same guy. But Jesus is more personable, ya know?"

"That he is," Trucker said softly.

"And you know what Jesus first said?" AK asked, waiting.

"I don't know," Trucker answered very delicately.

"He said that missing time — ya know, from when I was in the kitchen havin' a snack and then feedin' Barkie — he said that a bunch of his angels came and got me and brought me to him. I had a one-on-one briefing with Jesus Christ himself. Just didn't know it. Wiped my memory, I guess."

Trucker didn't say a word.

"Jesus had so much to say through the rods," AK explained. "But it was limiting, ya know? He could only answer yes-or-no questions that I had to think up."

"Yeah," Trucker said sincerely. "That is limiting."

"So, I scrounge around online," AK became hyper and dropped to the floor of his booth. He pulled up a quartz crystal attached to a shoelace and a wrinkled piece of paper with letters and numbers scribbled on it. "This stuff right here. This was the answer. And there were tons of videos online showing how to use 'em."

AK handed the paper and crystal pendulum to Trucker.

AK excitedly went on. "No more yes-or-no questions. I could just say, 'Jesus, what do you want me to do?' And he would answer. Spell out instructions plain as day."

Trucker asked, still ever so delicately, "What did Jesus tell you to do?"

"Oh, lots of stuff. Eat healthy. Go vegan. Exercise more. Save some lady from breast cancer. Write the new Bible," AK explained. "Now, I haven't gotten around to all of it. Jesus spelled out breast cancer lady's name and gave a description, but I don't know anyone fittin' the bill. And trust me, I tried and tried to find her," AK paused and thought for a moment. "And the Bible writin' . . . well, the Bible writin' is on hold . . . because —"

AK became overwhelmingly sad and violently grabbed the crystal pendulum and wrinkled paper from Trucker.

"This stuff stopped workin'. None of it works anymore," he waved the paper back and forth.

AK hopped behind the booth and chucked the crystal and pendulum against the wall. He picked up the rods and shook them intensely, nearly bending them in half.

"None of it works anymore. Nothing!" AK shouted.

Trucker stood up and put his arms out as if to calm a wild animal. He watched AK flail in his nameless camping booth.

"I was enlightened! I was talking to Jesus!" AK sobbed. "And now he's not answerin'. He's gone! It's all gone." He quickly swung from sobbing to thrashing and back again. He wiped tears from his face and said to Trucker, "I've tried everything to get it back. I've meditated, gone to retreats, read every book, watched every video, done yoga for hours, fasted for days, attended too many churches to count — tried mushrooms, acid, 2C-B, 5-MeO-DMT — and none of it . . . none of it has worked."

AK continued his emotional whiplash, "But that's why I'm here. I'm here to get it back. Get it all back. They say online, in the videos, that the energy created in this place — with all of these seekers and truly enlightened ones," AK gestured to the booths around them with the half-bent dowsing rods, "they say this space can realign you. This place can bring it all back . . . and then maybe Jesus will answer again."

Trucker looked around at the other booths and vendors and exhibitors and attendees moving about Ascend-A-Palooza. No one noticed or reacted to AK's outburst. None of them.

Trucker sat back on the table and patted the spot next to him. "Hey, AK. Wanna pop a squat for a moment?"

AK hopped up and sat next to Trucker with his bent rods.

"Let's just chill for a sec. Slow things down," Trucker said, "You okay with that?"

"Yeah," AK answered. "I'm cool with that."

"Okay," Trucker said, and the two of them sat without a word for a few minutes. Just watched the crowd of attendees move around them.

"I am not so sure," Trucker broke the silence. "I'm not so sure these people have it any more figured out than anyone else. Seems to me —"

Trucker paused and pointed to a booth with a banner that read: *NeuroLight Wand*™ — *Recalibrates your inner aura! $19.99* with a man waving what was clearly a cheap plastic knock-off lightsaber.

"Seems to me that most of these people are just selling a bunch of junk. Notice that?" Trucker asked.

"Yeah," AK answered calmly.

"Seems this place is no more enlightened or spiritually in tune than anywhere else," Trucker said. "Maybe even less so."

"Yeah," AK answered.

"I'd even go as far to say this place has the opposite effect. I don't know how long I have been here — feels like both six minutes and six days — but whatever enlightenment or insight I had before I walked through the doors is slowly being sucked out of me."

"Yeah," AK answered. "Thank you, Rōshi."

"I'm not a Rōshi. I'm not a teacher or a master," Trucker said warmly. "I'm just a guy."

Trucker didn't mean to, but he accidentally set off another episode from AK.

AK jumped behind his booth again, flailed about, and yelled, "That's right! What do you know? You're just some guy! You're not enlightened! What do you know?!"

AK kicked his cooler, and the water and melted ice sprayed everywhere. The spoiled sandwiches exploded against the wall. He grabbed half of his hammock and ripped it down violently. He was about to drop-kick a can of SpaghettiOs all the way to the Luminal Nexus Stage and knock out IronSpirit's lead singer. That is, until Trucker let out an ear-piercing whistle and barked, loud and clear.

"Hey! Hey!" Trucker scolded. An intense controlled rage in his eyes. "AK! AK!"

AK paused mid-drop-kick.

"I am one of *them*," Trucker said.

AK stood solid and completely motionless as if he were a garden statue.

"I am one of *them*," Trucker repeated.

"I knew it!" AK yelled, thrilled.

"I am one of *them*, and I was sent here specifically by Jesus Christ himself to get you out of here," Trucker said.

AK began to cry. "I knew it . . ."

"Drop the SpaghettiOs and pack up your shit," Trucker said like a drill instructor.

"Yes, absolutely," AK said and began rolling up his half-torn hammock.

Trucker grabbed the wrinkled piece of lettered paper used to communicate with Jesus, and flipped it over. He snagged a pen, with a HERA Network logo from behind the ear of an attendee who happened to be walking past.

The passerby stopped and asked, "What's the deal, dude?"

To which Trucker replied, eyes locked and intense, "Keep. Fucking. Walking." And the now penless attendee did.

Trucker took the HERA Network pen to the back of the pendulum paper and wrote down a phone number and address. He waved it at AK, who was quickly dismantling his camping gear.

"You have a new mission," Trucker said to AK with the same intensity but less rage. "Your mission is to go to this address and say, 'Trucker S. Holmes sent me.' You are to tell a man named Doctor Parker that I sent you."

AK nodded.

"What's my name?" Trucker asked.

"Trucker S. Holmes."

"What's your mission?"

"Go to the address you wrote down and tell a man named Doctor Parker that Trucker S. Holmes sent me."

"Good," Trucker dropped all the intensity, all the rage, and asked, "Can you do this?"

"Yes."

"Are you sure?"

"Yes."

"Good. I'd take you out of here and deliver you myself, but I am on the clock. A mission from God, as it now seems to be. Multiple missions," Trucker held up his phone to the half-manic, but currently stable, AK. "Have you seen this kid?"

To which AK responded, "Yes. Yes, I have."

8

SOUL GATEWAY GALLERIA

"This had to be the heart of it," Trucker mumbled to himself as he stood before the Soul Gateway Galleria. Its original name was the Crystal Ballroom, and he thought it odd that they'd renamed it. The original handle fit the festivities fine enough.

He leaned against the railing of the mezzanine level and peered down into the abyss. If what he had seen so far at Ascend-A-Palooza was merely strange, *this* was where that strangeness climaxed into a shimmering fever dream of delusion.

The hotel ballroom sprawled out into a carnival of madness, and the rows upon rows of booths appeared to be assembled like a giant rat maze, haphazardly, as if designed by architects who'd dipped into AK's stash of military-grade, high-powered mushroom powder.

Every third booth had a speaker or a microphone. Someone was always talking. Someone was always healing. Someone was always whispering to a spirit, or an alien being, or God only knows what. One man stood on a table shouting about divine light codes while a woman in an LED hula-hoop spun nearby in a silent, euphoric trance.

The lighting was both too bright and somehow not enough. Glittering, soft-colored spotlights bounced off crystals, glass, and iridescent fabrics, creating a kind of optical chaos that made it impossible to focus for more than a few seconds. It was both overwhelming and numbing.

There were too many people to even consider estimating the total attendance. Something near infinite seemed like a real possibility to Trucker. Some of the attendees moved with a purpose. Some wandered like they were waiting for a sign — any sign at all — to tell them where to go next. And there were just as many selling make-believe maps to get there.

"Ed was in here somewhere," Trucker said to himself. Of course, the only confirmation of this was questionable at best. But it was the only lead he'd had since arriving at the Convergence Conference.

AK had told Trucker he saw Ed go this way with a pretty girl. Or that he *thought* he saw him go this way. Could have been this way, and it could have been an hour ago, or it could have been a day ago. AK had seemed a little more settled when he provided the information, but any tip from someone who believed Jesus told them to write the new Bible through a dime-store crystal had to be taken with a mountain of salt. Still, AK seemed completely convinced that he'd seen Ed with the mystery girl while waving goodbye to the angel messenger, Trucker S. Holmes, on his way to Doctor Parker.

There was a tap on Trucker's shoulder. He turned around, and there was an elderly woman. All of four-and-a-half-feet tall and staring up at him with a kind of peculiar interest. She could have been his own grandmother. Anyone's grandmother.

"Excuse me," anyone's grandmother asked. "Do you know how we went from monkey to man?"

The question seemed to be asked with sincere curiosity, so Trucker answered in the same spirit.

"I don't know, evolution," Trucker said. "Via God, in general, maybe?"

"No," she said, answering her own question with absolute sincerity. "Beings from the Sirius star system came and turned most of the monkeys into men. They left a few monkeys around, though, because not all humans like bananas. So they thought, 'Somebody's got to be around to eat 'em.'"

"That was not going to be my next guess," Trucker said, not knowing if this was a joke or if she was just trying to spread the word. But, given the circumstances, he was heavily leaning toward her believing she was an important emissary of truth. He held up his phone, "Hey, have you seen this kid? He might be with a pretty girl. Not the woman in the photo?"

Anyone's grandmother looked closely at the photo and answered, "No."

"Thanks," Trucker said.

Anyone's grandmother shuffled over to another nearby attendee, and Trucker heard her repeat the monkey-to-man question.

Trucker turned back to the mezzanine railing and again looked down into the abyss.

"I don't know if I can go down there. I am standing up here out of the fray, and I am still catching alien origin monkey-to-man questions from little old ladies," Trucker said to himself under his breath.

He did a visual sweep of the massive, frenzied pit of foolishness, squinting as he studied the chaotic scene playing out below. Maybe he didn't have to go down there. Maybe he could just lean here for a little while, set up a makeshift overlook post. Maybe grab a cosmic coffee and an astral funnel cake from the Third Eye Celestial Café. Do a little old-school stakeout.

He kept poring over the sea of booths, vendors, exhibitors, and attendees. And then he saw him.

He saw the hard-boiled egg man in the military vest with neon orange trim standing in the middle of the Soul Gateway Galleria. He was motionless in an aisle within the maze of booths — a river of humanity flowed around him — and he was looking directly at Trucker.

"What is this guy's deal?" Trucker mumbled to himself, thinking it was too bad this guy's mom hadn't shown up at his shop this morning with ten grand in hand to find him. His body type alone was so irregular that he actually stood out in a crowd of hundreds. Even without the reflective road-construction-crew stripes on his camo vest, he could be spotted in seconds from a mile away.

But why was this guy evidently so obsessed? Had he followed Trucker into this funhouse of fringe from the beginning? Was it related to the case of the one missing Edward Young? Or was it something Trucker had done in the past that had caught the ire of this odd individual?

Trucker shook off these questions. If they needed to be dealt with in the future, then he'd handle it, if or when it came up. For now, he continued to search the Galleria crowd for Ed from his mezzanine perch.

He found it increasingly difficult to remain focused on the task at hand. With each booth, he saw another goofball exhibitor presenting their "truth" to the world, and attendees offering up their credit cards to purchase and validate that "truth."

Trucker figured he had the vendors' motives nailed down. How they packaged their image or product didn't matter: wise old pseudo-Buddhist bald monk offering courses on his own handcrafted path, middle-aged woman, who wouldn't look out of place behind a counter in Macy's, selling her ethereal essential oils. The slick young businessman, who probably lost his job at the car-dealership last week, pitching EMF shielded boxer-briefs. The vast majority were straight up con artists.

His real curiosity was directed at the attendees. He imagined how each of them might have gotten to this point in their life. Were some like AK — a perfect storm of past trauma and mental illness, coupled with random self-indoctrination that birthed a belief system destined to destroy the believer without intervention?

Maybe some had just been subjected to a series of unfortunate, random events and were now hopeful they could turn the tide by any means possible. Maybe some were born into this sort of thing. While at a young age, their parents taught them that powerful beings called Lemurians lived in a mythical city under Sausalito, and they only got a scoop of peppermint ice cream if they accurately recited the Lemu alphabet.

Or maybe it was just the overall decline of the education system, producing a massive deficit in critical thinking that allowed people to grow up assigning meaning to coincidence on a grand scale.

And maybe some — maybe even most — were like the father and daughter duo wearing Velcroed dragon-wing backpacks, their faces painted in bright airbrushed designs, laughing and smiling, who had simply bought tickets to this circus on a whim to spend some fun, quality time together, inside an air-conditioned hotel, to beat the heat on a hot and sweltry Southern California afternoon.

Trucker allowed himself a small smile as he watched the father and daughter duo skip and weave playfully through the crowd. The young girl stomped gleefully on the flyers and pamphlets littering every inch of the floor. She played a kind of hopscotch on the poorly designed teal images of bodies in the lotus position.

The two happy attendees settled at a booth too far away for Trucker to make out what its banner read. Whatever was on offer, the daughter really wanted to have a try. She tugged on her dad's arm, and in response he gently tried to redirect her attention. Not unlike a child wanting to play the ring toss at a carnival for the big stuffed animal, while the parent knows the game is rigged from the start. The father was no match for the daughter's smiling and arm-tugging.

The dad relented and hesitantly pulled out his credit card. The young girl sat down in a chair in front of the booth, and an exhibitor gently fitted her with a repurposed plastic bicycle helmet and a pair of goggles wired to a nearby laptop. Trucker was too far away to see, but he doubted the wires went anywhere.

The exhibitor began typing dramatically. The theatrics were rather impressive. Probably not worth the price, but it was quite a show. And dad kept a watchful eye over the whole operation.

The exhibitor looked intensely at the laptop's screen, waved his hands around, and appeared to be happily telling the daughter and father how special she was. Or Trucker hoped that was what the con artist was telling her. Because from his mezzanine perch, he could see the specialness, joy, and connection this father and daughter had between them.

A machine started cranking printouts behind the exhibitor, he spun around with flair, grabbed them, and handed them to the father and daughter as the daughter removed the helmet. The exhibitor was in a state of pure delight. Trucker assumed the delight was from the fact that he just sold three worthless pieces of paper and three minutes of time for a charge on dad's card.

But Trucker let his cynicism die for a moment as he watched the father and daughter duo stroll off, laughing as they read the printed results. The pages eventually slipped from her fingers and floated gently to the floor, quickly forgotten. Unbothered, they skipped away into the current of the Galleria crowd.

Trucker's attention fell from the duo and remained on the three freshly printed readouts. They lied atop the smashed pulpy mess of abandoned teal pamphlets and flyers. They were noticeable. They stood out. And those simple pieces of paper gave him an idea.

"It's gotta still be open. The hotel wouldn't shut it down for this conference. And it couldn't be rebranded or renamed. What would they even change it to?" Trucker said to himself as he shuffled across the mezzanine level, changing directions twice in a half-manic hurry. "But where is it? Hmm . . . I don't think I've ever used it before. Had no need."

He flagged down a HERA Network security officer.

"Yes, we appreciate all of our Auralite Twenty-Three Pass hol —" the officer began cheerfully, but Trucker cut him off.

"— Yeah, yeah, we're the best," Trucker said quickly, trying to stay polite. "Hey, do you know where I can find the hotel's business center? Need a computer and a printer."

"Yes, Mister Irwin Jessica Fletcher," the officer replied. "The business center is below the Elysium Level."

"So . . . first floor," Trucker confirmed.

"Yes," the HERA officer said, beginning to point and direct. "You'll need to go back by the Luminal Nexus Stage, down to the Spirit

Resonance Welcoming Zone. Then cut through the TempleWave Tunnel. The business center is just past the Hempire Threads Emporium. On the right."

"Okay," Trucker clarified, also pointing to repeat the directions. "So . . . back to the lobby, hallway past a clothing store, and it's on the right?"

"Correct," the officer confirmed.

"And it's still intact?" Trucker asked.

"Intact?" the officer's cheer gave way to confusion.

"You guys haven't replaced all the computers and printers with quantum mind portals or whatever?" Trucker asked, not meaning to be disrespectful, though a hint of offense was taken.

"No," the officer said plainly. "We have not replaced the computers with quantum mind portals. I don't even know what those are."

Trucker gave the officer a grateful slap on the shoulder. "Yeah, me neither. You've been a big help." He turned to race off toward the lobby level but turned back for a split second and held up his phone to the HERA Network security officer. "One more thing, don't suppose you have seen this kid? He might be with a girl. Not the lady in the photo."

"No, I haven't," without cheerfulness or sternness, but a mild quizzical perplexity.

LAX ROSEWOOD HOTEL BUSINESS CENTER

The room had remained entirely intact. It was a fallout shelter of corporate normalcy in the storm of alternate rationalities branded as Ascend-A-Palooza.

Time here was functional and sensed in the standard fashion. A minute was a minute, and an hour was an hour, displayed by round devices featuring thin metallic strips that appeared as lines and moved in the customary clockwise direction. With every second, there was a small, satisfying, and relaxing *click*. There were no orgonite hourglasses, no past-life egg timers, no timeline fork indicators. Just two standard-issue, boring old clocks on a wall painted in a color that had surely come from a can labeled "Business Blue."

Workstations were organized and set up in a sane and conventional straight-line style, constructed of walnut veneer and brushed-metal fixtures. Average, unremarkable office chairs slid into each standard stall, all of which were equipped with garden-variety computer towers, keyboards, mice, and monitors. No quantum soul sockets, just USB connections.

A simple, laminated, clearly printed instructional poster hung above a large printer-copier combo that sat in the corner beside a walnut table offering hotel guests caffeinated and decaffeinated coffee served in paper cups. There were no packets of reiki'd or chakra-leveling creamer.

The two speakers near the ceiling played classic, recognizable muzak versions of '80s hits at a volume that was not annoying, but just loud enough to induce calm productivity.

Trucker slipped into the business center fallout shelter. He took a deep breath, and his shoulders sagged as if he were a character in a horror story who'd just outrun the monster. He shut the door behind him and peered through the small vertical frosted window that looked out into the TempleWave Tunnel.

He leaned against the door and said to himself, "Okay, let's get to work."

There was a clattering and rustling from one of the workstations, followed by a set of keys hitting the floor and quiet voice muttering, "Shoot."

Trucker was not alone.

"Hello?" he called out.

"Hello?" the voice echoed back.

"Hello," Trucker repeated, friendlier this time.

A mop of curly red hair popped up from behind one of the workstations. "You're not one of *them*, are you?"

"You're gonna have to be way more specific than that," Trucker said.

The tuft of red hair rose with its owner, a pale, wide-eyed man who glanced nervously toward the direction of the lobby, not unlike AK when he looked toward the heavens.

"Oh," Trucker said. "No, I am not one of *them*."

"Then what's with the pass around your neck?" the red-haired man asked, clearly shell-shocked.

Trucker looked down at his Auralite Twenty-Three Pass and held it up. "Yeah, I had to get one. But I'm not one of *them*."

"That's exactly what one of *them* would say," the man replied.

"I don't know about that," Trucker said. "They seem awfully proud of who they are."

The red-haired man just stared at him.

"Look, I'll prove it to you," Trucker said. "Science is studying the structure and behavior of the physical and natural world through observation, experiments, and testing theories against real evidence. Then replicatin' it — doin' it again and again — and sayin' 'Yeah, that seems to make sense . . . for now. Until someone comes up with a more accurate way to look at it. Then we accept that and gain a better understanding.' Repeat until the end of time."

"Not sure exactly what that means. Kinda sounds like something *they'd* say," the man said, eyeing him. "But you don't *seem* like one of them. What are you doing here?"

"I'm on the job," Trucker said, holding up his phone. "Seen this guy around here?"

The red-haired man relaxed slightly and stepped closer to get a look at the photo of Ed and Heather. "No, I haven't seen them," he said. "But I've been basically hiding for the last two days."

"What are you doing here?" Trucker asked.

"It's a long story," the man said.

"Give me the short version."

"I have the worst luck of anyone alive."

"Okay, you can probably expand on that if ya want," Trucker said as he moved to a workstation and fired up a computer.

"I flew in two days ago after my flight was delayed five hours," the man continued while Trucker plugged in his phone. "When I landed, my luggage didn't land with me. The airline said they'd send it to the hotel. That hasn't happened."

"You know the guest Wi-Fi password?" Trucker asked.

"Yeah. 'WelcomeGuest' — and the numbers two, zero, one, five," the red-haired man replied, then continued, "I get to the hotel — and I have stayed here before. Many times."

"Thanks for the password," Trucker said. "And yeah, I've stayed here before, too."

"I walk into the lobby, and it's THAT," the man said, throwing his arms in the general direction of the rebranded atrium. "I can't even find the front desk. It's now some 'trans-dimensional quantum portal' or some other kind of nonsensical name sponsored by some company I've never heard of."

Trucker clacked away at the keyboard and nodded. "I'm listening." Then, moving to the printer-copier combo, he asked, "Hey, you got a room code I could borrow? I need to print a few things. I'll reimburse ya." He started to pull a hundred from his stash, but the red-haired man stopped him.

"Room 1307," he said.

Trucker punched in the numbers, and an enlarged version of the photo of Ed and Heather rolled out of the machine. He pulled out his stolen HERA Network pen and scrawled a phone number on the eight-and-a-half-by-eleven-inch photo with the message: *MISSING!* across the top. And *Ed Young! Call this number!* across the bottom.

He flipped open the copier lid, placed the poster on the glass, and hit the copy button.

"You sure you don't want some money?" he asked the man. "I'm gonna run this thing till I'm outta paper."

"No, it's fine," the man replied.

"Okay, let's hear the rest of your story," Trucker said as the posters began piling up.

The red-haired man explained that he was a private consultant. No support system. No assistant. He had to handle everything himself. He assumed that when he booked a hotel, especially one he'd used before in a major city, it would still be a *hotel* and not . . . whatever this had become. He blamed himself. He should have checked. But it never occurred to him that something like this could even exist, let alone happen at the LAX Rosewood.

His client presentation was in his lost luggage, and he now had to recreate the entire thing from scratch. The client had been forgiving and pushed the meeting back a few days — but it wasn't a good look, and he needed the business.

So now, he was trying to rebuild a crucial presentation while the Convergence Conference circled around him. On top of all that, he believed he had been cursed by an actual witch. He'd accidentally bumped into a woman on the way to his room, and she'd said something strange and stuck a sticker on him. Since then, things have only gotten worse: stubbed toes, cold showers, wrong breakfast orders.

"I swear, Irwin," he said. "I think she cursed me. And I already seemed to have upset the man upstairs anyway."

Trucker held up his own stickered hand as the copier spat out the last of the missing Ed posters. He tapped the warm stack of paper into alignment and said, "You didn't upset God. And the lady you ran into wasn't a witch. Doubt it was the same one who stickered me. But none of them are witches. Witches don't exist."

"Sure feels like I'm cursed," the red-haired man muttered.

"I don't know. You sound an awful lot like *them*," Trucker said, nodding toward the lobby with a half smirk.

"I can't see any other explanation," the man said.

"Sure ya can," Trucker replied, voice reassuring. "You're just upset and stressed and surrounded by people who don't think clearly — and it's rubbin' off on ya."

The man was quiet.

"Your delayed flight and lost luggage aren't divine wrath. Flights get delayed; luggage gets lost. That's life. You're a busy guy; you didn't check the convention schedule. No big deal. Even if you had checked and saw 'Ascend-A-Palooza,' I doubt you'd imagine this fiasco."

The man nodded slowly.

"Bad things happen. Randomly. And sometimes all at once. You already know this. You've known this since you were a kid. But sometimes we need remindin' because we forget things when emotions flair," Trucker said. "I don't know you. But you seem like a rational, kind, good guy. And for some reason, this convention has a way of just taking all of that from people," He paused. "You're strong. Resilient. You'll get through this. You'll give your presentation, go home, and keep going."

With a near-ream of missing Ed posters in hand, Trucker turned toward the door. He leaned into it with his back and kicked it open at the bottom, spilling out into the TempleWave Tunnel.

"They're not witches," Trucker called back over his shoulder. "They're vampires."

10

RETURN TO THE
SOUL GATEWAY GALLERIA

As far as ideas went, Trucker's wasn't bad. It wasn't Edison's light bulb or the vaccine for polio, but it also wasn't half-ply toilet paper or leaded gasoline. It landed somewhere in between. Maybe not as impactful or important as those historical highs and lows, but it mattered to Trucker in the moment. And he came up with it. That's usually what mattered most to people; he was no different in this respect.

He could put away his phone, avoid any and all conversation, and just hand out the missing Ed posters to everyone he passed. If they ignored the poster and dropped it immediately, so be it. He didn't need to rely on others' empathy or attention. The bright white paper would fall to the ground and stand out against the teal trash. They'd sit there like little beacons announcing, "Ed, your mom is looking for you." And maybe, just maybe, somebody who knew something would see one. Maybe even Ed himself. The HERA Network's lack of janitorial staff and the crowd's propensity to litter would be used to Trucker's advantage.

He walked down a staircase from the Elysium Level mezzanine, a giant ream of missing Ed posters in his arms, and began to run the gauntlet of the Soul Gateway Galleria.

It started out well enough. He peeled posters from the top of the stack and handed them out as he moved slowly and methodically through the claustrophobic, shifting crowd. Some of the attendees and exhibitors shook their heads in the negative. A few even offered support, "Hope you find him" or "Hope you find her," before eventually dropping the paper to the floor.

But then something changed.

The horde began to push back, or at least that's how it felt to Trucker. He swore it was as if the mass of attendees and exhibitors had all turned an internal dial to *zombie* mode, and they could sense the living, functioning brain in his head.

For every poster handed out, he was met with a face, up close and personal, that shouted some absurdity or announced a painfully un-insightful insight.

It started with the first proclamation:

"My aura's allergic to fluoride!"

But that was just the first slow chomp at Trucker's brain, a warning, an announcement for the waves to come.

And within a blink of a third eye, the first wave was upon him.

"DNA is just God's QR code, man!"

"Sacred geometry can manifest your dreams!"

"Don't breathe too hard — it disrupts the portal grid!"

"I asked for turtle in the pre-existence! Why am I human!"

"I only date people from my soul pod!"

"It's not a rash! It's a mark from a spiritual download!"

. . . and more.

They came fast and relentlessly. Trucker moved out of the middle of the crooked aisle, now flooded with people he felt belonged in an asylum or at the very least the waiting room of a therapist's office.

He caught his breath as the bodies of the attendees surged past, then leaned against the front of an exhibitor's booth. The bespectacled exhibitor tapped him on the shoulder and said, "I do free initial consultations but don't work on contingency. Although I am available to keep on retainer."

Trucker looked up at the booth's banner: *Larry's Luminous Litigation — Sue your past self. Settle dharmic debt.*

"I'm good," Trucker exhaled heavily. He placed a missing Ed poster on the booth's table next to a sign-up sheet and a law degree from the University of Sentience. It appeared the exhibitor went through their chiropractic program as well.

Trucker hesitantly moved back into the crowd and pushed deeper into the Galleria.

Another wave hit.

"Sales tax is satanic!"

"The illuminati put magnets in my chakras!"

"Vaccines cause the 5G demons to activate!"

"The Earth is hollow and holds the real Garden of Eden! We must get there!"

"Every time you blink, reality shifts!"

. . . and more and more.

Trucker stumbled out of the aisle again. He hadn't made it far. Only a third of his posters had been handed out, and he was becoming increasingly disoriented and dysregulated.

He leaned against the nearest booth, and the vendor eagerly clarified, without prompting or a question from the sweaty and out-of-breath Trucker, "We also help adults. In hindsight, I kinda screwed up the marketing."

Trucker looked up at the banner: *Quantic Spoon-Bending for Teens — Change Reality Through Collapsing Cutlery.*

He slapped a missing Ed poster on the table, sending cheap spoons, forks, and knives scattering everywhere.

His heart began to palpitate, skipping a beat here and there. Each breath shortened. A slight dizziness set in. He was having a legitimate physiological response, overtaxed by the sheer number of rapid assaults on his rational mind. But he had to keep moving, keep executing the plan.

He jumped back into the fight.

But before Trucker could even peel off the top poster from his stack and hand it to a passerby, a man with shoulder-length curly brown hair — wearing nothing but a speedo — grabbed Trucker hard by the shoulders, shook him, and declared emphatically, "Your spirit is not in your body! Your body is in your spirit!"

The nearly naked man had a giant logo tattooed across his chest for Laughing Yak Yoga studios.

While Trucker struggled to wrestle free from the man's surprisingly strong grip, he wanted to scream, "That is nothing but gibberish, crazy man! Put some pants on!" He fell to one knee and came face-to-Speedo with a laughing yak head printed across the swimwear.

Trucker crawled out of the aisle again and pulled himself up to a booth. He wobbled to his feet and dropped his stack of posters beside a clipboard sign-up sheet and a mug filled with pens — naturally sponsored by the HERA Network.

The smiling couple behind the counter said to Trucker, "It is a thousand-dollar deposit, and our next departure sets sail in the fall."

Trucker looked up at their banner: *Flat Earther Global Cruise Tours!*

Thoughts formed in Trucker's mind, but the words couldn't come out. It was as if his own verbal communication system rebelled and threw in the white flag. The larynx and vocal cords got together and said, "Look, Trucker. We know what you want to say. But telling these people about how their boat would need to use GPS, how that works, and blah blah blah. It just wouldn't get through to them. Not worth our time and effort. They have *global* written on their banner, for Christ's sake."

Trucker picked up his stack of posters, still wobbly but determined, and headed back into the aisle.

But then . . .

The next wave hit, and for some unexplainable reason, it had one singular theme. It was as if he'd entered a pocket of shared similar psychosis. It could have been called the messiah wave.

"I am a prophet of Jesus!"

"I am Jesus!"

"I am a prophet of God!"

"God is my prophet!"

"I am writing the new Bible!"

"I am in the Bible! Page four hundred and thirty-six!"

"I am Jesus! I am God! I manifested all religious books ever written!"

Trucker's heart and mind raced. Even knowing none of it was true — that these people weren't zombies or vampires or gods — his body didn't seem to care. He was sure every organ was malfunctioning. He had never had a heart attack nor a brain injury, but it felt like he was having both at once.

The Galleria zoomed in and out, panned right to left, and tilted back and forth like he was peering through a malfunctioning spyglass on a rocking and sinking ship at sea. He couldn't continue. He needed out.

He stumbled back toward a staircase leading back to the Elysium Level mezzanine and pulled himself upward slowly, step by step, fighting his spinning brain and pounding heart. All the while thinking: Too many Jesuses. What's even the plural of Jesus? Jesuses or Jesii?

He crawled back to his original perch, the spot where he'd planned to hunker down with a coffee and funnel cake and settle in for an old-school stakeout. Half the missing Ed posters were still under his arm. The mission was a half success; he could see the scattering of white pages dotting the parts of the Galleria below.

But it had taken its toll. He was not functioning properly. He almost started to believe he did have Quantum Fatigue Syndrome or some other made-up disease that only these people could fake-cure. But deep down, somewhere in that scrambled brain, he knew the truth: the symptoms matched all the hallmarks of a classic panic attack.

And now, panic gave way to paranoia.

He looked across the mezzanine and saw him again — the hard-boiled egg man. Just standing. Not moving. Just staring at Trucker. He was beginning to wonder if this odd, stalking figure was a figment of his imagination. Or maybe not. Maybe he should get a HERA Network security officer and sort it out.

He scanned the Elysium Level and down into the Galleria abyss. He spotted an officer in the all-black get-up. But then the flicker of paranoia caught flame — the officer was staring directly at Trucker. Not moving. Just staring. Another officer came into view. Also, just staring.

Two HERA Network security officers.

And the stalking, military-vested hard-boiled egg man.

All staring at Trucker.

The panic grew. His hands were sticky. His breath short. His heart beat like a drum at war.

"What . . . is going on?" he mumbled, trying to take a slow, grounding breath. But it wouldn't take hold. *Inhale, count to four. Hold, count to four. Exhale, count to four. Hold, count to four.* But while his mind was trying to attempt the simple countdowns, the numbers themselves were shifting into paranoia. *One lunatic oddball stalked me.*

Two black-clad weirdo goons. Three, possibly four, hours I've been stuck in this energy-healing hellscape.

And then he saw her.

Jennifer.

The out-of-place pretty woman in the light blue sundress who had helped him gather his runaway hundreds outside this madhouse. She didn't belong here. He knew it. She had a clear kindness. She hadn't asked questions or tried to sell anything. She didn't offer up conspiracies about the images on the hundred-dollar bills. No claims of a hidden "mark of the beast" in stonework of Independence Hall or that Benjamin Franklin was an alien. And she didn't sneak one into her pocket when she clearly could have. She just helped. She was the opposite of everything happening in this torture chamber of anti-truth.

Her presence had calmed him before, in mid-panic, when the wind tried to steal his money. And her presence now, at a distance and without her knowledge, began to relax Trucker. She was able to drop his heart rate, settle his breath, and bring his body back under control — even now — as she appeared to glide, not walk, toward the escalator to the third floor.

With his half-stack of missing Ed posters under his arm, Trucker had another idea.

He would ask Jennifer for help. Ask if she could help find Ed. Join the search. He'd split the bounty with her, and she could bring her *je ne sais quoi* to the whole mission. The two of them navigating this mad world of woo together. If she wanted to, of course. It wouldn't hurt to ask. She had helped before, maybe she'd be up for helping again.

And then, after they found Ed and sent him home, they could go get pancakes or cinnamon rolls and talk about the weirdness of the day.

If she wanted to.

Trucker watched Jennifer disappear up the escalator. He had to move quickly if he wanted to catch up to her.

His panic and paranoia had faded as he gripped the half-ream of his last big idea and looked over the mezzanine railing into the Galleria. He could see the missing Ed posters he'd managed to hand out, dotting the teal landscape here and there.

He looked toward the third-floor escalator, then back into the Galleria. He bounced the stack of paper in his hands once, inhaled deeply, took a big step forward, and with all of his strength, he heaved the stack far over the railing and into the open air above the ballroom.

The half-ream broke apart midair. The missing Ed posters dispersed and fluttered downward, drifting into the abyss below.

11

SERAPHIC REALM

"Pass?" the HERA Network security officer asked in a flat, unamused tone as Trucker stepped off the escalator and onto the third floor.

The officer examined the Auralite Twenty-Three Pass more closely than any other had before. He flipped it front to back, gave it a light squeeze, then let it fall back around Trucker's neck. His tone didn't change. "Enjoy your time in the Seraphic Realm."

"Hey, did a woman come through here? Short brunette hair. Blue dress. Kinda pretty?" Trucker asked.

"No," the officer replied, showing no care or emotion of any kind.

"Really?" Trucker said. "She just came up the escalator a minute or two ago."

"Didn't see her," the security officer said.

"Hmm," Trucker said, "She was —"

"I can't help you, sir," the officer cut him off. "Have a pleasant stay in the Seraphic Realm."

Trucker walked forward slowly, then glanced back. The officer was staring at him.

"Hmm," Trucker said again, looking down each direction of the third-floor concourse. "Left or right?" He looked once more at the officer, already knowing any further questions would be useless.

"Right, it is," he said — then stopped. "No, left."

A few yards from the escalator and the unhelpful HERA Network security officer, Trucker found an open door to a meeting room. An easel stood out front, propping up a dry-erase board that had been wiped clean and rewritten dozens of times, each layer leaving ghost trails behind it. It read:

Hollywood Stars Reveal The Real Truth!

Rex Del Mango

Tammi St. Vrain

Echo Kensington

& (name removed)

Brought to you by the HERA Network

Trucker had kinda-sorta heard of two of them. Possibly. He'd need to see their faces to be sure. He was almost curious about what "real truth" these celebrities were dishing out. This curiosity was probably residue from his time at the conference. Normally, celebrity opinions did not rank high on his list of cares. This would be another box to check on the list titled *How Many Ways Can the Convergence Conference Change a Person?*

Regardless of curiosity, he needed to know if Jennifer or Ed were inside.

He quietly entered the Hollywood panel discussion and slipped around a security officer leaning against the back wall. Trucker couldn't tell if the officer was asleep or just suffering from the same flat enthusiasm as the escalator pass checker.

Rex, Tammi, and Echo sat behind a long felt-covered table, each with a paper name card in front of them — which helped because

Trucker still couldn't tell who was who. Seeing their faces didn't help much. It just bumped his "kinda-sorta" to a strong "maybe."

He scanned the ninety-odd attendees for Ed or Jennifer, thinking this would be quick work. In and out.

Then Rex Del Mango pounded his fist on the table and shouted with emotional force, "Like I have been trying to say! Movies are real, people!"

Trucker did know Rex Del Mango. Well, he didn't *know* know him. But he had seen his movies. That room-chewing outburst was Rex's trademark, not a good one, but a trademark nonetheless.

Rex had been in a ton of TV shows before shifting to movies about twenty years ago. But nothing for a while. His face had been so surgically reworked that he was nearly unrecognizable. Trucker thought he should head to Heather Young's doctors, but figured the damage was already irreversibly done.

"Movies are real," Rex declared dramatically. "Transmitting truth to the public in plain sight. Especially the so-called —" he made air quotes, "— bad movies." Rex dropped his head to the table, then jerked it back up. "Those are rips in the curtain that reveal true reality. All of this is orchestrated by the cabal. Questions?"

There were two standing microphones in the aisles, which made Trucker smile. Lines were already forming.

A man at a mic asked, "So that movie about the colored pills and how we're all in a computer . . . that real? Cause it's a pretty good flick. Are we in a computer?"

"Absolutely," Rex replied, while Tammi and Echo looked like they were dozing off. "Next?"

A woman at the other mic asked, "Those romantic movies . . . with the vampires and the werewolves that aren't werewolves . . . are those real?"

"Yes, the most real," Rex said flatly. "Next."

Trucker heard a few attendees whisper, "I knew it" and "Makes sense" and "This is old news."

An elderly gentleman approached a mic. "Thank you for putting yourself at risk to bring us the truth."

Rex nodded, "It needs to be said. Do you have a question?"

"No," the elderly gentleman replied. "I just want to thank you for your work and service."

"You're very welcome," Rex said, trying to summon fake tears by subtly pinching the side of his cheek, "This mission has cost me greatly." The small tear vanished as he continued, "One caveat. Documentaries. They're all misinformation campaigns. All lies. Especially the good ones. Once again, orchestrated by the cabal. Next question."

Trucker stepped to the mic. He scanned the crowd and asked, "Is there an Ed Young here? Or a Jennifer?"

No man in attendance spoke. But five women raised their hands.

"My name is Jennifer," one said.

Trucker glanced at them, "Wrong Jennifers, but thank you."

"What are you doing, man?" Rex dropped the theatrics. "Do you have a real question?"

"Umm," Trucker stalled. "I really liked you as the voice of the squirrel in that animated movie. You had to find your missing confidence, right? That was you . . . I think."

"Yes!" Rex lit back up and kicked up the dramatics to eleven. "One of the most powerful and impactful performances of my career. I *became* Squirrelly. Very proud of that work."

"Is it real?" Trucker asked. "Do squirrels lack confidence?"

"Yes," Rex said with another fake tear. "I think we all could use a little more confidence. There's a little bit of Squirrelly in all of us."

The five Jennifers and the rest of the room rose to their feet in applause. Rex stood and accepted his standing ovation.

The roaring applause followed Trucker as he left the Hollywood Panel on the Real Truth and wandered further into the third-floor concourse, the Seraphic Realm. He thought about Squirrelly's message and the reason for Rex's standing O. It sure sounded good. Everybody should be more confident in who they are, right?

But how accurate was that message, really?

What if who they are is an absolute lunatic aardvark — or worse, an already-wannabe crocodile confidence man or woman, like many of the folks peddling mumbo jumbo around this joint?

They didn't need to be more like Squirrelly. They needed to be a whole lot less.

Trucker supposed there probably already existed an animated movie about a real piece-of-work walrus searching for his humility. But if it didn't, he'd like to see it made. Just not by him. He couldn't draw worth a damn.

LEGENDARY DOUG MARTINO CHANNELING KHALOOD!

A doorman stood outside the closed hall where the legendary Doug Martino was channeling *Khalood!* Or so said all the signage and marketing materials. It appeared to be unaffiliated with the HERA Network or at least wanted to appear that way. It was one of the few areas not stamped with the corporate name.

The doorman didn't seem to be associated with the black-uniform-obsessed network either. He looked to be about fifteen years Trucker's senior and could easily pass for the maître d' at a restaurant worth going to. There was an edge to his eyes, and his hand rested loosely on a portable point-of-sale credit-card reader strapped to his waist.

"Hey," Trucker approached. "Excuse me, umm —"

Doug Martino's doorman cut him off, though Trucker was having a hard time forming a useful thought anyway. "You don't look so hot, chief."

"Been a long day," Trucker confirmed, pointing to the poster of Doug channeling *Khalood!* "How much?"

"Three twenty-five plus tax," the doorman said dryly, with a thick East Coast accent.

"Martino," Trucker said, still looking at the poster. "Isn't he the brother of that singer?"

"Cousin," the doorman corrected.

"Right. What's he do in there?" Trucker asked.

"Gives advice."

"As an alien?"

"Yeah," the doorman said, doing air quotes not unlike Rex. "*Channels* him."

"Don't you find that . . . strange?" Trucker was pushing his luck, but he had a feeling.

"Yeah, but not really," the doorman replied. "It's decent advice. He stays away from medical stuff for the most part. Simple things. Don't forget to brush your teeth. Be a better person."

"From a channeled alien named *Khalood*?"

"Yip," the doorman said. "Don't forget the exclamation mark. Part of his extraterrestrial birth name, I think. And trademarked."

"Gotcha," Trucker said.

"Apparently, he tried it other ways," the doorman went on, "but people wouldn't take advice from the second cousin of a singer-songwriter from the fifties. Or at least not pay for it."

"I don't know. I think a few people around here would pay for advice from a toaster," Trucker said.

"True," the doorman agreed.

Trucker glanced at the doorman's shoes. "On the force?"

"Thirty years back east, retired," the doorman confirmed. "You?"

"Nah. Couldn't pass the physical."

"Really? Not that hard."

"Gotta show up to pass it."

"Right."

"Hey," Trucker said and pulled out his phone, "I'm looking for this kid for his mom. But I don't want to pay the —"

"He's not in there."

"Thank you," Trucker said, about to leave, but stopped. "Oh, didn't happen to see a brunette woman walk past here? Pretty. Blue dress."

"No," the doorman said. "Good luck finding the kid. If I see him, I'll send him home to mom."

"Thanks again," Trucker said sincerely.

"No problem."

RAINBOWS: GOD'S CHEMTRAILS

The door to the meeting room, a few yards down from the *Khalood!* doorman, was closed tight. A customary HERA Network dry-erase board on an easel stood just outside.

Doctor Bill Diotellavi, DC

Author of

Rainbows: God's Chemtrails

Trucker's left eyebrow twitched and rose involuntarily as he read the board.

"I mean, I gotta go in. Jennifer or Ed may be in there," Trucker said to himself while he reread the board and looked around the concourse. "Helllloooo?" he called out to no one, though he half-expected a HERA doorman to appear from the shadows like a corporate ninja.

He peered through the door's narrow frosted window. He couldn't see much, but he could tell the discussion was already underway. A man stood on stage behind a mic'd lectern beside a pyramid-shaped stack of books. Trucker figured shaping them into an actual rainbow would've taken too much effort.

He glanced around again, just to make sure no one was going to pop out and stop him.

No one did.

"Yup. Here we go," he said as he swung open the door. He was so focused, determined, and single-minded about what lay ahead that he didn't bother closing it behind him.

A HERA Network usher just inside placed a hand on his shoulder and said, "Sir —"

Trucker cut him off. "I know, I know, I'm running late, but —" he waved to the man at the mic'd lectern, who gave a slow, confused wave back. "See? Bill knows me. Like I was saying, I know I'm running late. But I'm here now. So I'll just go on up and join Doctor . . . Dostoevsky? . . . now."

"Diotellavi."

"Exactly," Trucker said. "I'm just gonna head on up now. Cool?" He gave the usher a thumbs-up, then turned to Doctor Diotellavi and gave him a thumbs-up, too. The doctor returned it, still confused. All three exchanged a string of awkward thumbs-ups as Trucker walked down the aisle and made his way to the stage.

He leaned in and whispered to the doctor, covering the microphone. "Doctor Diooo . . ."

"Diotellavi."

"Yes, Doctor Diotellavi," Trucker said smoothly. "I let Jeff back there —" he gestured to the usher, who waved again, "— I let him know I was running late, but I'm here now."

"And who are you?" Diotellavi asked.

"Who am I? I am Doctor Irwin Jessica Fletcher, renowned rainbow expert," Trucker explained.

"I wasn't aware there would be anyone joining me for my discussion," Diotellavi said.

"Yeah, Jeff said he forgot to tell you about your surprise guest," Trucker gave Jeff another thumbs-up. Jeff returned one on cue.

"I don't need a surpr —" Trucker gently placed a hand over Diotellavi's mouth.

"You wanna sell some books, Billy?" Trucker whispered, forcefully but cheerfully, like a discount cruise ship pitchman. "I move units. My audience is far and wide. My publications regularly hit the top twenty in Bhutan, Grenada, and both North *and* South Macedonia. I am also featured heavily in magazines and blogs like *Bunking the Debunkers* and *Skeptics Schmeptics*."

He stared into Diotellavi's eyes.

"I could go on with my credentials, but I can see I've clearly impressed you."

Trucker slapped the lectern. A screech of feedback jolted the room.

"Let's sell some books, Bill. Let's do this thing."

Doctor Diotellavi took a slow step back, then gave a little shrug, and waved an arm toward the lectern in a gesture of reluctant surrender. He added a polite clap. Jeff the usher joined in, followed by the audience, giving Trucker a warm welcome as he took the mic.

"I'd like to thank Doctor Bill —" Trucker tried to pronounce his last name but gave up on the butchered attempt. He covered the microphone, leaned over, and whispered to Diotellavi, "You a real Doctor, Billy?" Diotellavi looked uncomfortable as Trucker continued. "Don't worry. I won't check the paperwork," Trucker winked.

He uncovered the mic and stood up straight.

Trucker spoke clearly and professionally into the microphone as he looked over the crowd of attendees for Jennifer and Ed, "I would sincerely like to thank the sponsor for this important discussion, the HERA Network. And of course, the fine doctor. Let's give them a hand." He started clapping, and once again Jeff, Bill, and the audience joined in. Trucker couldn't see Ed or Jennifer anywhere in the room.

"Now, to the matter at hand: rainbows," Trucker's tone shifted to something a little more serious but warm and passionate. "I have not yet had a chance to peruse Billy's work here," he gestured toward the pyramid of books. "Can anyone get me up to speed?"

Doctor Diotellavi leaned forward to respond, but a young man in priority seating beat him to it.

"The doctor was saying the Greek goddess Iris isn't a myth. She's real. And she lives within the rainbows themselves."

Trucker looked at the doctor, who nodded in affirmation.

The man continued, "And that her mission of sending messages from God has never ended."

More nods from the doctor.

"And that all we need to do is touch the rainbow. And we will receive downloads or direct messages from God through Iris."

The doctor continued nodding.

"He said he's technically a prophet of Iris. And that he has followers all over the world set on the mission of touching rainbows. All of them posing as storm chasers."

Another nod from the doctor.

"He asked us if we'd like to join his organization. To become storm chasers and talk to God."

Trucker looked at the doctor, then at the crowd. He could leave — Jennifer and Ed weren't here — but the search was only one reason why he'd walked into this room. There was another.

"Prophet of Iris? Followers? That sounds an awful lot like a cul—" Trucker stopped mid-word as he noticed Jeff, the thumbs-upping usher, was now giving a very pronounced thumbs-down with his face.

"Regardless," Trucker said, "let's talk about rainbows. I like rainbows. Always have since I was a kid. Tried to chase a few down myself," he added kindly and noticed the audience members were paying attention.

"So, I like rainbows. Always have. At some point, I stopped chasing them and started looking into what they actually were." He paused. "Turns out, humans have the whole rainbow thing figured out. A lot of smart humans, smarter than me. They nailed this one."

"Aristotle laid the groundwork. He noticed the sunlight, the moisture, and the same shape and direction every time. He didn't have the tools to figure out much more, but solid attempt from ol' Aristots."

"In the Middle Ages, rainbows were seen as neon signs from God. A promise — 'Hey, sorry about that water-based mass-murder genocide thing. Noah and the boat? Won't do that again. Here's a colorful pinky promise in the sky.' Meanwhile, a fella named Ibn al-Haytham —" Trucker pronounced his name perfectly. "— was working on optics. Laid some serious scaffolding on Ari's rainbow foundation."

Trucker thought he might be losing the attendees, but he wasn't. He also noticed a new member of the audience. Jennifer was standing just outside the doorway. Leaning on its frame and listening intently.

"So here comes the Renaissance. A couple of friars and monks — Bacon and Freiberg — start sorting things out. Get shockingly close to our modern understanding of the rainbow."

"Enter René Descartes and Isaac Newton, about three hundred years after our smart, friendly friars and monks. Rene's running experiments, doing math, working out all the angles. Newton rocks a prism, not to summon ghosts, but to split white light into a spectrum."

Doctor Diotellavi stood and moved behind Trucker. The usher didn't look thrilled, but he also looked unsure about whether tackling someone mid-rainbow-lecture was policy.

Trucker knew that his time was limited. And that much like The Velvet Elbow bar, he was about to get tossed out of here. But he pressed on.

"A couple hundred more years pass. More smarties refine the understanding of rainbows." Trucker paused and looked over the crowd and at the doorway to Jennifer directly.

"All of that doesn't tell you how you should *feel* when you see a rainbow. If you feel blissful . . . warm and fuzzy, then that is wonderful. But it doesn't mean there is a leprechaun with a pot of gold on one end. Or a winged goddess beaming down divine downloads."

"What it does mean is that light hit water just right. It refracted — bent. Reflected inside that little water droplet, played a little game of hopscotch, then refracted, or bent, again on the way out. Each bend a different wavelength of light, from red to violet. And that is a rainbow."

He paused and looked at Jennifer.

"And you *should* feel warm and fuzzy. Because if a ray of light hitting a drop of water and creating a spectrum of beauty across the sky isn't miraculous, nothing is. But it's not magic. It's not mystic. It's not a goddess. It's explainable. It's science. Started by Aristotle, and its understanding has been refined for thousands of years by smart people, people who were really good at math, who probably wouldn't pay hundreds of dollars to hear how their dog was Moses in a past life," Trucker looked toward the door, but Jennifer was gone.

"It is impossible . . . physically . . . scientifically . . . impossible to touch a rainbow. But if you'd let it, a rainbow can touch you."

Silence.

"Any questions?" Trucker asked as Doctor Diotellavi firmly pushed him away from the lectern.

"Yes, I have a question," said the man in priority seating as he stood. "Doctor Diotellavi? Will we get our own storm-chasing cars? And can I pick a new name for myself? I would like to be known as Thunderbird Jones."

Trucker ran up the aisle and out the door before the doctor, the usher, or any of the future storm-chasing cult members could admonish his highly accurate, if not all-encompassing, speech on rainbows. He spilled out into the third-floor concourse of the Seraphic Realm.

But Jennifer was gone.

He looked up and down the concourse, but she was nowhere to be found. Someone else, however, was lurking. That someone turned the corner and marched straight for Trucker.

It was the hard-boiled egg man, still donning his military vest with road-construction trim.

"Good gawd," Trucker mumbled to himself. "Here we go."

The odd individual had Trucker in his sights and stomped to within an awkward few inches of him. He was so extremely, inappropriately close that Trucker could smell his hot breath. A mixture of a school cafeteria, a morning cigarette, and a six-pack of light beer. His voice was slow and low.

"You look familiar, dude. I saw you at the Appalachian Mountain Conference, or maybe it was Connection in the Desert," he said.

"Pretty sure that's not possible," Trucker replied.

"No," hard-boiled egg man said. "You were there."

"Nah," Trucker said. "I haven't been to those. Haven't even heard of them."

The hard-boiled egg man grabbed hold of Trucker's Auralite Twenty-Three Pass. "Nah, I remember you. Even remember your name, Irwin Jessica Fletcher. It's a weird one." He dropped the pass. "We were on a panel together. The impending forced vaccines, ghost containment, and UFO disclosure. We did some good work."

"That's quite the combo of topics, and thanks," Trucker said, "but you've got the wrong guy."

"No," hard-boiled egg man insisted. "It was you. I know what I am talking about. I remember."

"I —" Trucker tried to think of a way out of the conversation without just pushing the guy over.

"We went to that Italian place afterward, Esterno," hard-boiled egg man said. "You showed me pictures of your kids. That red-headed waitress was flirting with us."

Trucker raised his eyebrows and exhaled slowly. "Sir, please don't take offense, because none is intended, but you are very confused. You've got the wrong person."

"You sayin' I'm lying?" hard-boiled egg man snapped.

"No, I said you must be confused," Trucker said, trying to bring down the temperature.

"You're calling me a liar!" hard-boiled egg man shouted, then reached inside his military vest as if about to pull a gun.

Trucker saw his life flash before his eyes. Every victory. Every defeat. Every love. Every loss. Every bad decision he regretted, and a few good ones that he was proud of. He wondered where the hell Ed Young really was. He saw himself as a young boy chasing rainbows, not knowing that years later he'd be taken out by a man who looked like an egg boiled to perfection at a convention filled with lunatics.

He saw young Trucker shaking his head at this ending — so old Trucker tried to prevent it.

He grabbed for the hard-boiled egg man's gun. They struggled for what seemed like forever, until somehow the hard-boiled egg man got the upper hand and Trucker fell hard to the ground.

Trucker looked up at the hard-boiled egg man and down the barrel of . . .

"Umm," Trucker said, confused. "What . . . is that thing?"

He clambered to his feet and brushed off his pants for some reason. He looked at the device pointed at him.

"What do ya got there?" Trucker asked carefully.

The hard-boiled egg man proudly showed it off. He displayed each side, top, and bottom of the contraption. It looked like a glue gun with three broken TV remote controls stuck to it.

The slight paradox of how someone hot-glued something to a hot glue gun ran through Trucker's mind. But only for a moment. He realized that this was the kind of man who would own a twelve-pack of hot glue guns.

The hard-boiled egg man bounced it in his hands. "Nice, right? It is also infused with homeopathic cannabis aromatics."

Trucker thought for a moment, "You smoked grass while gluing it together?"

"No," hard-boiled egg man explained. "I baked pot brownies. But left the oven cracked open."

"I see," Trucker said wryly. "Smart."

Hard-boiled egg man admired his invention, "It is just like we talked about. Perfect."

"Listen, this is the first time we've spoken," Trucker said. "But . . . what is it?"

"It's a handheld ghost detection device," hard-boiled egg man said. "Also tunes guitars and heals skin cancer, psoriasis, 5G EMF poisoning, kidney stones, migraines . . . and some studies suggest fibromyalgia."

"You've already had studies done on . . . this thing?" Trucker asked.

The hard-boiled egg man ignored the question. "This is just the prototype. Almost sounds too good to be true, doesn't it?"

"It does," Trucker confirmed.

"Right? It's amazing. Can't wait to get them into production."

"Right. And how much you thinkin' about sellin' these for?" Trucker asked for some reason.

"Well," hard-boiled egg man said, "that's where you come in. We talked all about this at dinner. I can't believe you don't remember."

"We've never had dinner. But go on."

"You invest in the original production line. About five grand."

"Umm-hmm," Trucker grunted.

"Then you get three friends to invest another five grand each," hard-boiled egg man smiled.

"Pyramid scheme," Trucker said. "You are describing a pyramid scheme exactly. Which is impressive. Most people around here dress it up a bit. You should track down one of the energy-healing sticker ladies." Trucker held up the back of his stickered hand. "Get some pointers. They're a little smoother on the delivery."

The hard-boiled egg man wasn't angry, just flustered. "There's a conspiracy against pyramid schemes!" he shouted. "*They* don't want the average Joe to know how powerful the pyramid really is. Dates all the way back to the nineteen-sixties, when the Lemurian Pyramid was discovered in the Arctic Circle."

Trucker sighed and relaxed, realizing he had only been stalked by an idiot trying to run a remote-control glue-gun scam, and not someone immediately dangerous.

"Ya know," Trucker said, "everything's a conspiracy if you don't really understand anything."

"Wake up," hard-boiled egg man pleaded. "That kind of talk sounds just like what *they* want you to believe. Where'd you hear that?"

"Bumper sticker," Trucker said. "On a Honda. In an Albertsons parking lot."

Hard-boiled egg man shook his head. "That's how *they* do it. Infest every corner of our lives. One bumper can take that message millions of miles."

"Millions?" Trucker asked. "It was on a Honda. Not a spaceship."

"How do you know the Honda wasn't a spaceship?" hard-boiled egg man asked intensely.

"Umm . . . yeah . . . I . . ." Trucker searched for a way out. "Oh — astral funnel cakes! I was gonna go check out the organic astral funnel cakes at the Third Eye Celestial Café."

"Me, too! We can try them together."

"I'm sorry, but this is a journey I must travel alone."

Trucker began walking away, then stopped. Held up his phone and sighed, "You haven't seen this guy, have you?"

"She's hot," hard-boiled egg man said.

"No, the m —" Trucker stopped himself. "Never mind. Good luck with . . . just good luck."

Trucker hustled down the third-floor concourse, away from the hard-boiled egg man. It had been an excuse to escape, but now he started to think an astral funnel cake would hit the spot. He hadn't eaten all day, besides the cookie-dough cone, and last night had been rough. His sleep had also been cut short thanks to the personal wake-up call from Heather Young.

All of which, he imagined, contributed to his early panic and paranoia. He could fight through the lack of sleep, as he had done before in the past — for more days than he could remember. But the growing growling in his belly made it clear that an astral funnel cake was required to continue the search for Ed.

Trucker had his postcard theme-park map out, flipping it one way and then the other, figuring out the fastest way to the Third Eye Celestial Café, when three HERA Network security officers approached.

"Hey," Trucker said. "Good, I was just gonna look for one of you guys. There's this oddball," Trucker pointed in the last known direction of the hard-boiled egg man. "This fella. . . super weird, and for this place, that's an achievement. Been stalking me for hours now. Don't worry though, he's only packin' hot glue."

"We're here for you. To talk to *you*," the security officer on the right announced with an air of authority.

Trucker paused and quickly tried to size up the situation.

"Hey, with a little hindsight, I know I shouldn't have tossed all those papers into the Galleria. Dumb move." He started digging into his stash of hundred-dollar bills, "I'll pay for the cleanup. You boys might accidentally pick up some of the other thousands of pamphlets lying around while you're at it."

"That's not why we need to speak with you," said the officer in the middle.

Trucker thought for another moment and looked back toward the *Rainbows: God's Chemtrails* sign. "I was out of line for hijacking the rainbow room?"

"That's not it either," said the officer on the right.

"Well, I probably offended the sensibilities of many," Trucker said, thinking hard. "Those preppers in the lobby? But I doubt they'd run to the law."

"The exhibitors from the Pre-Ascension Prep Portal did file a verbal harassment complaint," said the officer in the middle, "but that's not why we're speaking to you either."

Trucker paused. "I could keep guessing, or we could kill the suspense. What did I do to get all three of ya here?"

"You stole a pen," said the officer on the left.

"A pen," Trucker repeated. "When did I — ohhh." He remembered writing directions for AK. "Yeah," he dug into his pocket, "I borrowed this from someone walking by. Here it is," Trucker pulled out the HERA Network pen and wrapped a hundred-dollar bill around it. "You can give it back to him. Right as rain."

"Are you bribing us, sir?" said the officer on the right.

"No," Trucker fumbled. "It's for the guy. Penless guy. Let's call it a rental." He looked at the unamused officers and pulled out another hundred, wrapping it around the first. "And late fee."

"Did you threaten the man when you stole his pen?" asked the officer in the middle.

"Threaten? I don't remember a threat," Trucker said honestly.

The officer in the middle pulled out a phone and played a video, security footage angled from the ceiling in the second-floor reception area near AK's camping booth. It showed an enraged Trucker pulling a pen from behind the man's ear and yelling at him before scribbling on the wrinkled pendulum paper.

"Did you curse at him," asked the middle officer, "and tell him to keep walking?"

"You know," Trucker said, "I did. It was a tense moment."

"You seem rather tense now. Is that moment over?" asked the officer on the left.

Trucker remained silent.

"We go to great lengths here at the Convergence Conference to create an atmosphere of ascension and abundance in all forms," said the officer on the left.

"Do you know who you stole that pen from?" asked the officer on the right.

"No," Trucker said. "How would I ev —"

"A Celestial Pass holder," said the middle officer.

"That's the one above —" Trucker held up his Auralite Pass. "That's the one above this one. The kid in the ticket booth said Celestial was only if I wanted a hotel room. No mention of a Star-Bellied Sneetches-style caste system. Might've upgraded."

"His pass status is irrelevant," the middle officer said.

"Well, you guys brought it up," Trucker pointed out.

"The guest you threatened is the nephew of someone very important to us at the HERA Network," said the officer in the middle.

"Which, in regard to the grand plan, is also irrelevant. But a part of the truth," added the officer on the left.

Trucker became slightly more concerned, enough to refrain from pointing out to the officers that they kept mentioning things they claimed were irrelevant.

"We go to great lengths to enhance and nurture the natural quantum frequency and overall energy harmonics of the Convergence Conference," said the officer on the left. "The consciousness and ascension of all attendees is our number-one priority."

"We are not asking you to leave," said the officer in the middle.

"We believe in change and transformation at the HERA Network," the officer on the right added, "not just for those within these walls . . . but the world at large."

"Change is possible, Mister Irwin Jessica Fletcher," said the officer on the left.

"We would like you to consider your behavior moving forward," he continued. "Join us — and the other attendees — in the process of ascension, transformation, and change."

"It is possible," repeated the officer in the middle.

Trucker looked from one officer to the next, "You know, thank you for this wake-up call." He was not thankful. His intuition was firing and misfiring like a car engine struggling to ignite. He didn't know about this change the officers were more than suggesting. But he did know he needed something to balance his system. And fast.

He pulled out the postcard map. "I think I just need to take a break. There's a lounge around here somewhere, right?"

The officer on the left smiled, "Yes, the Lapis Lazuli Lounge." He pointed down the third-floor concourse.

"Thank you, gentlemen," Trucker said and took his leave in the direction the officer suggested, without waiting for their approval or dismissal.

"Enjoy the rest of your time at the conference," one of them offered, but an unusual hallway echo made it sound like all three had said it at the same time. Trucker raised his star-stickered hand, waved farewell without looking back, and continued to the Lapis Lazuli Lounge.

12

LAPIS LAZULI LOUNGE

The curved banquette in the far corner had been turned into a sale station for *ethical* and *enlightened* hard seltzer. Two varieties were available: something called *ElixEarth* and *Luna Fizz*. A vinyl sign poorly wrapped around the corner section of the wall laid out the reason for purchasing a can or three: Made with alkaline water and sacred sound resonance. It claimed to be liquid mana of the divine and boasted moonlight-infused, bio-holographic living water, ultraviolet ozonation, and vortex-induced something or other.

The man out front, cans in hand pitching the seltzer, was either an aged rock 'n' roll guitarist whose bandmates no-showed on him — or he wished that were the case. His name was Tony Temple, so said the dialogue bubble above the life-size cardboard cutout of himself that stood just off his left shoulder. He had a gravelly, cracked voice that barked at Trucker as he walked into the lounge.

Trucker raised his hand to the twin Tonies in the universal "I'm good" gesture, but it leaned more toward "Stop. Don't even try."

The third-floor hotel bar was normally known simply as the Rosewood Parlor. It was a somewhat hidden-away spot, and the interior was as simple and elegant as the name suggested. That was before its temporary transformation into the Lapis Lazuli Lounge. Of all the changes made to the hotel for Ascend-A-Palooza, Trucker felt slightly more affected by what they did to the Parlor. Not for any profound reason other than he had visited the bar far more often than he had ever had reason to stay at the hotel.

Along with Tony Temple's sales corner, the namesake-carved furnishings had all been covered with teal, purple, and semi-psychedelic-patterned drapery. Small sheer sacks filled with deep-blue stones were tied together with plastic meditating figures and assembled into cheap-looking centerpieces that held temporary drink menus. Trucker had no desire to read them. He had reached his limit of pseudo-scientific-spiritual gobbledygook by the time he'd finished reading the bus-bench advertisement for the conference. Everything after had been thrust upon him against his will. He didn't need to know what the HERA Network was calling a martini.

The lounge was not brimming with activity like the rest of the conference, but it did have a handful of patrons milling about here and there and a few at the bartop. Trucker moved around them, found a spot to himself, pulled out a stool, and half-collapsed.

He straightened up as a bartender wearing a standard LAX Rosewood uniform greeted him promptly with a napkin. Much like the business center itself, the Rosewood Parlor's professional staff remained untouched and unaffected by HERA. Trucker assumed the bartender had been spared a teal shirt and apron thanks to the local hospitality union. Really, he didn't care why. He was just grateful for a drop of normalcy.

"What are you having today?" the bartender asked. "Cocktail? Beer?"

"Nah," Trucker said. "Quit drinking ten years ago."

"That's great," the bartender said sincerely. "How about a soda? Glass of water?"

"How about a glass of unenlightened water," Trucker said.

"Sure thing," the bartender filled a glass with ice, hit it with plain water from the bar gun, and set it neatly on the napkin.

Trucker pulled out a hundred and slid it to the bartender, "I won't need anything else. Just gonna sit here for a bit and rest."

The bartender thanked him, took the money, and left him in peace.

Before Trucker could enjoy a single sip of water in silence, Tony Temple saddled up next to him and slammed a can of *ElixEarth* and a can of *Luna Fizz* on the bar top, one after the other, with a startling **thump, thump**.

"This stuff right here," Tony said with his raspy, nearly unintelligible radio-announcer inflection and delivery. "It will change your life."

"It's not true," Trucker said, staring straight ahead.

"Oh, it's true, brother," Tony insisted. "Scientists have actually been shocked by our moonlight-infused, alkaline, and bioholographic living-water fermentation process."

"I'm not talking about your shitty seltzer," Trucker said without looking at him and took a drink of his water.

"It's not true," Trucker quietly repeated, ignoring the wannabe rock star. "I tell people I quit drinking ten years ago, but that's not really the truth. It's only kinda true."

He took a sip of water and continued, "After walking through this place today — whatever the hell this thing is — and coming face-to-face with the sheer number of people who, for one reason or another, have a spurious relationship with the truth at best . . . and flat out ignore it at worst," he paused. "Kinda true isn't enough. And I realize it never should have been enough."

Trucker inhaled deeply and exhaled slowly. "I don't want to be that way anymore. I don't want to knowingly be *kinda* true. About anything."

He took another sip. "I quit drinking ten years ago. Quit drinkin' 'round the clock, day after day. It was so long ago I don't even remember exactly why I stopped. But I did. For a while. Years."

Another sip. "But then sometime, somehow, I started again. Not every day, not like I used to. But enough. I don't remember when or why it happened — but I pretend it didn't."

"I still tell people I quit drinking ten years ago. Because it sounds good. And it's kinda true," Trucker said. "And I've said it so often that even I believe it."

He took a big drink of water, "Then I run into people who remind me that the truth exists. That I was blind drunk yelling about rainbows. Or that I peed in their enchanter's cauldron." He paused and shook his head, "I wake up half-hungover and still mostly drunk this morning and agree to help a lady find her son because she flashed a stack of money at me. And I can't say *no*."

Trucker finished the last of his water, "Hell, I'm probably still kinda drunk now. Don't remember much about last night."

"This is no way to live," he said. "Living in a permanent state of kinda true. Which, in the end, is just a lie."

He didn't know when Tony Temple wandered off to his next victim, and he didn't care. Trucker pulled out his phone and flipped through the photos of Ed and his mother. "I'm gonna find ya. And I'm going to get you home."

He waved down the bartender, held up his phone, and swiped through the photos. "Seen this kid? Not the lady — the kid."

"Haven't seen him."

"How about a pretty, short-haired brunette woman in a blue sundress? She has a way —"

"— Jennifer," the bartender said. "I don't know her, but I know who you are talking about. She's right down the hall," he said, pointing. "Few doors down."

"Thanks," Trucker put another hundred on the bar top and walked out of the Rosewood Parlor.

13

THE RADIANT WAY

"One . . . two . . . three . . ." Trucker had always assumed that a few meant four, but he couldn't see any of the usual signage he'd come across earlier in the hallways of the Convergence Conference. There was no HERA-approved easel or dry-erase board indicating anything was occurring or being discussed as he came closer to the fourth doorway.

But there she was — Jennifer. She stood in front of a group of attendees.

He stood in the doorway and watched her. Her audience was small. Far smaller than the near-death superhero psychologist's congregation, smaller than the hyper Hollywood almost-icon Rex Del Mango's fanbase, and even fewer than the misinformed meteorologist's storm-chasing wannabe cult members.

Jennifer had no books for sale. No stage. No lectern. She didn't even have a microphone. Just her kind, warm, and passionate voice for those that gathered.

She saw Trucker, smiled, and gave him a small, cutesy, discreet wave, motioning for him to come in. Then she continued:

"There is nothing wrong with you. You are not broken. Others may make you think you are broken, that there is something wrong with you. That little voice may be saying the same thing. That you are broken. That there is something wrong with you. But none of that is true."

Trucker didn't want to be a distraction. Though there was open priority seating available in the front, he thought it best to just find a spot in the back. And then, when she was finished with her presentation or speech or whatever this was, he'd talk to her. Let her know he could use her help again. That he'd like her to join him in the search for Ed. Two heads being better than one, and all that. They'd split the fee. And maybe, after they'd found Ed and sent him on his way, the two of them could go have pancakes or cinnamon rolls to celebrate.

He quietly excused himself and apologized as he maneuvered past the knees of those in the back row. He found a spot and sat down.

Scanning the room, he looked for Ed. Maybe he and Jennifer could skip straight to the celebration.

There was no sign of Ed. But everyone else? Riveted. They hung on her every word.

Trucker listened.

"The world is broken around you. It's okay to see that. Okay to admit that there is something wrong with the world. That brokenness makes the little negative and judgmental voice inside yourself louder, makes it seem more important. It makes the voices of others louder, too. And there are plenty of people — even here at this very conference — who feed those voices."

The woman next to Trucker was struggling to stay awake. She kept brushing against him like she was fighting to stay upright.

Trucker kept listening.

"I can help you lower the volume of those voices. But really, I would just be reminding you of something you already know, but maybe have forgotten. Your gut, your internal compass, the broken world throws it off. I can help you help yourself to reignite that . . . to reignite your intuition.

Now Trucker was more than interested. He was equally riveted.

The woman to his left was struggling to not involuntarily count sheep and catch the Zs that were desperately trying to take over. She jerked suddenly and hit Trucker's stickered hand hard. She turned to him, wide-eyed and apologetic.

"I am so, so sorry," she whispered.

Trucker turned to whisper back, "No worries." Until he saw him over the sleepy woman's shoulder.

Ed.

"Oh my gawd, oh my gawd," Trucker whispered. He reached over the sleepy woman, slapped Ed's knee, and whispered louder. "Ed! Ed!"

Ed turned slowly. Bloodshot eyes, sunken eyes. Like he hadn't seen a pillow since long before The Velvet Elbow.

The sleepy woman swatted Trucker's hand away and whispered, "Knock it off! I said I'm sorry!"

Trucker ignored her and tried to get Ed's attention again as he turned back toward Jennifer. He kept trying to slap Ed's now-found knee as he whispered, "Ed! My name is Trucker. Your mom sent me to find you."

The sleepy woman kept trying to stop Trucker's slapping hand, while Ed turned back, confused, and said, "You're a trucker?"

"No," Trucker tried to explain quickly and quietly. "My *name* is Trucker. Your mom sent me to find you. She's worried."

The sleepy woman grabbed a hold of Trucker's arm and asked in an almost slur, "How do you know my brother? What did Mom do?"

"Brother? Mom?" Trucker asked, confused, and then held up his phone to the sleepy woman. He showed her the photos, motioned toward the door, and whispered, "Let's sort this out. Hallway."

Trucker stood up, joined by the sleepy woman who helped Ed to his feet, and together the three walked out into the hallway of the Seraphic Realm.

Jennifer had continued her speech through all of the slapping, whispering, and walking out. She appeared unfazed by any of it. "The truth matters," she had said. "Language matters. We can't just pretend that there are no weeds in the garden. In the world and within ourselves. Because just a few weeds can overrun everything. And then nothing of value can grow. I can help you. I can help you find a way through this crazy mad weed-filled world. I like to call this way *The Radiant Way*. But really, it doesn't need to have a name. You can call *The Radiant Way* anything you'd like. You can make it your own."

Trucker, Ed, and the sleepy woman who was desperately trying to wake up all stood in a small huddle just outside Jennifer's doorway. The sleepy woman and Ed looked exhausted. Their eyes were red, bloodshot, and puffy, with lids that hung in the shadows of dark circles. Their skin was pale, dry, and dull with dehydration. Trucker had seen this face before, in his own mirror. They both seemed drunk, but he knew they weren't.

"What is going on?" the sleepy woman asked. "Who are you, and why do you have pictures of Ed and Mom?"

Ed was completely zoned out and stared back into Jennifer's room.

"Maybe you should start," Trucker said to the sleepy woman.

"No," she snapped. "You're the one with the problem here."

"Okay," Trucker relented. "My name's Trucker. I am not a truck driver, but that is not the first time that mistake has been made. I am an investigator. Ed's mom showed up at my . . . office . . . this morning and hired me to find him." He glanced at Ed, who hadn't moved, then turned back to the sleepy woman, "Now you. Who are you? And what is going on?"

"This is just like her," the sleepy woman said, shaking her head.

"Just like who?" Trucker asked.

"This is just like Mom," the sleepy woman said. "Ed's fine. I am fine, too."

"You're Ed's sister?" Trucker asked.

"Yes, genius," the sleepy woman said, "I'm Ida. And we are both fine. Her baby is gone for a few hours, and she flips out. Don't suppose she hired you to find me, too, did she?"

"Look, you two are not fine. It has been over two days, not a few hours," Trucker said, then added something that could be considered a kinda truth, "and yeah, the fee covers the both of you."

"Two days?" the sleepy Ida was beginning to wake up.

"Yup," Trucker said, glancing at Ed who moved closer to the doorway and was still locked on Jennifer's voice

Ed listened closely as Jennifer spoke from inside the room: "I have such a love for everyone in this group. A love I cannot properly express. You all have a desire to become better. A desire to raise the standards of your lives. You all have come close. But together we can help one another complete the journey of becoming better and remove all that limits us."

In the hallway, Trucker turned to Ida, "Why don't you start from the beginning?"

"It hasn't been two days?" Ida didn't believe it and shook her head. "No."

"It has," Trucker confirmed. "It's Saturday."

"No. No. No," Ida began to pace and panic, becoming more alert and angry with every step. She pulled out her phone. Dead. "It can't be."

"It can. And it is," Trucker quietly and adamantly confirmed.

Ida collapsed to the floor and leaned against the wall outside the doorway. "My dissertation proposal . . . hearing," she was in shock. " . . . it . . . was . . . Friday."

"Hey," Trucker said gently, "Focus. What happened?"

Ida was despondent but eventually said, "Ed . . . Ed and I went out on Thursday afternoon. I had some time. A few hours. I am a PhD student . . . third year at UCLA. Or — I was." She put her head in her hands.

Trucker kept checking on Ed, who was not coming out of his wobble and still listening to Jennifer from the doorway.

"I was going to meet some friends, but they canceled. So, I called Eddie. I love Eddie," Ida said. "But he has to get out of that house. And Mom . . . is Mom. It's all unhealthy."

"Love you, too, Sis," Ed said as he kept his attention on Jennifer.

Ida continued to piece things together for Trucker and herself, "So, we go out to a bar on Thursday afternoon. Have a few drinks. I needed to get back, but Eddie wanted to talk to some psychic he saw on the way into the bar. So, I humor him, and we go see a couple of old ladies with their tired routine. Eddie loved it."

"I've met Madame LaBu," Trucker said.

"Real performer, that one," Ida said. "So, I get Eddie out of there before he buys Mom some expensive junk ring. And we go get a cone across the street. I love their cones."

"Mine was good," Trucker agreed.

"Then Eddie sees an ad for this place. Ascend-A-Palooza," Ida looked off to the side. "I don't know exactly why I agreed. Maybe I thought he needed some more time and space from Mom. I don't know."

Trucker kept Ida on task, "So you came here. Then what?"

"Ed bought a couple of these absurdly expensive passes," Ida said, pulling at the Celestial Pass hanging around her neck. "We wander around. Check out the nonsense. Ed was having fun and actually, so was I. It is so bonkers ridiculous . . ." Ida thought hard for a moment, "Then . . . we ran into Jen. She and Ed seemed to hit it off."

"And?" Trucker asked.

"I don't really know. Kind of a blur. We met some of Jen's friends. They had rooms. We hung out. Checked out more of the conference . . . it is all . . . fuzzy," Ida looked down. "I can't really explain it."

Trucker didn't push it, "When was the last time you slept?"

"I don't know," Ida said. "I don't remember. Maybe I haven't? How has it been two days? I cannot believe I was so irresponsible. Can't believe I let this happen."

"Hey," Trucker said. "Don't feel bad. Don't beat yourself up. It isn't your fault. It really isn't. I have been here for a few hours — I think

— I don't even know for sure. And I feel like I have lost half of my mind. I swear this . . . thing . . . this nonsense . . . is contagious. This place does something to you. There is too much stimulation, too much information, and none of it is true. But it is laced and layered with things that either sound real or you would hope are real." Trucker paused. "It would be comforting to know I could talk to the aunt I love that has passed away or a glue gun or sticker can cure cancer and make you wealthy without effort. But it's not real, none of it, and almost everybody in here is selling something on your hope that it is. Doesn't matter who you are. If you are subjected to this stuff long enough, it seeps in and infects you."

Trucker snapped his fingers in front of Eddie, grabbing his attention. "Eddie? Buddy?"

Ed turned to Trucker, "Yeah?"

"We're getting out of here," Trucker said.

"Why?" Ed asked.

"Because this place isn't good for ya. For anyone. Need to get out of here."

"That's not true," Ed said. "Jen's here. She's good. She cares. I'm gonna stay."

"Ed," Trucker quickly thought about how to approach this, but his intuition started to misfire. "Ed . . . this is not up for debate. All three of us are getting out of here. Now."

"Yeah, Eddie," Ida added. "We need to go. It has been TWO DAYS."

"You two leave," Ed said, looking into Jennifer's room. "I'm staying."

Trucker closed his eyes and inhaled sharply through his nose, "No, Ed. You're not. You're going home."

"Why should I listen to you? You're just some guy. Why do you even care so much?" Eddie angrily asked, "Huh? Why?"

"Because, Eddie, I got a problem," Trucker said. "I actually have many, many problems. But one of them is that when I say I am going to do something, I do it. When I say *yes* to something, then it is a commitment. A promise. And I do not stop. You may think that's not a real problem. But it is. I'm an on/off switch. There is no in between and . . . that is not a healthy way to be. I can, and have, said *yes* to the wrong things, and *no* to the right things, often. And it takes an act of God to stop me."

Trucker paused.

"Why do I care, Eddie? Because I said yes to your mom. I clicked 'yes.' I promised her I would find you and send ya home. And I never would have stopped till I found you."

Trucker paused again. Held up his phone showing the photos of Ed and Heather to Ed.

"She paid a lot of money to make sure you were okay. She's worried about you. You should go see her and let her know you are safe."

"Yeah," Ed rubbed his eyes and asked Ida, "Two days?"

"Yes," Ida said. "And it pisses me off."

As Ed was coming around, Jennifer's speech had ended. She walked out into the hallway, joined the trio, and said, "Edward, Ida — we will be beginning our group meditation now. Mister Trucker, you will be joining us, I hope."

Ed smiled at Jennifer, and Trucker whispered quietly into Ida's ear, "Your mom didn't pay me to find you because she knows you have something she never will. She knows you will always be okay. And yeah, she may hate you for it. But that's her problem. Not yours. Now get him out of here. Don't stop for astral funnel cakes. Front door. Now."

Ed started to walk back into the room with Jennifer.

Trucker put his stickered hand on Ed's shoulder, stopping him cold, and said to Jennifer, "Hey. I have been looking for you half the day."

Ida put her hand around her brother's waist and began walking with him down the hallway of the Seraphic Realm.

Jennifer watched them go, then turned to Trucker and gently placed her index finger into the center of his chest, "I'm glad you were. And here we've found each other again."

"Hey, hold up," Trucker called out to Ed and Ida as they walked away.

He reached into his pocket and pulled out the small cardboard box, the packaged mood rings from LaBu's psychic shop.

With an easy underhand toss, he sent it airborne their way.

"It's a gift. For a job well done. Also, for the love of gawd, next time you go missing, tell your mom to use the app."

Ed caught the jewelry box, the soft thump of it landing in his palms sharper than expected. He looked down at *The Aura Authority* stamped in silver foil, then clutched it tight.

The two siblings gave Trucker a final wave goodbye.

Trucker turned back to Jennifer.

"I just wanted to thank you for helping me earlier," he said, pulling a hundred-dollar bill from his stash and offering it to her.

She took his hand, folded his fingers around the bill, and peeled off the star-shaped energy-healing sticker. Then, gently pressed his hand toward his chest, "Keep it."

"Are you sure?" Trucker asked.

"I'm sure," Jennifer said. "You are quite special. Did you know that?"

Trucker didn't answer as he watched Ed and Ida walk away.

Jennifer continued and suggested, "Why don't you come in and meditate with us."

"Oh, no," Trucker said. "I have to get out of here."

"Come on," Jennifer smiled. "Will do you some good. Ten minutes. Get refreshed for the trip home."

"Ten minutes?" Trucker asked while looking at Ed and Ida as they disappeared in the distance.

"Ten minutes." she said while looking deeply into his eyes and still holding his unstickered hand.

"Okay," Trucker said. "Sure, why not. Yes."

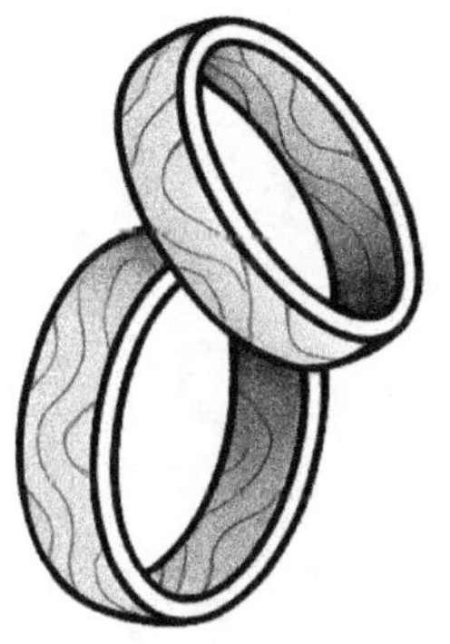

14

TEN YEARS LATER

It was twelve minutes to noon, late July, with the sun trying to break through the wide oak window blinds that ran the length of the office. The space was warm but minimalistic, painted in a muted terracotta palette of light taupe with deep cerulean blue accents. Soft white light from recessed ceiling lamps blanketed a simple, cozy couch in the corner and three plush but structured armchairs angled toward one another.

A clean, plain desk — free from clutter except for a closed laptop and a flipped-over cellphone — stood in the shadow of the blinds.

Shelving filled with books, an assortment of kintsugi bowls, and small abstract wooden statues was offset by gradient charcoal sketches on white canvases, hung next to a framed diploma that read:

University of California

. . . have conferred upon . . .

Ida Joyce Young

the degree of

Doctor of Philosophy

in

Clinical Psychology

. . . with all the rights and privileges thereto pertaining.

"And how does that make you feel?" Ida asked the young woman sitting across from her, with a wry smile and a knowing look.

The young woman, somewhat confused, somewhat incredulous, smiled then laughed.

"I thought you'd like that," Ida's half-smile turned bright, and she laughed with the client. "Where do you feel it?"

"Whenever I have the floating thoughts — the fantasy reminiscing that I know isn't true — there's a tightness in my chest, a drop in my stomach," Betsy explained both with words and hand gestures. "And a slight metallic taste in my mouth."

"And you label it?" Ida asked.

150

"I label it, work through it," Betsy said. ". . . and it eventually fades. And happens less and less."

"Good," Ida said. "You are doing it right. It is hard and takes time; that's just how it is. But you're doing better each time I see you."

"Thanks. I feel safe. Or . . . safer," Betsy said, ". . . and feel like things are changing for the better."

"The timing of all of this couldn't be better," Ida said as she shifted slightly back in her chair.

"I think so, too," Betsy said as she stood. "Thank you again. Today has been good."

"I agree," Ida said as the session drew to a close and they exchanged goodbyes.

Ida moved behind her desk and opened her laptop to document and make notations on her session with Betsy. A notification popped up in the bottom right corner: six new emails from Edward Young.

"What now?" Ida asked aloud, shaking her head. She flipped over her cellphone. Seventeen missed text messages from Ed.

"Jesus," Ida said under her breath and returned to her laptop and work. But now she was distracted. What could Ed possibly want this urgently? Urgent to Ed could be anything. There was the time he watched the movie *Chef* and wanted to start a food truck. Then realized he couldn't cook, so he changed it up to an ice-cream truck before remembering he couldn't drive. There was the time he binge-watched *Mad Men* and wanted to go into advertising. But called it off immediately after realizing he didn't smoke or drink. She was thankful that Mom didn't let him watch horror movies.

But what could it be this time that he desperately needed Ida's attention? Anything could spur a fifteen-text blowup.

She scoffed, picked up her phone, and tapped on his contact name.

The first messages were nothing but exclamation marks and shocked face emojis, then a link to a national news broadcast from two weeks ago, followed by a few more shocked-faced emojis. The last two texts were "We have to go get him!" and "We have to save him!"

This did not help Ida. The exclamation marks. The random newscast link. The pleas to go get someone and save them, meant absolutely nothing to her. Get whom? Save whom? She quickly texted him, "Working. What do you need? Important?"

She went back to her laptop and continued to work, but kept glancing back to her phone, waiting for a response.

"Damnit, Eddie," she grumbled, exhaled sharply, picked up her phone, and called her brother.

On the first ring:

"Hi!" Heather Young answered.

"I need to talk to Eddie," Ida said. "Why do you have his phone? He was just texting me."

"Hi, Mom!" Heather said, bubbly and sarcastic. "It is good to hear your voice, Mom."

Ida rolled her eyes, "It is good to hear your voice, Mom. Now where is Eddie? Put him on."

"He's using the potty," Heather said.

"Well, have him call me back," Ida said. "I gotta go."

"Don't want to talk?" Heather asked.

Ida clacked on the keys of her laptop, multitasking. "Fine, sure. What do you want to talk about?"

Heather had nothing to say, and Ida kept working through the painfully awkward silence — until there was a crash and clatter in the background of Ed's phone.

"Is that Sis?!" Ed could be heard rushing to his phone. "Here, Mom. Give it to me. Mom! Is that Sis?"

Ed commandeered the phone while Heather chirped, "It was great talking to you, Ida! Should come by the house more often."

"Sis," Ed said, now on the line and speaking a mile a minute. "We gotta go get him! We gotta save him! We gotta go get him out!"

"Slow down," Ida said. "Are you watching *Saving Private* —"

"Stop it," Ed interrupted then asked. "Did you watch the video I sent?"

"No," Ida said. "I'm working. At work."

"Watch it!!" Ed said, emphatically.

"Why don't you just give me the highlights," Ida suggested.

"Trucker," Ed started. "We have to save Trucker!"

"Who?" Ida asked. "A truck driver needs to be saved? Why would we need to save a truck driver? Ed, what are you watching?"

"Ida!" Ed yelled. "You're the smart one!"

"Eddie," Ida yelled back. "I'm at work. What do you want?"

"Agggh," Ed groaned dramatically. "Ida. Please. Just watch the video. Please."

"Okay, fine. Calm down," Ida said. "I'll watch the video in a little bit. I promise."

"No," Ed snapped, then laughed. "You gotta watch it now . . . with me on the phone."

"Goodbye, Eddie," Ida said. "I'll watch it later and call you back. Don't let Mom go through your phone. *Boundaries*, Ed."

"No, you have to watch —" Ed began, but Ida cut in quickly, "I love you. Bye," and hung up.

Ida flipped her phone face down and returned to her laptop. She opened her schedule, confirmed the next client, swapped to the corresponding file, and glanced back at her phone.

"Godamnit, Eddie."

She kicked back in her chair, put her feet up, and scrolled to the video link Ed had sent. It was a national news broadcast from two weeks ago. She paid close attention but couldn't understand what Ed was so worked up about. Flooding in the southern United States. A plane crash. Ida doubled the playback speed. The anchor's voice turned chipmunklike as images flew past. Politics. President. Economy. Immigration. A Yankee hit a home run. A prison escape.

And then:

"Influencer or cult leader?"

Something about that line sent a shiver down her spine and goosebumps across her arms. But she wasn't sure why. She slowed the video back to normal speed and rewound.

"Influencer or cult leader?" the news anchor repeated, this time in their normal voice while a social media post of a striking brunette woman in her late forties flashed on screen.

Ida hit pause.

Her chest became tight. Her stomach dropped. Her hands lightly trembled, and she could taste metal in her mouth. It was her. It was Jennifer, from a decade ago. Jen from Ascend-A-Palooza and the Friday that disappeared into thin air.

Ida's face turned pale as memories involuntarily floated back and flashed in her mind. That Friday wasn't just a random day. It was the day her dissertation proposal hearing had been scheduled. And she ghosted it. She no-showed. She had been busy listening to the woman now frozen on her phone screen.

It was a vanished Friday that nearly derailed all her hard work and carefully laid academic plans. And it wasn't the kind of situation where she could pound out an email and write: *My bad. How about Monday?* It had been a one-time scheduled event. A major milestone in her educational trajectory. One she couldn't screw up.

And she had.

The fallout from that screw-up took everything Ida had to recover from.

She had to contact and meet personally with the dissertation committee, her chair, and the director of clinical training. Some of whom were nearly impossible to track down as the committee disbanded. But she eventually did. She took full responsibility, offered no excuses, and worked to convince them she wasn't burnt out, she hadn't dropped out, and her mental health was stable.

She was required to take a brief oral examination and attend several academic probation meetings.

They eventually allowed her to file a formal petition to reschedule the hearing, which took months and cost her a practicum slot. Everything was delayed, and she had to fight and claw her way through it all.

In the end, it made her more driven. More focused. But it was a trial that nearly crushed her — a moment in time she would never forget, even if she wanted to.

She hit play to continue the newscast.

The segment wasn't long, and Ida was shocked that the cult leader angle seemed like an afterthought. *Influencer or cult leader? We vote influencer* seemed to be the broadcast's takeaway. It was almost an advertisement for Jennifer's *Radiant Way*.

Jennifer, whose last name was apparently Smith, but Ida questioned that, along with everything else in the three minutes of footage.

Fourteen years ago, Jennifer Smith had created an online presence with a video channel titled *Jen's Jenius Jems*. Yes, it was intentionally misspelled, or so she claimed — but Ida questioned that, too. The Jenius Jems were simple platitudes like "love yourself," "take time for you," and "make good choices." It was all advice borrowed, or stolen, from hundreds who came before her in the self-help world. All of which were nothing but ideas that could be taught by a half-decent kindergarten teacher or somewhat-attentive parent figure. It made Ida groan, but people ate it up.

Her harsh judgment did get put quickly in reserve, as Ida remembered she herself had fallen for it.

Not only that, but she fell for Jen's subtle coercive schtick while in an intensive PhD program for clinical psychology.

Anyone could be susceptible.

The packaging helped. Jen was a conventionally attractive woman with some exotic features and a quality that was hard to teach — and an approach that, as Ida understood it, had nothing to do with intellect and everything to do with instinct.

Again, anyone could be susceptible.

Including one Trucker S. Holmes.

"Trucker," Ida said to herself. "How could I forget Trucker?" She regretted not immediately recognizing the name when Ed had said it.

She may have gone through academic hell to rebuild her reputation and future, but none of it would have been possible without Trucker. If he hadn't shown up, woken them up, and pulled them away from Jen's coercive control, who knows where they might be now.

As the video played, she saw what Ed must have recognized on first watch. In the background of nearly every social media clip was a man who looked very much like Trucker. Skinnier, with a shaved head and an immaculately groomed long beard tied neatly in a knot at the end, but it could be him.

Ida squinted at her phone and asked the man in the background, "Trucker, that you?"

The video ended.

She rewound it and watched it again before calling Ed.

"Hi!" Heather Young answered on the first ring.

"My gawd," Ida said. "Stop answering his phone."

"He's busy," Heather replied. More crashes and clattering pans could be heard in the background.

"I'm here!" Ed shouted. "Mom, give me the phone!"

"Ed?" Ida asked. "You there?"

Out of breath, Ed panted, "I'm here. I'm here. I was baking cookies."

Ida was going to ask an obvious question, but Ed answered before she had the chance, "I've been watching *The Great American Baking Show*. I think I'm a baker."

"That's great, Eddie. I watched —"

"You watched the video!" Ed excitedly cut her off. "Isn't it crazy? It's totally messed up. We have to save Trucker, right? I mean — we *have* to."

"Slow down," Ida said. "We don't really know anything yet."

"Come on," Ed said.

"We don't know what is going on with Trucker. Or even if that is Trucker," Ida said. "And all we know about Jen is from a news broadcast."

"Bullcrap," Ed said. "It's Trucker. Ya know, the saint, the angel who saved us? And Jen is a crazy monster. So messed up. She gets millions of views online."

"*Crazy monster* isn't a technical classification I can just throw out after watching a three-minute news snippet," Ida explained. "*Crazy monster* is not a clinical classification at all."

"Well, it should be," Ed paused, frustrated. "So we do nothing?"

"No," Ida said. "We look into it. We find out what's going on."

"That's one plan," Ed said. "How about this one? We go save him. We go get him *right now*. That's my vote. It is what he did for us."

"I have work, Eddie," Ida said. "I can't just leave on a whim — or bake cookies in the afternoon."

"Unfair," Ed said.

"I apologize," Ida replied. "But I still can't just leave to go rescue a stranger, right this second. We don't even know if he *needs* or *wants* rescuing."

Ed was exasperated, "Ida . . . are you kidding me?"

Ida scrolled through her schedule and knew what she was about to find. A chunk of free time coming up in ten days. A planned vacation that she had taken time off for, but never actually got around to planning. "I might — *might* — have free time in ten days or so."

"Ten days!" Ed shouted. "Trucker's organs could be harvested in ten days!"

"Eddie, he's made it ten years," Ida said. "He can make it another ten days."

"Fine," Ed relented. "But if he's missing a kidney or a spleen, I'm telling him it's your fault."

"It'll give us more time to figure out what's really going on," Ida reassured him.

"Okay," Ed agreed. "So . . . ten days?"

"Ten days," Ida confirmed.

15

SEVEN DAYS LATER

It was nine minutes to noon, early August, and the sun broke through in wide, expanding horizontal beams past the partially opened window blinds that ran the length of Ida's office.

Ida was once again seated across from her client, Betsy, giving her space and safety.

"Sometimes I wonder when this all will end. When I wake up and go a day without thinking about what happened. Or a week, or a month," Betsy said absent of frustration or sadness but sprinkled with a dash of curious hopefulness.

"It is a process that —" Ida began but was cut off by Betsy.

"I know it is a process," Betsy said. "Just wish the process could be sped up."

"With time and distance —" Ida tried again.

"If you say 'time heals all wounds,' I am going to throw up," Betsy smiled.

Ida returned the smile, "Time doesn't heal all wounds, and neither does distance. It is what you do with the time and distance that matters. And you are doing all the right things." She leaned back in her chair.

Betsy seemed to relax and said, "I won't see you for two weeks. Going on vacation?"

"I had a vacation planned," Ida said. "But something came up. Need to help my brother with some things."

"Family is good," Betsy said.

"It can be," Ida said as the two stood up.

"Enjoy your time off," Betsy said. "I should be okay."

"You will be great. But if something comes up, you have all the numbers," Ida explained. "And there is the messaging service."

The two exchanged goodbyes, and Ida rushed behind her desk, picked up her phone, and called Ed.

The moment the call connected, Ida blurted out, "You're right! She *is* a crazy monster."

She glanced sharply at her office door and hoped Betsy hadn't heard her inappropriate squawk. She listened closely — thankfully, Betsy seemed to be out of earshot beyond the door.

"I am *not* a crazy monster," Heather said playfully on the other end of the line.

"Mom, get Eddie," Ida instructed. "And quit answering his phone."

"Who is a crazy monster?" Heather asked. "You know I love some good gossip."

"Get Ed, please," Ida insisted.

"Is that Ida?" Ed could be heard as he came to the phone. "Ida? Sis!"

"Yup," Ida answered.

"That chick is a crazy monster, right?" Ed asked.

Ida had spent her free time over the last seven days attempting to watch and read everything Jennifer Smith had ever put online. Fourteen years' worth of content. What started as observational curiosity had become a forensic-level breakdown of her belief system. A crash course in who she was and how her *Radiant Way* came to be.

Ida had taken meticulous notes:

THE RISE OF JENNIFER SMITH AND THE RADIANT WAY

It had started simple enough: Jen began uploading poorly produced videos with an innocent new-age wellness vibe. She sat in poor lighting on a yoga mat and revealed that she suffered from past trauma and chronic illness. She wanted to share her healing journey and offered awkward affirmations and platitudes with an amateurish delivery through a cheap microphone and awful audio recorder. *"You attract what you are." "Raise your vibration." "The universe is listening."* She regurgitated self-help clichés that had been repeated, recycled, and plagiarized so many times that finding who originally said them was an impossibility.

But she had three undeniable assets: she was beautiful, she was charming, and she believed. Those qualities alone racked up subscribers and views. Early comments all echoed: *"She seems nice." "Gorgeous."*

Ida noted that this was as close to normalcy as the entire thing would ever get. Nothing truly unusual.

Things gradually escalated over the months, but the foundation of normalcy remained. She was viewed as insightful, special, and magnetic, as her delivery shifted from awkward to eloquent, matching her aesthetic appeal and growing confidence. She ditched the yoga mat and splurged on a better camera and set of lights. The subscribers and followers hung onto every message, which became more spiritual, unique, and revealing.

Then, Ida noted a major shift.

Jennifer Smith branded her belief system. She called it *The Radiant Way*, and those who liked, subscribed, and followed her she christened her *Radiants*.

The number of online Radiants skyrocketed along with the production quality. It all became a pristine package for the online scroller to buy into. In more ways than one. Views and subscriptions were good. But direct donations were better.

From the random clicker to the "just one more video before bed" viewer. From trauma survivors looking for meaning, to the grieving, the ill, the heartbroken, the lonely, the disillusioned, the recently divorced, the laid-off. And the spiritual seekers, new-age wanderers, reiki practitioners, yoga teachers and students, astrology enthusiasts, and those bored with mainstream religions.

It became a place for all of them and more. A place to become a better person. A place to heal themselves and others. A place bigger than themselves. A place to belong. A radiant place.

They only had to believe and give. A few dollars was nice. But *everything* was ideal and more than welcome.

Over the following years, the intensity of Jen's messaging increased dramatically, and Ida noted a clear pattern emerge.

Jen would idealize, flooding someone or entire audiences with love. *"If you found this, you're not here by accident. You are one of us. You are special. You are chosen. Our spirits and hearts are connected."* This created bonds, parasocial or otherwise.

Then she would devalue and demean, sometimes individuals, sometimes an entire group. *"You are not doing enough. Some of you will always be stuck and diseased with overthinking. Even Radiants can be infiltrated, fall, and cause resistance. You are not worthy."* She induced shame, confusion, fear, and doubt. It pushed followers to reinvest and prove themselves.

And then, in a calculated fashion, she would either discard people or offer faux reassurances through conditional affection and coercive guidance. She gave non-apologies that sounded like sincere mea culpas and promised a reward or a utopia that was yet to come — if only the Radiants did this or that. If they just gave more. Of themselves and from their wallets.

The pattern had flashed and blared like an alarm in Ida's well-trained, highly educated mind: idealize, devalue, discard, repeat. Sometimes overt and obvious. Sometimes covert and subtle. But always there. And never-ending.

Eventually, the cycle became sprinkled with paranoia, persecution, and mystical prophecies. Jen invalidated other teachers' and scientists' points of view as *"dark"* and delivered rants about *"attacks"* on her by some mysterious *"evil enemy."*

The Radiant Way became the only way. The only truth.

There were more videos. More to watch. But Ida had seen enough. She now felt she understood the clinical, pathological framework of Jennifer Smith. Especially after the last video she watched, where Jen alluded to having lived millions of lives and hinted that Jesus personally anointed her a prophet.

Jennifer Smith had a personality structure that had been studied and documented for decades, if not centuries. The same operating system used by abusers, con artists, and cult leaders since the first account was ever recorded. And Ida knew how dangerous it could be.

Ed asked again, "She's a crazy monster, right?"

"Right," Ida said, skipping the drawn-out explanation and reasoning behind her extremely accurate educated guess.

"And you're sure?" Ed pressed. "Don't you need to sit down with her? Do all that shrink stuff? Not to kill the fun, but isn't there a rule against you calling someone *crazy* who isn't your patient?"

"Ed," Ida replied, slightly annoyed, "first of all, I don't call any of my clients *crazy*. And yes, there is an ethical rule against offering a public professional opinion on someone unless you've examined them and received consent to make a formal statement." She took a breath, "But if my brother asks me if I think some lady is a crazy bitch, then yeah — I'm ethically clear to confirm the craziness."

"Cool, cool. Didn't mean to give ya a hard time. Was just curious," Ed said. "It is so easy to see, right? I mean, who she is and what she is up to. She is pretty much made of red flags. Shocked she has a single follower. And Trucker, of all . . ."

"Umm," Ida said. "We were *this* close to being exactly where Trucker is now."

"Right," Ed ended the confirmation with a sharpness.

"Anyone is susceptible to being caught in the trap of someone like Jennifer Smith. She is a predator that uses love, lies, and coercive manipulative control to get whatever she wants."

"Right," Ed was set on repeat.

"And she doesn't want weak or unintelligent people. She wants qualities she can exploit. Idealism, vulnerability, a desire for change, meaning, and purpose," Ida said. "These people — her supply, her targets — have to also have something to offer. So she can take that from them. And that makes her a monster."

"Right."

"And after I watched her claim to be a personally appointed prophet, she gets the crazy label thrown in there, too," Ida said. "Do you want the clinical terminology for all of this? And how it is a self-sealing system that cannot be broken? Or no?"

"I think crazy monster is good enough," Ed answered.

"Yeah. Me, too," Ida agreed.

"Okay, let's go save Trucker!" Ed said, back to his enthusiastic self.

"It's not so simple," Ida said. "But yes, let's try and save Trucker."

"While you have been up to your clinical mumbo-jumbo, I have been doing a little research myself," Ed said proudly. "A little investigation." He gave himself a round of applause.

"Don't tell me; let me guess what you've been watching," Ida pondered. "*The Maltese Falcon* . . . or . . . *The French Connection*?"

"Wrong. I don't even know what those are," Ed said. "Although I have watched *Who Framed Roger Rabbit*, Bob Hoskins, Christopher Llyod. And *Clue*. Tim Curry and Llyod again. Ya know. To set the mood."

"Of course," Ida said.

"Through my investigation into one Miss Crazy Monster Jennifer Smith, I've found that she and her *Radiant Way* have four properties. Four!" Ed said. "Can you believe that?"

"Yes," Ida said flatly. "I can."

"Oh, hang on," Ed corrected himself. "I mean, three. They have three properties. One in southwest Florida, a little ways off the beach. Another in Colorado, some sort of campground thing. They sold the one in California — it was a defunct cannabis farm. And then, there is a spot outside of Kamas, Utah. Not far from Salt Lake."

"We're not visiting all of these, I hope?" Ida asked, then clarified. "Sorry — I should have said, *I hope you know* I'm not visiting all of these."

"Oh, I know. Your time is valuable. Thankfully, you're not charging by the hour," Ed said.

"This is all pro bono," Ida said. "For the greater good."

"I know what *pro bono* means," Ed replied. "Anyway . . . I wasn't just watching *Who Framed Roger Rabbit* and *Clue*. I was also watching Jen's latest livestream. It was . . . interesting. She was taking audience questions from all over the world and 'channeling' a straight connection to the universe for answers. I don't think *she thinks* she's a prophet of God anymore. Pretty sure she believes she *is* God."

"Yup," Ida said. "The closed system escalates until it's forced into collapse by things outside of her control. Normally a judge or —" Ida cut herself off, then continued, "and then it just resets and starts all over again."

"Yeah, real whacko," Ed said. "So, during this livestream from her Kamas, Utah, compound . . . guess who showed up?"

"Trucker," Ida said.

"Bingo. Big money to you. He wandered in and out of frame in the background," Ed said. "So, Trucker is in Kamas. Right now. Let's go get him."

Ida groaned, "Why couldn't it be the beach?"

"Oh, I hear ya," Ed said. "But this is no vacation, Sis. We're on a rescue mission! A mission from God. Let's go. Right now."

"Slow down; we can't leave right this second," Ida said. "I've got clients and appointments for the next three days."

"Skip 'em," Ed implored.

"Umm. No," Ida said dryly.

"Okay," Ed said. "Then we'll leave in three days. Chuck has a new motorhome and said we could borrow it."

"Umm," Ida said, raising an eyebrow. "Two questions. Who's Chuck? And why in the world do you think I am driving Chuck's RV to Utah?"

"Chuck is New Dad," Ed explained. "He's super nice and said we could borrow his new ride. It's luxury. You'll love it."

"Ed," Ida said, "I'm not driving Chuck's toilet on wheels. We'll fly to Salt Lake, rent a car, and get an Airbnb. Also, thirty-two-year-olds don't have *new dads*."

"Sure they do. Why not? Chuck's a great New Dad. You'd like him," Ed said. "He and Mom were sealed a couple months ago. He converted for her."

"Lovely," Ida said unenthused. "She's piling up quite the harem of husbands for the old celestial kingdom. Or whatever level of afterlife she is shooting for."

"Sis," Ed said. "Don't be that way. Mom is good, and Chuck is a nice guy. I also don't think sealings work that way anymore. But I could be wrong. The rules are a little confusing sometimes."

"I'm not sure how it works, either. Left the church so long ago, it feels like a dream. Or a nightmare. Or . . ." Ida trailed off, then refocused. "Okay. Doesn't matter. Chuck's motorhome stays in the driveway. Keep an eye on the crazy monster's livestreams. If anything changes, let me know. In the meantime, I'll book us flights to SLC, and get us a place to stay. We're leaving in three days."

"Yay!" Ed excitedly announced. "Rescue mission. Let's do it."

"Three days," Ida reminded.

16

THREE DAYS LATER

At the end of an absurdly long ticket counter line in an overcrowded, chaotic LAX terminal, Ida leaned against her small piece of luggage and went over the rescue plan in her mind.

She had overcome the ludicrous proposition of saving a stranger from a situation he may not want to be saved from. Because he wasn't just a stranger. He was the man who had relentlessly gone out of his way to save her and her brother.

He had saved her future.

She felt obligated to return the favor.

But ten years of coercive control and undue influence couldn't be undone just by showing up and saying, "Hey, you're in a cult. Let's go."

She knew his mind was not his anymore. And that no one could get it back or undo *The Radiant Way* programming but him. He had to see the situation for what it really was. He had to see the true face of Jennifer Smith.

She and Ed had to somehow help him do that. And they had little time to do it. But she had a plan.

The clock was ticking, and the ticket line inched forward.

"This place is a zoooo," Ed exclaimed as he greeted his sister with a hug.

Ida squeezed him back. "It's good to see you. Ready?"

"Oh, you know it," Ed said, adjusting his carry-on backpack. "I also had a great idea on the way here."

"What's that?" Ida asked.

"I saw the LAX Rosewood while I was coming in," Ed began.

"Yeah. Me, too," Ida said. "Gave me flashbacks I'd rather forget."

"Oh. Me, too," Ed nodded. "But it also gave me an idea! That HERA Network — those people who put that thing on every year?"

"Yeah?" Ida prompted.

"Well, they're a whole thing now," Ed said, waving his phone. "They've gotten even bigger. Like, big. Huge operation. Media company with tons of online channels and all that."

Ida waited.

"So, I go check 'em out. You can subscribe to their stuff. Including . . . including . . . their entire back catalog of events and videos."

"I can't believe you'd give those people a single penny," Ida said with disgust.

"It was actually a little over a hundred dollars," Ed said.

"That's crazy."

"A month," Ed added.

"Jesus."

"But wait — wait," Ed said. "They record everything. *EVERYTHING*. And their back catalog — their archive — has everything. *EVERYTHING*."

Ida stared at him.

"Hey, smarty," Ed said. "We can watch the footage from the 2015 Ascend-A-Palooza. We can see what happened to Trucker. Get some intel. I've learned that intel is pretty important in investigations. *Knives Out.* The first one."

"That's not a bad idea," Ida admitted.

"I know, right?" Ed said with pride.

The ticket line finally brought them to the counter.

"I'm sorry, but your flight has been canceled," the agent said.

"What?" Ida groaned.

"It's a sign from God," Ed said, pulling out his phone. "I'll call Chuck and have him gas up the —"

"I can get you on a different flight," the agent interrupted. "D1777. Departs an hour later."

"D1777!" Ed exclaimed. "It's a sign from God. Seven, seven, seven. I don't need to tell you the importance of sevens in the scriptures," Ed nudged Ida.

"Please don't," Ida said, then turned to the agent. "We'll take them."

SIX HOURS LATER

"You could've gotten something a little nicer," Ed said from the passenger seat of the rented Nissan Sentra. "I don't know. Maybe something . . . European? Leather seats at least."

"When you learn to drive, you get to have an opinion on the car," Ida said, sticking her tongue out. "Regardless, I think spending dumb money on an expensive rental is a waste. But when you get that license someday, spend your allowance however you like."

"Unfair, but not false," Ed said. "I just hope this isn't a sign of things to come with the accommodations you have picked out for us."

"It's fine. It's an Airbnb," Ida said. "It'll be fine."

Ida's sensible Nissan Sentra peeled east through Salt Lake City toward Jennifer Smith's compound on the Wasatch Range, whose peaks still clung to snow in the deep August heat.

The city of Salt Lake sat in the valley like a colossal and catastrophic contradiction. A supposedly divinely inspired location with a drying toxic lake that smelled of brine and rot, its shores littered with dead birds and an arsenic-laced dust that, when caught by the wind, spread its poison to the faithful and unfaithful alike.

A manmade, gridded Cartesian city with its massive main temple as the origin point. But try as the holy construction crews might, their temple would never reach the heights, or the beauty, of the natural, jagged, and wild mountains that surrounded them, carved by ancient volcanic violence.

The central temple itself was a contradiction in its own right. Atop, its steeples looked torn from a fairy tale, with ornate Gothic spires and buttresses, adorned with symbolic ornamentation, and crowned by a literal golden angel named Moroni — blowing his horn to the heavens. But below, the structure stood on thick, bare Romanesque fortresslike walls as if designed to withstand a siege. And maybe it was built with that in mind, as the sacred and secular waged a cultural cold war within the city's grid. Just a minute's walk from the temple's front steps, a man or woman could step into a tattoo parlor and get inked with the angel Moroni blowing whatever they imagined. Four minutes farther, they could push open the door to a pub and drink whiskey until they proposed to the bartender and ranted and raved about rainbows.

The contradictions were comprehensive. Reverence versus repression. The faithful smiled politely while professing clean, family-friendly views. But underneath the façade there was depression, plastic surgery, secret pill bottles in glove boxes, and incognito browser tabs that told a different story. Faith versus fear. The prophet and president of the church spoke for God, but questioning him could get you excommunicated and quietly erased from the community.

All of it sat directly on the Wasatch Fault Line, a natural ticking time bomb, overdue for the earthquake that would swallow it whole.

And . . . Ida hated that it was all so gorgeous.

Ed peered out at the city and mountain landscape.

"This just feels like I am home. Ya know? It feels like we belong here," he continued craning his neck, looking at everything around him. Taking it in. "I don't understand why Mom and Dad ever left."

"Well, after Dad graduated from university," Ida said, "he eventually got a great job in California, and they had to move. Simple as that."

"Do you remember much about Dad?" Ed asked.

"He was smart. He was a super genius," Ida said, glancing at Ed. "He was a literal rocket scientist."

"I know that part," Ed said. "But . . . do you, like . . . remember him?"

"I do," Ida said with her eyes on the road. "He was kind, compassionate, and would do anything for anyone. He was a rock, Ed. And I miss him."

Ed remained quiet for a moment. "I don't remember him. Except that . . . he was smart. And . . . loved movies. But that's it."

Ida looked at him, "That's not your fault. You were young. I got a couple extra years with him."

"I would've liked to have those years," Ed said.

"I would've liked to have even more," Ida replied.

Ed wiped away a few tears that were welling up, and he cleared his throat, "But it was God's will. He needed him. And he's up there looking down on us now. We're on a mission from God. And Dad."

Ida stared straight ahead at the road. Silent.

A moment went by before Ed said, "Not to sound too cheese-irific, but I can see why Brigham said, 'This is the place.' Ya know? Just look at this view, Sis."

Ida knew that now was time to enact Phase One of her plan.

"The guy with fifty-seven wives? *That* Brigham?" she asked, eyes still on the road.

"That was a long time ago," Ed said.

Ida swiveled her head around, looking in every direction, "Pretty sure that big university Dad went to is around here somewhere, with Brigham's name plastered all over it. That's pretty impressive for a racist despot who only went to school for, like, a week."

"Ida, Brigham was a man of his time," Ed said. "But still divinely inspired. As the prophet and president, he received revelations from Heavenly Father."

"Funny how God was such a racist, polygamist, and pedophile back then," Ida said. "Heavenly Father seemed like a real jerk. Luckily, he changed his ways . . . kinda."

Ed looked at Ida while her eyes stayed on the road, "What are you doing? Why are you being this way?"

Her eyes never left the road, "Do you trust me?"

"Yes," Ed said.

"Implicitly?" she asked, glancing at him and then back to the road.

"Of course," Ed confirmed again.

While Ida's sensibly rented Nissan Sentra made its way toward Trucker, Jennifer Smith, and *The Radiant Way* compound, she commenced a relentless verbal assault on the Church of Jesus Christ of Latter-day Saints. She started with things she knew Ed was already aware of — thanks to his love of TV shows and movies and a general pop-culture addiction. Nothing she said was anything he couldn't have come across in cartoons, reality television, or docudramas.

The well-worn sentiment that Joseph Smith was a grave-robbing con man who made up the Book of Mormon because he didn't want to work on his family's rock farm. She skipped over the fact that the gold plates Joseph claimed to find defied physics. That the bottom pages, or plates, would be crushed so flat by those on top, that nothing written on them could possibly be legible. Because regardless of Ed's external appearance and sometimes dim-witted behavior, she knew their father's genetics were swirling around in there somewhere. She didn't want to cause a legitimate crisis of faith. That was actually the exact opposite of what she intended.

She continued to shame, ridicule, and harshly, sarcastically dismantle Ed's Mormon belief system. She aggressively threw out what many consider faith-breaking facts. The impossible and inaccurate translations. The divine details that were both plagiarized and anachronistic. Stolen rituals from known Masonic practices.

But with every belief bomb and bullets she dropped and shot, Ed countered them with ease. Offering up answers anchored by church authorities and apologetics. Ida's assault wasn't weakening his faith, his belief. It made him hold onto it even tighter.

She pivoted to attacking, in her words, a *pioneer sex cult's* prophets and presidents. She pointed out that every so-called new revelation from God conveniently helped the church grow and adapt for survival.

The U.S. government said, "You can't be a state if you're marrying a million wives." What do you know, the prophet just had a little powwow with Heavenly Father. He said: "Hey, let's ditch the polygamy." Blamo, Utah becomes a state.

Civil rights takes hold in the country through marches and movements. What do you know? Heavenly Father just called an emergency meeting, "Black people are cool with me now."

None of this fazed Ed. Not even a little. Which was exactly what Ida wanted.

Part of the plan, that Ed could not know about, was Ida's attempt to make the most Mormon Californian she knew even more Mormonified. She needed his armor of belief, no matter how nonsensical she found it, so strong that nothing could penetrate it.

And Ida's plan was working.

It was not a plan she came to lightly. She firmly believed the facts she was spitting at Ed. She remembered, when she was younger, being labeled difficult by the church and its members for speaking her mind. She remembered believing as strongly as Ed did, until the final straw broke that belief and shattered it.

She had wanted to believe everything her elders told her. She wanted to believe the people she was told to respect and trust. But on the very first day of her Mormon mission, in a far-off country, she witnessed baptisms she found reprehensible — against everything that she stood for, and that she thought the church stood for. Impoverished children and families with hot, bare feet were lined up and sprayed with a garden hose and tapped on their head. That was it. Whammo. New Mormons.

She spoke up. She was sent home. Bampf, one less Mormon.

Later in life, she'd learn accurate terms to describe what she witnessed: *undue influence and lack of informed consent.*

She didn't like that the only plan she could devise required pushing her brother deeper into a faith she found not only apocryphal, but so hypocritical it made her stomach churn.

She avoided hammering on Ed about the hundreds of billions the church was currently hoarding. Money that could actually be used for good. Or their treatment of the LGBTQ community. Because she knew their father's genes were in there, and that compassion would not withstand the cognitive dissonance the modern church's actions would create.

As they cut through the Wasatch Range, Ed said, "This country is absolutely stunning."

Ida agreed with a smile, but said, "That's how they get ya. Love-bombed by mountains."

ONE HOUR LATER

The Radiant Way ranch was nestled on forty-odd acres of naturally sloping hills that rose into steep, jagged rock along the ridgeline of the Wasatch Back. Tucked away from prying eyes, the formerly charming family-style retreat had been transformed into something different, something subtly sinister. The property was fenced and walled off, with the exception of a natural ravine to the west that did a better job of keeping out wandering hikers and hunters than the manmade mini-fortifications.

The main house sat centered on a flattened section of the acreage. What was once an elegant wood-and-stone, ranch-style mountain home had been modified with a green steel roof and a series of additions that clashed in almost schizophrenic architectural fashion: an adobe-spackled sunroom, a colonial-style annex, a half-finished granite turret, and a salvaged Gothic arched doorway bearing the motto *Leave Resistance Behind. Let Radiance Flow.* painted across the threshold.

A small pebbled walkway behind the residence led to a greenhouse of equal size and similar chaotic modifications — partial original glass mixed with plastic shells of bubbled panes, held together by haphazard duct-taped repairs.

A curious, windowless structure made from five welded-together cargo-containers sat a couple hundred yards from the main house. Three containers formed the first floor, with the remaining two stacked on top to create a second level. Each container was painted with large, childlike murals and had its doors swung open, unbolted padlocks hanging loosely from the outside.

Farther up the mountain was a ramshackle solar array with fractured panels and exposed wiring, situated beside a ski tow rope and a small zip-line course that were likely artifacts from the previous owner but seemingly still functional.

At the entrance to the eerie off-grid compound stood an industrial, solid-iron gate streaked with rust. There was no keypad or visible mechanism to open it from the outside. The gate was anchored to thick I-beam posts, graffitied with indecipherable symbols, as if a child had painted them. Atop the posts, cameras pointed at a perfectly squared patch of loose cobblestones framed in concrete.

Standing within the square of cobblestones were three men, all wildly different in age and apparent backgrounds. One looked like a retired schoolteacher, another a young active-duty Marine in uniform, and the third a middle-aged office manager still in his business attire. All three stood at attention, facing the closed gate, while a fourth man in a dirty T-shirt, jeans, and sneakers lay curled in a fetal position just outside the square.

A hundred yards down the private drive from the gate, on the passing country road, Ida and Ed rolled by at a snail's pace in their sensibly rented Nissan Sentra. They both leaned to catch a better glimpse of the entrance to *The Radiant Way* Utah compound.

"What are those guys doing?"

"They're waiting to be accepted," Ida said as she inched the rental forward.

"Can't see much," Ed replied. "But any surveillance can be useful. *Enemy of the State*. Will Smith. Gene Hackman."

"Right," Ida said, squinting down the drive. She noticed the camera mounted on the gatepost just as the massive slab of rusted iron began to creep open.

"We're gonna need a better layout of the place when we sneak in," Ed said, as Ida accelerated down the road, out of view, and toward the Airbnb cabin she had reserved.

"Mm-hmm," Ida replied.

17

A HALF-HOUR LATER

Homebase for Ida and Ed's rescue mission was a small, cozy cabin seven miles down the country road from *The Radiant Way* compound. Cozy, as often described in real estate listings, was a cute way of saying the smallest livable space allowed by law for a human being. One could sit on the toilet, fry an egg in the tiny kitchenette, read the welcome note the owners had left on a tiny desk, and lock the front door — all at the same time. It seemed the only plausible way the bunk beds got inside was that the cabin had been built around them. Still, it had a charm and smelled of warm cedar.

"This place ain't so bad," Ed said as he jumped up to the top bunk and dug into his backpack.

"It was cheap and available," Ida said. "Off-season."

"Well, I love it." Ed bounced on the bunk then lined up two iPads and his phone on the bed. "Perfect spot to launch Operation Save Trucker. Stone's throw from the crazy monster's house."

While Ed started up his multi-screen portable entertainment center and command post, Ida sat at the tiny desk and unfurled her laptop.

"I'm going to keep digging through Jennifer's *Radiant Way* content," she said. "Get a better understanding. If that's possible. And maybe find something we can use."

"Cool, cool," Ed said. "While you do that, I'm going to go through the HERA Network's video archives. 2015 Ascend-A-Palooza. Let's have a race to see who finds something useful first."

"And?" Ida asked.

"And what?" Ed looked over.

"And what else are you watchin'?" Ida asked.

"Oh, *Rush Hour*. Jackie Chan. Chris Tucker," Ed answered unashamed.

"Which one?"

"All of them."

"Good choice."

The two young siblings watched away on their devices, looking for anything that might help them in their rescue attempt of Trucker S. Holmes.

Ida knew the difficulties they faced, and they were beyond simple obstacles. They were attempting to get an almost complete stranger to exit a coercive system of control, while said stranger was in the actual isolated compound, near the controller herself.

If she were to hold a weeklong conference to discuss the situation with the best-trained and most-educated psychologists and interventionists available, she imagined the resulting consensus would be: "Can't be done. It's impossible."

In order to help someone leave a cult, abusive relationship, or high-control group, a few things needed to happen, and they were all equally important.

One: There had to be genuine trust and rapport between the person under undue influence and the one trying to free them from their metaphorical, but very real, chains.

Two: They needed to be reminded of their pre-cult self. Before they became subjected to covert coercion and gaslighting and eventually gave up their agency to meet the needs of the leader who bound them. *Remember that one time we used to do that one thing. Boy, that was so much fun.* Reconnection with their authentic self was critical.

Three: The person trying to break the chains had to introduce information gradually, gently, and indirectly. They needed to encourage the person under control to think critically and regain their autonomy and ability to reality-test their current situation. This required time and a safe, neutral environment.

Four: The chain-breaker could and should offer detached perspectives of other known groups or relationships clearly identified as psychologically dangerous and destructive. *Hey, those guys Jim Jones and Charlie Manson. Real screwballs, huh? Ever heard of that lady Lori Vallow? Real piece of work.* This allowed the person to begin recognizing parallels and cultlike dynamics for themselves, on their own terms.

And even if all of that happened perfectly, the odds still weren't great for the chains to be broken.

They didn't know Trucker. They didn't know his past. Their only exposure to him had lasted twenty minutes at most, when he saved them from the fate of *The Radiant Way*. It was a slim chance he'd even remember them. And even if he did, those twenty minutes were up against a decade of a monster's manipulation, on her home turf.

It would be like trying to get a random heroin addict to quit doing heroin while they were in a heroin den, actively using heroin, surrounded by other heroin addicts who kept giving them more heroin. Even kidnapping the heroin addict would work for only as long as it took them to run back for more heroin.

Ida had already contemplated all of this days ago and still chose to make the attempt. But it was becoming very real now, as she imagined the stranger named Trucker — who once went out of his way to save her future — trapped in the crazy monster's house a mere seven miles away.

She continued her research on Jennifer Smith, combing through the online content Jen had been posting over the last fourteen years. Maybe there was something more. Something useful. She hadn't found it yet, but the videos had already solidified her earlier assessment, formed from a distance.

Jennifer exhibited a mix of Cluster B personality disorders accompanied by fixed delusions. Narcissistic traits beyond the very human narcissism everyone has to some degree. *Do I look good in this dress? I wish this pimple would clear up.* What Jen had was a clear inflated sense of self-importance, an unhealthy need for admiration and validation, a lack of empathy, and obvious exploitative behavior — and even though she would never admit any of it, she also had a fragile self-esteem under the mask.

Ida could connect the dots on Jen's antisocial personality traits. The name itself frustrated Ida; it gave the impression that it described someone who didn't like parties. When in reality, it described someone who saw morality and rules as optional when they weren't convenient. Jen spun the truth in self-serving ways. Showed little to no regard for others' needs or pain. Weaponized charisma to get inside people's heads or their wallets. Guilt rarely registered, and she carried rage in a handbag. Promised everything. Delivered nothing.

Jen's delusions were trickier. Did she actually believe the things she was saying? Or was it all manipulation? If she'd believed them for as long as she had, then they were likely fixed. And she would be considered functional but diagnosable with delusional disorder. She could fully believe that she was having conversations with Jesus himself and still go to the grocery store, complain to the clerk about the state of the raspberries, and flirt with the manager for a discount.

Were the delusions real?

The famous Kurt Vonnegut quote popped into Ida's mind: *We are what we pretend to be, so we must be careful what we pretend to be.* And Ida decided it didn't matter. One personality disorder fed and supported the other, completing a sealed system — closing it off, making it impervious to intervention.

Ida's eyes were getting tired by the time she came across a video uploaded on May twentieth a few years ago. It was Jennifer Smith's birthday. Ida watched as Trucker and several men presented Jen with a cake covered with candles. As Ida observed, she mentally checked off borderline and histrionic personality disorders from her theoretical list, watching Jen swing from elation to rage to weeping gratitude and back again. All in six minutes.

The intense outbursts, emotional whiplash, and dysregulation seemed to be triggered by the flavor of the cake, or the number of candles, or something equally absurd. But Ida didn't care anymore. She shut her laptop and rested her head.

"Find anything new?" Ed asked from his top bunk command post.

"No. Still a crazy monster," Ida said. "Wait." She opened her laptop again. The video was frozen on the title and date. "Her birthday is May twentieth. That's something, I guess." She shut the laptop again. "How about you?"

"Jackie just vaulted over a fence and kicked a bad guy while Chris cracked wise," Ed said. "They're about to rescue the kidnapped girl."

"Anything else?" Ida asked.

"Oh, yeah. Tons," Ed smiled and hopped down to the bottom bunk with an iPad, then patted the spot next to him. Ida joined him and leaned on his shoulder. They both watched the screen as Ed scrolled.

The iPads had multiple video players open in split-screen mode.

"What do we got?" Ida asked.

"So, the HERA Network 2015 footage from Ascend-A-Palooza covers presentations and some of the performances at the conference," Ed explained. "Trucker actually pops up a few times." He tapped "play" on the first video player.

The first clip featured Doctor Robert Thompson, the subject of the book *Revelations of Splendor*, a psychologist preaching about his near-death experiences and the powers they gave him.

The siblings watched as the doctor calmly explained how he communicated with sentient office furniture, who, according to him, judged human adultery harshly. Ed pointed out a very uncomfortable-looking Trucker in the front row.

"Let me find the right spot," he said.

Ed scrolled ahead. Doctor Thompson was mid-sentence, telling a story about dark demons entering the top of a man's head, when Trucker began coughing loudly. An usher approached. Ed and Ida watched as Trucker was escorted out, while coughing and yelling, "Ed Young!" and "Your mom is looking for you!"

"That's him!" Ida said excitedly.

"I know!" Ed matched her enthusiasm.

"I think that nutty doctor is a respected Mormon, by the way," Ida added.

"Stop," Ed groaned. "Also, it's *LDS*."

"Just sayin'." Ida smirked. "Best and brightest."

"Okay," Ed said, ignoring her. "Moving right along." He swiped and tapped open the next video player.

A HERA Network employee had recorded the performance of the aging glam rock band IronSpirit on the Luminal Nexus Stage. As the leather-pantsed lead singer belted out a ballad, Trucker could be seen weaving through the crowd, holding up his phone, and doggedly interrogating attendees. Ed paused the video just as Trucker's face turned toward the camera. He looked frazzled.

"Doesn't really help us a whole lot," Ida said.

"Sis, any intel is important," Ed replied. "More information is better than none. We know he isn't a fan of . . . what was the band's name?"

"Iron something," Ida answered.

"Right," Ed nodded. "And look at him."

"I know."

"Doesn't matter how much Mom paid him," Ed said. "He cares. He does."

"What's next?" Ida asked.

Ed opened the next video and hit play.

An exhibitor on the floor of the Soul Gateway Galleria was demonstrating his new lightworker spirit-cleansing technique. He moved his hands in fluid motions and announced his full course was $49.99. In the background, Trucker could be seen on the second-floor mezzanine tossing half a ream of paper onto the crowd below — making it rain missing-persons posters. Ed scrolled back and replayed the moment repeatedly.

"Look at him go!" Ed said, pausing the video. His and Heather's face were visible on several of the posters floating in mid-air.

"Still doesn't tell us a lot," Ida said.

Ed glanced at her, then started the next video. It was from the panel discussion *Hollywood Stars Reveal the Real Truth!* He fast-forwarded through Rex Del Mango's rant about how movies are real life, while Tammi St. Vrain and Echo Kensington tried to stay awake.

"I think all three of those people are dead," Ida said. "May they rest in peace, and all of that."

"Rex was pretty good in *Battle Bugs 4: Return of the Battle Beetle*," Ed said. "I mean, it wasn't black and white or from a hundred years ago, so you haven't seen it."

Ed slowed the playback as Trucker stepped up to the Q&A microphone, looked over the crowd, and said, "Is there an Ed Young here? Or a Jennifer?"

Ed hit pause and looked at Ida.

"He's *looking* for Jennifer now, too?" Ida asked.

"Right?" Ed said. "Why? What happened? How does he know her?"

"Trucker doesn't look the greatest, either," Ida added.

Ed fired up the last video. It was labeled *Rainbows: God's Chemtrails*. He and Ida watched as Trucker said something off-mic to the main speaker and usher.

Then Trucker took to the lectern, and Ed turned up the volume.

"Regardless," Trucker said, "let's talk about rainbows. I like rainbows. Always have, since I was a kid. Tried to chase a few down myself in elementary school."

Trucker paused, smiled toward the doorway, and continued.

"So, I like rainbows. Always have. At some point, when I was young, I stopped chasing them and started looking into what they actually were," He paused again. "Turns out, humans have figured rainbows out. A lot of smart humans. Smarter than me. They nailed this one."

The recording then had a clear jump cut, editing out a large section, and the main speaker was back at the lectern. "Yes, you can be known as Thunderbird Jones," he said.

Ed stopped the video.

"That's it?" Ida asked.

"That's it," Ed said.

"So, what we know," Ida recapped, holding up her fingers one by one. "Trucker has the tolerance to sit through a Mormon — sorry, LDS — quack and his disciples," she raised her pointer finger. "He's not a fan of the band Iron something," she raised her middle finger. "At some point, he started actively looking for the crazy monster, Jennifer," she raised her ring finger. "And he really likes rainbows. Chased them as a child," she raised her pinky finger.

"Yup," Ed said. "That's four more things we didn't know before."

"Not bad. Good work," Ida said.

"Might be useful when we sneak in," Ed added. "Who knows."

Ida moved back to her tiny desk. It was time to let Ed in on her plan.

"I'm not sneaking in, Eddie."

"What are we gonna do then?" Ed asked. "You saw that front gate. They're not just gonna let us waltz on in."

"I'm not going in at all," Ida said.

"What do you mean?" Ed stood up. "We're here. We came this far. You can't back out now."

"I'm not backing out," Ida explained. "I just can't go in."

"You want me to sneak in alone?" Ed was not happy. "I can't do it alone."

"I don't want you to sneak in," Ida said.

"Then —" Ed started, then cut himself off.

"I want you to join *The Radiant Way*," Ida said.

"Are you out of your freakin' mind?!" Ed asked.

"Maybe," Ida said. "But this is the only way I could find. It's the only way any of this can work. And trust me — I've thought of everything."

"Well, then let's think of everything *more*," Ed said.

"Look, there's no way into that compound and effectively reach Trucker, other than acceptance into *The Radiant Way*," Ida said. "I would do it myself, but I wouldn't be accepted. Men are her focus. The only women I've seen in any of the videos are few and far between. I'm guessing they're relatives, old friends from her past, or complete sycophants she picked up at conferences like Ascend-A-Palooza."

"Ida! She nearly got me before. You send me in there, and all it's going to do is give her another follower," Ed said. "And then you'll be on a rescue mission for two people. Or at the very least need to forward my mail from Mom's house."

"No," Ida said. "She's not going to *get* you. You're protected."

Ed slowly sat back down on the bottom bunk and processed the reality of the situation.

"You can do this, Eddie," Ida encouraged.

Ed sat in silence for a moment and quietly said, "It's gotta be me. This is my calling. My Heavenly Father's will."

Ida looked at her brother and could see a bit of fear in his eyes, "Yes, it is, Ed."

She moved back over to the bottom bunk and sat next to him. "It's not going to be like it was ten years ago. I'm going to send you in there armed with information. Knowledge. I'm going to teach you everything anyone could possibly know about people like Jennifer Smith — how they do what they do, why they do what they do, and everything you'll need to know to help Trucker break free."

"But Jen is smarter than me," Ed said. "She'll —"

"She's not smarter than you, Ed," Ida explained. "What she does has nothing to do with intelligence. These people have an innate ability to manipulate and exploit. It's wired into them for many reasons. That, combined with Jen's delusional disorder, doesn't make her smart. It makes her clinically pathological." She added, "The 'con' in 'con artist' stands for *confidence*. They're not called IQ artists."

"Okay, but what if she recognizes me?" Ed asked.

"It was ten years ago. But it won't matter. People like her don't really see people the way you do. They just don't," Ida said.

"That's strange," Ed said.

"It is," Ida agreed. "Now, are you ready for your crash course?"

"Isn't there like a documentary or something I could watch instead?" Ed asked.

"Ya know," Ida said, considering, "there probably is. But we're doing it my way. Cool?"

"Cool."

Ida spent the next few hours teaching her brother a rapid-fire series of lessons: *Jennifer Smith 101*, *Coercive Control 201*, *Cult Dynamics and Exit Strategies 301*, and *Psychoeducation 401*.

Ed listened intently, and Ida began to wrap up her session with a final short list of what not to do when dealing with Trucker.

"Logic won't work alone," she explained. "The control involves emotional, social, and psychological manipulation — it's not just faulty logic. Empathy and patience are more important than facts alone."

She continued, "And whatever you do, don't directly attack Jen or the belief system that has been instilled in him. It'll just validate her narrative that outsiders are evil. It'll strengthen Trucker's connection to her and the group. Don't ridicule or shame her or *The Radiant Way*. He's with her because of emotional needs — not because he's stupid or gullible. If you go in with mockery, he'll just dig in harder."

"Wait," Ed stood up and walked the three steps to the tiny desk and sat down. He thought for a moment. "This is why you've been such a big B since we got here. You've been on a full, rather annoying rant about the LDS all day. You were —"

"— trying to make you a super Mormon," Ida admitted. "Your beliefs are yours. I think the whole thing, the church, everything is messed up," she paused, "but you are a good man. I know you would be a good man regardless of your faith. But in this case, what we need to do, what you need to do . . . your faith is going to protect and save you."

She continued to explain without going deep into psychological frameworks. "Jennifer Smith has chosen to create a belief system and use it to manipulate, exploit, and indoctrinate anyone she can. To make herself a prophet and god, to take whatever she wants or needs. And she is very good at it."

Ida took a breath. "Your faith must be stronger than the crazy monster's coercion. So I tried to give you a Mormon suit of armor she hopefully can't penetrate."

"It's *LDS*," Ed corrected. "An LDS suit of armor."

"Whatever," Ida said.

"You could've just told me to strengthen my testimony."

"Didn't think that would be as effective."

"Pretty messed up, Sis," Ed said. "Actually, pretty manipulative."

"For the greater good," Ida replied. "Sometimes you have to train your soldiers by any means necessary to survive and defeat the enemy."

"I forgive you," Ed moved over to Ida and gave her a hug. "Love you."

"Don't try and wash my feet," Ida pleaded, then added, "Love you, too."

"So," Ed sighed. "How do I join *The Radiant Way*?"

Ida squeezed her brother tight and said, "You just walk back to her compound. Stand in the cobblestones and wait. And pray that she takes you in." Ida meant *pray* not in the religious sense, but as a figure of speech: to hope or even beg. But she knew Ed took it the other way. Which was fine.

She added, "You can't take anything with you. Although I doubt she'd object to some credit cards or a pile of cash. But leave everything here."

"Okay," Ed said. "I can do this. I'll take off in the morning."

18

THE NEXT MORNING

Ida woke up on the bottom bunk in the cozy cabin, extremely groggy and with a bit of brain fog. She sat up and could hear her brother above in the top bunk. All of his devices were turned off. He was quietly praying:

"Dear Heavenly Father,

I come before Thee in humility, asking for strength and guidance.

Please help me to do Thy will.

Bless me with courage, with discernment,

And with love for those I'm trying to help.

I don't know if I am strong enough, but I trust Thee.

Please let Thy Spirit be with me.

In the name of Jesus Christ, Amen."

Ida looked up and said, "Amen."

"You're up!" Ed said excitedly, hopping off the top bunk fully dressed.

"I'm thinkin'," Ida said, rubbing crumbs from her eyes. "We don't have to do this."

"Nah. We have to do this."

"We really don't. We might be biting off more than we can chew. Actually — I know we are," Ida said. "Trucker's been under her control for ten years. We don't have to rush. We could come up with another way to help him."

"This is the way. It's my calling," Ed said. "I feel the Spirit within me. Guiding me. This is what I'm supposed to do."

Ida didn't roll her eyes and refrained from explaining to Ed that the Spirit he was feeling was a cocktail of biological chemicals surging through him: a dash of dopamine lighting up his system, a splash of norepinephrine with adrenaline heightening alertness and internal significance, an ounce of oxytocin providing connection and a feeling of rightness. Drops of endorphins delivered that fleeting sense of hope. All the while, the brain's default mode network took a breather, the "self" dissolved, and Ed became a vessel for the Spirit.

"I love you, brother," Ida said. "If you're ready and want to go."

"I do. And I'm ready right now."

"Okay," Ida was frantic for a moment. Then opened a small cabinet in the kitchenette, grabbed a trash bag, and shook it open with a snap. She pulled six bottles of water from the mini-fridge, dropped them in, and handed it to Ed. "For the walk."

Ed hugged Ida as she wished him good luck, and he left the cozy cabin, shutting the door behind him.

Ida collapsed at the tiny desk. "This is a horrible, awful idea," she said to herself, once again imagining the risky, utterly impossible nature of his task.

She then, just now, decided she was going to give him four days. No. Three days, tops. Then she would ignore all expert guidance, break into *The Radiant Way*, and grab both Ed and Trucker from the compound. She wondered how well a sensibly rented Nissan Sentra would hold up against a giant iron gate. She wondered if she remembered to take the comprehensive rental insurance.

She set a three-day timer on her phone and watched it start counting down from seventy-two hours. Then swiped through the phone and scrolled for the sensible rental agreement when the door to the cozy cabin flung back open.

She shot straight up.

"I almost forgot!" Ed said. He climbed to the top bunk, dug into his backpack's side compartment, pulled out something small that Ida couldn't quite see, and slid it into his pocket. "Gonna smuggle in a little contraband. Might be a secret weapon. Might be silly. Who knows."

Then he jumped down, kissed his sister on top of her head, and raced back out the front door.

"Good luck!" Ida yelled through the closing door and whispered, "May your Heavenly Father protect you. And all that."

SEVEN MILES LATER

Three full water bottles weighed down the bottom of Ed's trash bag knapsack while three empties rattled around on top. The bag swung back and forth as he walked along the edge of the country road toward *The Radiant Way* compound. He'd made good time, walking, jogging, then walking again. He repeated that cardio pattern for about two hours, all while preparing himself for what he called a mission from God . . . and his Dad.

He thought about the footage of Trucker he'd watched the night before. Trucker, relentlessly searching for him. Never giving up.

He also thought of Jackie Chan and Chris Tucker from the *Rush Hour* movies, never giving up on their investigation either. He performed a little hand chop and leg kick as he jogged.

And then he thought about what his sister had told him. That anyone could fall under the spell of someone like Jennifer Smith. That he had fallen prey to Jen once before, nearly taken in, before being saved at the last moment. He wondered how it happened to Trucker. How he got *got*. He wondered if Jackie Chan and Chris Tucker could be pulled in too, while trying not to think about the fact that they were fictional detectives.

All of it played on a sort of mental shuffle during his two-hour trek until he came to the private entry drive of *The Radiant Way*.

He looked down the short rocky drive leading to the iron entrance gate. Of the four men he and Ida had seen during their earlier drive-by, only two remained. The retired schoolteacher and the young soldier. Both stood wobbly in the cobblestone patch.

Ed took one step toward the gate and whispered under his breath, "Nephi, two, two. Thou knowest the greatness of God, and He shall consecrate thine afflictions for thy gain." The plastic trash bag of water bottles trembled in his hand. "Doubt not. Fear not."

He took a few more steps up the drive and then whispered to himself again, imitating Detective Carter from *Rush Hour*, "Do you understand the words that are coming out of my mouth?"

As he reached the cobblestone patch, he paused at the edge of the concrete square, looked down at his feet, then at the two men, both of whom were still staring at the iron gate.

"Hi, guys. This is the place, huh." Ed then stepped onto the cobblestones.

The men didn't respond. Ed looked each of them over and quickly concluded that they were not doing well. Their deteriorated state made him think about his pioneer ancestors who had journeyed from Iowa and Nebraska to the Salt Lake with nothing but handcarts filled with their possessions. Handcarts not pulled by oxen but by the pioneers themselves. It seemed like an insane endeavor to Ed but was also an example of what was possible through absolute faith. Ed also correctly guessed that Ida probably knew some horrific facts about the handcarts and faithful cross-country slog.

Ed dug into his trash bag and pulled out two full water bottles. He offered one to the soldier, whose eyes never left the gate.

"Take it," Ed said.

The soldier didn't react.

Ed shook the bottle gently. "Come on. You need some hydration."

Without looking away, the soldier grabbed the bottle and chugged the entire thing in one go, water spilling down his chin, then dropped the bottle at his feet.

"Thank you for your service," Ed said, then turned to the retired schoolteacher and offered the second bottle.

The schoolteacher accepted it without hesitation but still did not remove his eyes from the gate. He took a sip and held it by his side. The bottle trembled.

"Thank you for your service as well," Ed said, then stood in silence with the men before he turned toward the entrance. He looked up at the camera pointed directly at them and joined in what was to be an unofficial gate-staring contest.

Boredom took hold almost immediately.

After a while, he wondered how long it had been. If he'd had a watch, he'd have known it had only been about five minutes. Five straight minutes of simple, uninterrupted silence. This was rare for Ed, aside from naptime or quiet moments spent in faithful contemplation inside a temple's celestial room. Five minutes without a movie, television show, or checking his phone.

In his mind, he replayed the footage of Trucker at Ascend-A-Palooza. He remembered flashes of what Trucker had said that helped snap him free from Jennifer Smith's clutches. And how he was never going to stop looking for him, or something like that.

Ed figured that if all he had to overcome was boredom, then that was doable. He had it easy.

He stared at the rust-streaked slab of iron in front of him. After so long, the constant focus on the single object started to feel . . . strange. The edges of his vision blurred. The gate seemed to breathe, inhaling and exhaling. Rust streaks twisted and streamed. It started to feel like something else and began to induce a mild altered state.

He blinked, trying to break the visual dissociation.

When he looked again, the wide gate reminded him of something different. A movie screen.

This gave him an idea. A plan to counteract the weird indoctrination effect happening to him before he'd even stepped inside the compound. He'd tap into his vast library of movie memories and project them onto the gate like an old-school drive-in theater. No cars. No projector. Just his brain. He would mentally reenact each adventure, scene by scene, to pass the time.

He queued up the first film that was still fresh in his memory, *Rush Hour*.

The soldier and the schoolteacher both glanced at Ed as he let out a little giggle and smiled at what he thought was a brilliant idea.

But before Ed could make it past the opening credits, the iron gate began to creep open.

There he was. Trucker.

He was thinner in person than in even the most recent *Radiant Way* videos. His head was still shaved to stubble, but his once-long beard was gone. His cheekbones were sharp. Eyes sunken, with dark circles like bruises from exhaustion.

An unbuttoned Hawaiian shirt hung limply from his bony, slumped shoulders. His exposed skin was sunburned. His blue jeans worn thin, and his tan work boots were scraped and tattered.

To Ed, he looked like a chunk of steak someone had tried to turn into beef jerky, without knowing what they were doing. Or so he remembered from an old episode of *Good Eats*.

Trucker had emerged from behind the iron gate with another man dressed similarly: unbuttoned Hawaiian shirt, blue jeans, and work boots. But this man was thick, imposing, muscular, and much younger. It looked like he'd been stealing from Trucker's food bowl.

The two of them, Trucker and his fitness-bro cohort, stood before Ed, the soldier, and the retired schoolteacher.

Ed wanted to shout, "Trucker! It's me! That guy from ten years ago! Let's go! Let's get out of here!" But that went against everything Ida had taught him. Still, he had to say something. But before he could, Trucker raised a finger to his lips.

Ed didn't know what it meant beyond the universally understood symbol for, "Don't speak." But he swore he saw something more. A flicker of recognition in Trucker's tired eyes. Maybe he remembered him. Maybe. Ed couldn't be sure.

The fitness-bro cohort stepped toward the soldier and said, "Go home. Maybe next time."

The soldier didn't move.

Then the fitness-bro cohort turned to the retired schoolteacher. "You, too. Get out of here. And there will never be a next time. She doesn't want you."

The retired schoolteacher didn't move either.

Through it all, Trucker stood a few feet back, detached, almost supervisory. He looked hard at Ed, who returned the stare with a soft smile and open kindness. Trucker looked down at Ed's shoes, then gave a slight nod to his fitness-bro cohort. The two of them turned and disappeared back through the gate as it slowly closed behind them.

The soldier and schoolteacher didn't move at all. Not right away.

Not until the soldier let out a guttural, primal scream and began walking back toward the country road.

The retired schoolteacher stood there and wept.

Ed looked at him and said softly, "It'll be okay." Then he turned his attention back to the iron gate, fired up his mental film projector, and started his movie memory marathon.

By the time the last *Rush Hour* movie had finished, Ed guessed, somewhat accurately, that a little over four hours had passed. Somewhere in that four-and-a-half hours, the retired schoolteacher had thrown in the towel and left the cobblestone patch, but Ed hadn't noticed.

Jackie Chan and Chris Tucker had kept him company just fine. Detectives saving the day had kept him focused and his mind busy. But he needed more. He had no idea how long he'd been standing there. He needed something more. Something to keep him sane and encouraged.

He looked away from the iron-gate movie screen, glanced at the security camera and then at the trees and countryside around him. One particular tree caught his eye. It appeared to almost have a personality. A twisted, exposed patch of bark looked like it had been healing for years. A couple of limbs reached out like arms. And Ed could almost see a face in the leaves. It reminded him of a character from one of his favorite films.

Ed smiled at the tree and said, "Oh my goodness, thank you. That's a great idea," he patted his pocket to check on his contraband, his possibly silly secret weapon. "I actually can't believe I didn't think of it."

He turned back to the iron gate and started up the first movie in the legendary heroic trilogy he'd seen too many times to count: *The Lord of the Rings*. Extended editions, of course. Total runtime: over twelve hours.

Ed began his mental retelling of the tale.

The somber orchestra score over a black screen. The voice of Cate Blanchett as the elf Galadriel, speaking Elvish, then English: *"The world has changed. I feel it in the water. I feel it in the earth. I smell it in the air."*

The beginning was burned into his brain. He couldn't recite the entire trilogy verbatim, but he was going to try.

He imagined the forging of the One Ring. Sauron's initial defeat. Bilbo Baggins, Ian Holms, finding the ring, and eventually leaving it to Frodo, Elijah Wood. Gandalf, Sir Ian McKellen, warning Frodo, "That ring's no good. Gotta throw that thing into a volcano."

Frodo gathered his buddies to go play volcanic ring toss. The most important buddy being Samwise Gamgee, Sean Astin. *He really does a lot of the heavy lifting,* Ed would periodically think.

The buddies set off and faced danger at every turn. Boromir, Sean Bean, bites it in a gloriously valiant and sacrificial manner. Ed almost let himself get distracted thinking about how many times Mr. Bean had died on screen, but he refocused. Frodo and Samwise split off from their buddies and continued the journey alone.

About a half hour into *The Two Towers*, the sun slipped below the horizon and Ed found himself in total darkness.

Bugs, wildlife, and the sounds of night began to stir. But Ed was not afraid.

He looked toward the dark silhouette of the tree with personality and whispered, "We've got a little ways to go till your part, Treebeard. I'll let you know."

Then he returned to his mental movie epic about the endurance of hope and the triumph of good over corrupting evil.

He pushed through for hours. Aragorn, Viggo Mortenson, and the army of free peoples faced off against the Dark Lord Sauron in the final battle at the Black Gate. A distraction to give Frodo a chance.

Ed kept going. The ring was destroyed. Sauron defeated. Aragorn crowned king. The hobbits returned home, forever changed. And Frodo sailed to the Undying Lands with Gandalf and his elf friends.

As the credits rolled in his mind, Ed found himself inspired. But the sun had still not yet risen.

So, Ed prayed to his Heavenly Father until it did.

An hour had passed, Ed's legs felt like rubber and he long finished the final sip from the last bottle of water. He didn't know if he could make it. He looked at the tree with personality and said, "Don't' know how they do it. Don't know how horses and cows stand around all day then sleep standing up." Ed looked around. "Maybe they don't sleep standing up? I don't know. But I can't do this much longer, Treebeard."

Luckily, only a moment later, the iron gate to *The Radiant Way* opened. Ed of course did not think it was luck, but rather an act of God.

Once more, Trucker and his fitness-bro cohort walked out, still wearing the same clothes as they had yesterday. Ed wasn't to judge. He didn't bring a change either.

"What's your name? Trucker asked.

Ed paused, then answered, "Chris Tucker. But I also go by Frodo."

Trucker looked at him with a curiosity until the fitness-bro cohort said, "Well, Frodo, now you are to be Zeke the Initiate."

"Why do I need a new name?" Ed asked.

Trucker stepped forward and said, "Normally, a question of any kind would mean immediate expulsion. Do you want to be part of a better future? Do you want to be part of Jennifer's *Radiant Way*?"

"Yes," Ed answered as sincerely as he could, while Trucker continued to look at him with a strange, thoughtful expression.

Ed added, "Gotta tell ya, I've always wanted be a Zeke. Perfect choice. Upset my *MOM* didn't pick it."

Trucker squinted at him.

The fitness-bro extended his hand. "Welcome, Initiate Zeke. They call me the Sam of Sams."

"Like Gamgee?" Ed stopped himself. "Sorry, that wasn't a question. Like Gamgee," he repeated flat-toned without a lilt.

"Who?" Sam of Sams asked.

"Doesn't matter," Ed replied.

"Let's go," Trucker said, and the three of them began walking toward the gate.

Ed looked over his shoulder at the tree with personality and gave it a thankful nod goodbye.

All three disappeared into *The Radiant Way* as the iron gate closed behind them.

19

INSIDE

If he didn't know any better — if he had absolutely no prior knowledge, if he hadn't been standing on a patch of uneven stones for over twenty-four straight hours, and if he wasn't sleep-deprived to the point of near-hallucination — Ed might have thought the property beyond the iron gate was idyllic. Approaching paradise.

Sure, the main house had additions and modifications that looked odd, but it was a quirky odd sprinkled with beauty, not a *run-in-terror-they're-cooking-people-parts-in-the-kitchen* kind of odd. The same went for the haphazardly repaired greenhouse, the large muraled cargo-container structure, the recreational area with ski tow rope and zip-line course, and all the other odds and ends.

And the Radiants walking along the flowered paver stones, moving here and there, wore smiling faces and radiated the outward expression of people who had found their sanctuary. Their Garden of Eden. Not souls on the ragged end of need.

All of it cradled in the undeniable natural beauty of the Wasatch Range and the fringe of the Uinta Mountains.

But Ed did know better. Ida had trained him well, and he understood that beneath it all, beneath the charm and polish, was a dangerous woman who, given the right circumstances, could be capable of anything. It didn't matter what was built on top of that foundation. Whether it appeared odd, beautiful, or even flawless, it would eventually collapse. And when it did, anyone nearby, or maybe even far off, would be in danger.

Ed had to get Trucker out.

He was following Trucker and Sam of Sams along a crooked line of paver stones toward the cargo-container structure when a high-pitched voice called out from the direction of the main house.

"Trucker! I need you."

Trucker patted Sam of Sams on the shoulder and jogged toward the main house.

Ed stepped up beside Sam of Sams and said, "Trucker. That is quite a name. Not that I'm complaining about Zeke. Love it."

Sam of Sams led Ed inside the cargo-container structure.

It was a bunkhouse. Or what *The Radiant Way* would call a bunkhouse, Ed supposed. It was what one would get if they threw a military barracks into a blender and set it on a psychedelic-spirituality spin cycle. Soda-can-sized holes were drilled sporadically across the upper walls, and dim string lights wove their way around the ceiling. The scent of patchouli, strawberries, and coconut hit Ed's nose the moment he stepped inside.

"Cozy," Ed said to Sam of Sams as he was led to the third bunk bed in.

Sam of Sams pointed to the bottom bunk. "Here's a spot you can call home for now. Get some rest."

Ed collapsed onto the mattress.

Under any other circumstances — say, traveling through the desert and stopping at the only roadside motel for miles — he would have asked the front desk to get him another room or hit the road. The mattress felt like a used foam slab pulled from a dumpster behind a third-rate hospital. One even Goodwill wouldn't accept. Which, to be fair, it was.

But under these circumstances, he was asleep in seconds.

Exactly thirty-six minutes later, Ed was woken by the face of another Radiant just inches from his own. It was the face of a sweet-looking old man in his mid-seventies with a good head of hair and a double chin.

"Zeke. Zeeeeke! Initiate Zeke!" The old man began with a whisper but ended in a nasally shout, gently shaking Ed's shoulders.

Ed, of course, didn't know he'd only been asleep for a little over half an hour. His brain was foggy, and he was beyond groggy. It took a moment just to remember where he was, let alone why a strange, kindly-looking grandfather was in his mom's house.

And then he remembered.

"Zeke," the old man said. "Good. You're awake. I'm Roman. Sam of Sams said you needed food. A few of us are having a picnic on the Heavenly Hill, so I was told to come get you."

"Wait . . . what time is it?" Ed asked.

Roman put a finger to his lips. "Questions are a big no-no for initiates. You know that. But don't worry — I won't tell anyone." He tried to guide Ed into a sitting position on the edge of the bottom cot. But was failing.

Realizing Roman was not going to stop, Ed leaned forward and sat up. "I'm really not hungry. Need to sleep."

"You'll love the food here," Roman said, still tugging gently. "It's fresh. Everything straight from the garden. No pesticides. No herbicides. Or any other kind of -cide's *they* don't tell ya about. Just pure radiance."

"Let's get you up and fed," Roman said.

As the old man kept tugging, Ed got the not-so-subtle hint that this was not an optional invitation. It was a command.

Ed stood up shakily, if for no other reason than to get the old man to stop pawing at him.

Roman beamed. "You'll love the Heavenly Hill. It's a great spot. Some of the others are already there."

HEAVENLY HILL

Roman led Ed on a short walk past the main house and the greenhouse and over the crest of a gently sloping hill dotted with wildflowers.

Ed was grateful for the elderly man's naturally slow pace. He was nearly asleep on his feet, barely fighting off the urge to collapse right there in the grass. He shielded his eyes from the bright sunlight and rested a hand on Roman's shoulder for balance.

When he looked back, the buildings were gone from view. Ahead of him, stretching across the horizon beyond an open field, was a sweeping panorama of the Wasatch Range. It was, indeed, a heavenly view worthy of the name. For a brief moment, it put him at ease. So much so, he contemplated doing a spin with his arms stretched outward and sing about the hills being alive with the sound of music.

In the middle of the field, they came upon a group of Radiants sitting cross-legged around the edge of a large round mandala-printed blanket. They were facing three closed wicker baskets laid carefully in the center.

"Hello, everyone," Roman said. "This is Initiate Zeke."

The five Radiants, four men and one woman, all turned to the very tired Ed and greeted him with enthusiastic, if not eerie, smiles.

"Hello, Zeke. I'm Levi."

"Hi, I'm Noah."

"Hey, call me Gabriel."

"Hello, I'm Isaac."

"Welcome to the Radiance, Zeke," the woman said. "My name is Ariel."

"Like the little mermaid," Ed said, trying to lift his eyelids past half-mast. His Disney princess observation received no reaction from the picnicking Radiants. They just kept smiling at him.

The Radiants scooched around to make space, and Roman sat down with Ed. The group reached for each other's hands and said in unison:

"We thank Jennifer for her guidance. We thank her for showing us *The Radiant Way*."

Isaac and Ariel opened the three wicker baskets in the center of the mandala blanket, made plates of food, and handed them to Levi one by one. The picnickers passed them along to each other in the circle until everyone had one.

Ed looked at his plate and was grateful it was actual *food* food and not imaginary cubes of radiant energy. It was vegetables. The freshest and most vibrant assortment he had maybe ever seen.

He picked up a carrot with his fingers, took a bite, and let out an involuntary "Mmm."

"Good, right?" Gabriel said.

"It is . . ." Ed took another bite. "It's like I've never tasted a real carrot before. You guys grew these?"

Levi's smile disappeared. He put a finger on his lips and stared at Ed with flatness. Not anger or malice, just an emotionless, piercing gaze.

Ed was confused. Did this Levi guy have a problem with carrots? Who could possibly have a problem with these carrots? Then it hit him. He'd asked a question. An innocent, even complimentary question, but a question nonetheless.

Roman coughed and placed a hand on Ed's shoulder. "I agree. These carrots are incredible. They're my favorite."

"They are good," Isaac added.

Ariel leaned forward and pulled two sealed Mason jars from a basket, each filled with a rough-textured, cream-colored liquid. She handed one to Ed.

She unsealed her jar and clinked it against his. "To you, Zeke. For leading yourself to the Way."

Ed unsealed his jar and looked curiously at the liquid, then at Ariel. He wanted to ask what it was, but there was no way to do so without breaking the "no questions" rule. He tilted his head, hoping for a hint.

"It's raw milk," Roman said. "The finest."

Ed swirled the jar and swore he saw the bacteria inside forming gangs to decide whether to give him salmonella or E. coli.

"Bottoms up," Ariel said, taking a long drink.

Ed felt he had no choice but to follow. He sipped the creamy liquid.

"Good, right?" Gabriel asked.

Ed actually agreed, it was good. But tastiness was not what concerned him. What concerned him was how close the nearest emergency room might be in case the milk decided to turn his insides inside-out.

"It's lovely," Ed said with as much joy as he could muster, lifting the jar to his lips without actually taking a drink.

Noah took a bite out of a tomato. Juice dripped down his chin, and he made no attempt to wipe it clean as he asked, "What helped you find the Way, Zeke?"

"A newscast," Ed said, chewing another carrot. "A couple — maybe a few — weeks ago, there was this broadcast about Jennifer and *The Radiant Way*. There was something about it. It caught my attention."

"And what helped you find the Way, Initiate Zeke?" Levi asked.

Ed wanted to ask, *What do you mean?* and say *I just told you.* But that didn't seem like a smart option. He also got the impression there wasn't any better clarification that would qualify as an acceptable answer. He took another bite of carrot and pretended to be in deep contemplation.

"What helped you find the Way?" Noah asked again.

Ed chewed slowly. "Like I said. I saw Jennifer on the news. It was a national broadcast . . . I think. Something about it caught my attention, so I looked deeper into Jennifer and what her Radiant Way had to offer. Watched some of her videos. They spoke to me." He swallowed the carrot.

"What helped you find the Way?" Levi asked again.

Ed looked at Levi, who was smiling wide. Roman glanced between them, clearly about to speak and break the awkward silence, but Ariel beat him to it.

"I'll tell you what helped me find the Way," she said, and proceeded like she was almost reading a script. "Growing up was a nightmare. My mother was an abusive narcissist, and my father was an alcoholic. I used to hide in the storage space of our house to avoid both of them. I kept hiding until I was old enough to find drugs and boys. Then I ran through both until I didn't know who I ever was or could be," Ariel smiled. "And then I discovered Jennifer and the Way. She has given me everything that I am."

Isaac reached out to Ariel and squeezed her hand and shared, "I was destroying myself until I found Jen and *The Radiant Way*. She taught me the evil that I was putting into my body. The food, booze, drugs, and cigarettes. She and her gift pulled me from the depths. I owe her my life."

Unprompted, Roman followed. "I used to be an attorney. I thought I had everything . . . a good, fulfilling life. And then I met Jen. Not on the web or those videos. But in real life. We had magnetic chemistry immediately." He smiled and was heartfelt. "She taught me how much more there was to life. Taught me how to give. How to be a philanthropist, so to speak. I've given everything. And I'll continue to give whatever I have. Because I am nothing without her radiance. It guides me. I love Jennifer."

Ed's innate empathy was going haywire. His hands tingled and his back started to ache while he listened to the two Radiants. His discomfort could have come from a number of things. The lack of sleep. Levi's unpleasant and incessant staring without blinking. The possibly dangerous bacteria now swirling in his belly. The unsettling radiant-made hodgepodge of a stone-and-brick barrier topped with barbed wire in the distance behind Levi. Or the not-so-subtle camera that he just noticed embedded in that barrier wall, pointed directly at him.

"Which of the videos of Jennifer spoke to you, Initiate Zeke? What did they say?" Levi asked, still with a smile and still without a blink.

There was a real fear racing through Ed on that Heavenly Hill.

He and Ida had been so focused on making sure he wouldn't be indoctrinated or trapped within *The Radiant Way* during the rescue attempt, they hadn't spent much time on what would happen if his real motives were sniffed out. Were these people violent? Ida had said Jennifer was capable of anything. Ed assumed that applied to her followers, too.

Were Levi and Noah, and their subtle sinister smiles, about to drag him to Jennifer and have him boiled in her kitchen?

How high was that barrier wall with the camera? Could he clear it with a good sprint and his best jump? He was awfully tired. His raw-milked gut was grumbling. And Levi's question still hung in the air.

Then Levi's entire demeanor shifted, along with the rest of the Radiants. They seemed to be overcome with respect and even a touch of fear. Ed thought his prolonged silence might have been taken as a sign of strength. That would explain their sudden deference.

But Ed sensed that wasn't the case. He turned around, and there was Trucker, standing behind him.

"She is receiving a download. Will be sharing guidance," Trucker towered over the cross-legged picnickers and said in a voice devoid of emotion, "Quickly finish your lunch, pack up your things, and show yourselves in attendance."

It occurred to Ed what had possibly just happened.

Maybe Levi and Noah would have stopped with their questions. Maybe Ed would have come up with a satisfactory answer. But more likely, they would have seen through him, and he would have cracked under their odd, smiley interrogation.

It was a very real possibility that Trucker had unknowingly just saved Ed for the second time in ten years.

The Radiants began tidying up the area and rolled up the mandala blanket.

"Roman," Trucker said. "How are you? Taking care of yourself?"

"Yes, Mister Trucker," Roman replied. "Doing very well. Thank you."

The Radiants started their way back toward the main house when Trucker said, "Initiate Zeke, walk with me."

Ed hustled to Trucker's side. "Yes, sir. What —" He caught himself before asking a question. "Can —" He stopped himself again.

"It has been decided," Trucker said. "I am going to personally oversee your initiation process."

"Thank you, Trucker," Ed said.

Trucker looked at him curiously, "We can tell you have a good soul. We believe you have a lot to give — that you can become your best self and achieve radiance with the right guidance. I will help you. Jennifer said this has been sent to her."

"Thank you, again," Ed said sincerely. "I can't begin to tell you how much I appreciate you. All of this seems too good to be true. Like truly unbelievable. I look forward to you pointing me in the right direction."

"Yeah," Trucker said, studying him closely. "I can . . . help show you the Way."

20

THE GUIDANCE

Back at the main house, Sam of Sams stood at the bottom step that led to the Gothic-arched doorway, painted with the motto: *Leave Resistance Behind. Let Radiance Flow.* He was holding a large wooden cube covered in indecipherable symbols and childlike drawings.

The picnickers returned with Trucker. Ariel and Isaac danced ahead of the group, with Roman hurrying to keep up behind them. They joined a large group of Radiants in the open area between the greenhouse and the cargo-container barracks while Trucker passed Sam of Sams and went up the steps into the main house.

Ed stood with the picnickers and was swarmed by smiling Radiants. They overwhelmed him with handshakes, hugs, and slaps on the back. It was disorienting, but he tried to take a headcount. Intel was intel, as he had learned from the movies. Better to have too much information than not enough. Who knew what might come in handy? He counted around forty men and ten to twelve women.

The Radiants settled down and turned to face the archway of the main house, where Trucker now held the front door open.

And then she emerged.

Jennifer Smith.

Dressed in a muted teal-grey sleeveless jumpsuit and with not a care in the world, she was deeply engaged with her phone. She offered no acknowledgment to the Radiants waiting for her, only a brief lift of her head and then back to her screen.

She turned to Trucker and whispered something. He, in turn, went back into the house, returned with a vape pen, and handed it to her. Without breaking focus from her phone, she took a deep inhale, held it, then exhaled a cloud skyward.

She smiled faintly at her screen as she descended the stairs.

Trucker followed her.

Sam of Sams followed Trucker.

She walked to the center of the gathered Radiants. Without pause, she took another drag from the vape pen as Sam of Sams set the cube on the ground. Trucker took her hand and helped her up onto it.

The audience of encircled Radiants looked upon her with quiet reverence. A reverence she had yet to acknowledge.

One of them shouted, "We love you, Jen!" and the rest followed with cheers.

She looked up from her phone, slipped it into a pocket of her jumpsuit, and slowly scanned the crowd.

Ed instinctively slid behind another Radiant, trying not to catch her gaze. Then he glanced at the picnickers, all of whom stood in awe.

He saw in their eyes the same look he'd seen in Ida's when they were kids on Christmas morning after she had unwrapped a new book. Or the look on his mom's face when she brought home a new dad. That look of hope. Of expectant joy. *This is the answer to all of my problems.*

He imagined Roman saw the true love he met very late in life — the one he'd give everything for, anything to spend another five minutes with. He imagined Gabriel saw a mother who finally cared. And imagined Ariel saw the big sister who saved her from her parents' storage space.

Ed saw none of this when he looked at Jennifer Smith standing on her box. He didn't see hope or joy or an answer of any kind. He could only see the truth, the manipulating monster under the mask.

He was no longer fearful of accidental indoctrination but was afraid he would be found out before he could save Trucker.

"I love you, too," Jennifer said. "I love you all. And what synchronicity . . . because guess what message I have received?" She did not wait for an answer. "That's right. It was pure love. Spelled out clearly. Tears poured down my face as the download, the guidance came through. I have never felt such intensity, clarity, and . . . love. I feel that same love now when I look at this circle of radiant souls. Each and every one of you."

"I am grateful for my gift — to receive the divine truth. Undiluted, plain, simple, and perfect. With no outside influence. No distortion. Only what is real," Jen let the words settle. "This gift of insight and revelation is a great responsibility. To teach. To lead."

"Others — outsiders — are jealous of this blessing I was given. Envy it." Jen turned slowly, her gaze sweeping the crowd. "They do not understand. They have not lived what I have lived. They do not know the battles I still fight."

"As you all know, I live with chronic illness." The Radiants nodded; Ed mimicked the motion half a beat too late. "I could barely get out of bed. Plagued by weakness. Fading."

The Radiants responded with sympathy, placing their hands on their hearts.

"Then the divine found me and showed me *The Way*. Showed me the radiance that was always mine."

"Even now, I fight through the illness. But I draw strength from all of you . . . and from *The Radiant Way*." She paused, looking from face to face. And those Radiant faces hung on her every word.

"And yet — I am attacked — by those who don't understand. Evil that fears and wants to destroy the light. It truly is us . . . versus *them*."

Her tone shifted. Colder. "I have received guidance that the real enemy is much closer." Jen's eyes locked on the picnickers and Ed.

All of the Radiants' eyes followed Jen's. Ed's body locked. His fight-flight-freeze response stuck on *deer-in-the-headlights*. His heart pounded; his feet went numb.

"I have been told," Jen said. "That one of us . . . is actually one of *them*."

Ed wasn't quite sure what these people would do to an evil other in their midst. He didn't really want to find out, so he weighed his options with a tired mind. None were good. Even if he made a mad dash this second, he'd be caught long before reaching the iron gate — which he'd have trouble climbing over even on a good day.

"Roman," Jen announced.

"Yes, sweetheart," Roman called out.

Jen's gaze hardened. "I have been told that you are not who you claim to be."

The Radiants slowly drew back from Roman in unison.

Ed didn't know exactly what was going on but was relieved he had avoided detection for now. He followed the Radiants' lead and stepped back from Roman. He also had the impression that he was the only one who didn't know what was happening, or about to happen. Aside from maybe Roman.

"What do you mean, not who I claim to be?" Roman asked. "By whom?"

"The guidance, Roman. The divine."

"I don't understand. You know me," Roman said quickly. "I love you."

Jen tilted her head, "Do I? Do you?"

"Yes, of course." His voice shook.

"The guidance says otherwise. Do you believe in the guidance?"

Roman sunk into himself, despondent, and the Radiants edged farther away.

"Do you believe in the guidance, Roman?" Jen repeated, sharper now.

"Yes," Roman said. "But . . ."

"It makes sense," Jen said coldly. "I've had my suspicions. Felt something was off with you for quite some time. Now the guidance confirms it."

"Jen, it's me. You know me. This is a mistake. The guidance must be wrong."

Around them, heads bowed down — except Ed, Trucker, and Sam of Sams, who snapped at Roman, "Are you saying Jen is wrong?"

A flick of her eyes silenced Sam of Sams instantly. He stepped back and nodded quickly in compliance.

"Wrong?" Jen's voice cut through Roman.

"No . . . that's not what I meant." He stammered and pleaded, "Maybe . . . it's from a different timeline? Dimension?"

"Maybe. Possible," Jen said, and Roman clung to that tiny shred of hope until she continued, "but I don't think so. It was very specific."

"No," Roman begged. "Please . . ."

"This is for the best. You have not shown proper support in some time."

The truth was, Roman had given everything he had to Jennifer Smith. Money, properties, cars, boats, time, love, and his very self. And the only thing left he had to give was that self. His physical presence. And now, by her decree, that was no longer needed or wanted.

"Jennifer," Roman pleaded, "please don't do this."

"It's not me," Jen said. "It's the guidance."

"No, please," Roman cried.

"Levi. Noah," she didn't need to say more.

The two Radiants stepped before Roman.

"Just go," Noah whispered to him. "Don't make us make you."

"Jen! I love you!" Roman grunted through tears. "This is wrong! Ask the guidance again! Ask again!"

Sam of Sams joined Levi and Noah, and the three men lifted Roman, carrying him toward the iron gate as his voice broke into a scream, "Please don't do this! I have nothing without you! Please don't!"

As Roman's pleas and screams faded into the distance, the temperature of Jen's expression shifted from calculated coldness to a warming reassurance. Her smile lit up; her eyes seemed to sparkle.

"I'm sorry you all had to see that. I'm sorry it had to be done. But it is what it is. The guidance is never wrong. It is divine. And it is proven right — always. As we just witnessed with Roman's doubt and questioning attacks. It infected him."

"*The Radiant Way* works one hundred percent of the time . . . but only when applied by someone who sincerely desires to improve their life, to uplift one another, and to heal the world. *The Radiant* cannot fail. Radiance does not fail. But you can — with overthinking, with selfishness, with questions, with doubt. It can infect you as it did Roman."

She stepped down from the wooden symbol-covered cube and moved slowly into the circle of Radiants. A hush fell over them as she passed. One by one, they reached out, brushing her arms, her shoulders, the fabric of her jumpsuit. As if touching her might transmit something divine.

She didn't speak. She simply moved among them, eyes soft, smile serene. Then, without warning, she stopped and wrapped her arms around a young woman. The others pressed in immediately. What began as a simple embrace became a cascade of bodies folding in from every side until the entire circle collapsed into one massive, reverent group hug.

"If we follow the guidance," she said from within the enormous huddle, "we can live in radiance. In love. Forever."

Ed found himself on the outer ring of the giant group hug celebrating the closeness and love of people who just banished a nice old man.

Roman's offense? As far as Ed could tell, nothing. Unless you counted meeting a monster, giving her all of his worldly possessions, and of course, waking Ed up after only thirty-six minutes of sleep. But in the end, none of those things were really Roman's fault.

The hug dissolved naturally, and as the Radiants peeled away like petals from a wilting flower, Jen stood in the center and fixed her eyes on Ed. She smiled wide and approached, light as air.

She extended her hand delicately.

It triggered momentary flashbacks within Ed. First, to the blurry day, ten years ago, when he'd first met Jennifer Smith, and further back to his Mormon mission in South America.

Back then, Ed had been taught that the Mission President possessed the gift of discernment: the ability to see a person's true nature through the power of the Holy Spirit. One handshake, they said, was enough to reveal error or evil.

Jen, apparently, did not have this power. Or if she did, Ed thought, she was hiding it well.

"It's a pleasure to meet you, Initiate Zeke," Jen said. "You have a familiar presence and a good energy. Welcome to *The Radiant Way*."

"Thank you for accepting me," Ed replied. "When I learned about you and what was here, I felt compelled to come immediately."

He couldn't tell whether she recognized him from all those years ago. There was a strangeness in her eyes he couldn't pin down. It made him look away out of pure reflex, and his stare landed on her vape pen.

She raised it slightly. "Medicine. For my chronic afflictions." She took a drag, exhaling a cloud toward the sky.

Ed nodded and smiled.

Her eyes swept over his clean-cut, slightly lived-in clothes. "This outfit just does not go."

Ed looked himself over, smiled, and said, "I don't know. It looked good on the mannequin at the GAP."

Her cheerfulness switched off like a light. "Does that make you angry? Does it make you angry that I don't think your outfit is fitting for you?"

Ed's eyebrows went up. "No. Not at all."

"You look angry."

"I'm sorry. I promise I'm not."

"You seem very angry."

Ed blinked, unsure what had just happened.

"If you can't take criticism," Jen said plainly, "then your time here may be cut short."

"Oh," Ed said, keeping his voice upbeat. "I can take criticism. I was just making a joke about the GAP mannequin."

"It came across as aggressive."

"I promise it wasn't. Was just a joke."

"Okay." Her smile flicked back on, warm and hypnotic. "Because we consider all feedback valuable. Even if you may not like it."

"I agree my clothes could use an upgrade. And I am here to be better in every way."

"Good," she tilted her head, "because I'd be heartbroken to lose you before we got to know one another."

"That'd be a shame," Ed said.

"It truly would."

Ed still didn't know what was happening. Only that, somehow, her one-on-one presence was pressing against his defenses, dulling the memory and knowledge of what she really was. At a distance, her influence could not pierce Ida's crash course in cult psychology or his own armor of faith.

But up close? It felt supernatural.

His fear of indoctrination flared again. A slow, spreading dread in his chest. He smiled, looked into her eyes, and something inside him began to falter. He knew better. He knew what she was. So why did her gaze make that truth feel so . . . remote?

He had to do something. Fast.

Panic pressed at the edges of his mind, but he pushed it back and mentally reached for something solid. Something true. He went back to the last trial he had to overcome. The iron gate. The cobblestones. The hours of waiting that were meant to break him. What kept the madness at bay?

And there it was. The answer was hidden in the mental movie marathon that saved him before. It would save him again. It was absurd. Perfect. Obvious.

Looking into her eyes he could see it: she was Sauron. A reasonably attractive middle-aged woman who also happened to be the evil, manipulating Dark Lord of Mordor from *The Lord of the Rings*.

It was plain as day.

Ed laughed out loud at this revelation.

"Laughing is good!" Jen said. "Laughing brings us closer to radiance. It transcends ego, connects us to our true selves, and protects us."

"That it does," Ed said. The fear slipped away. He could anchor himself in the truth whenever she looked into his eyes. She was Sauron. He was Frodo. And Frodo wins. Good wins.

Ed took pride in resisting what felt like a magical assault on his mind. He barely registered her prattling on about connections and divinity when distant movement caught his attention. Someone was running toward them from the main house. Small. Quick. Not a hobbit, but close.

"There's a kid here!?" The questioning, emphatic words tumbled out before he could stop them. He quickly corrected himself. "That wasn't a question. I need to work on my tone and inflection. I meant — there's a kid here! That's great!"

The boy ran straight to Jen, hugging her and burrowing in. She hugged him back hard. He kissed her on the lips repeatedly, and their fingers interlocked as they held hands.

"Initiate Zeke," she said, "this is Saul. My son. He is an old soul that has lived millions of lives. Has had many powerful reincarnations."

"Hey, Saul, nice to meet you, buddy," Ed said kindly to the boy.

"Are you new?" Saul asked.

"I am," Ed answered.

"Are you my new best friend?"

Without hesitation, Ed said, "If that's what you'd like."

"Yay!" Saul shouted. "Mom, let's do the zip line. Zeke, you wanna come?"

"I'm sorry, honey," Jen said, "Zeke has work to do. But we can go play." She turned to Ed, "I'm glad you're here, Zeke."

Jen and Saul sprinted up the hill toward the ski tow rope and zip-line course. Ed watched and noted that her sprinting speed was remarkable for someone with chronic illnesses who supposedly struggled to get out of bed without divine intervention and guidance.

Ed watched Jennifer and Saul clamber around the zip-line course, their laughter echoing through the trees. At first glance, it might've passed for a normal mother-and-son outing. But from Ed's vantage point, it was just one more unsettling entry in the growing catalog of dysfunction on display.

It wasn't that the Lady Dark Lord of Mordor had a child. Anyone could have children. It was *how* she behaved with him. They didn't move like parent and child. Not really. More like siblings at best, partners at worst.

They cavorted through the obstacle course until Saul — either by accident or something less innocent — struck Jennifer across the face. Even from a distance, Ed could make out the sharp cries of pain, followed by a volley of rage:

"This is just like your father!"

"Do you want to be like him!?"

"Men always do this to me!"

"Do you want to be like all men?!"

Saul withered. Ed watched as the boy tried to make it right, leaning in for a hug, saying something inaudible. And within a minute, like nothing had happened, they were both locked back into a strangely intimate rhythm again. Hugging and kissing and comforting.

It wasn't the screaming or emotional whiplash that got to Ed the most. It was the twisted closeness. The entanglement. Watching it stirred something familiar and unwelcome. He couldn't help but think about his own mother.

Not because of the verbal abuse. But because of the intensity. The emotional fusion. The sense that he was her confidant, her surrogate partner. Even now, it was hard to sort out where she ended and he began.

He exhaled slowly. Ida would've had a term for all of this. Probably several. Too bad she couldn't have infiltrated Mordor instead. She could've set up shop and filled a thousand notebooks with the psychological wreckage on display.

"Initiate Zeke," Trucker said, jolting Ed out of his trance and snapping the thread of thought that had been caught in the off-kilter mother-son dynamic.

"Yeah," Ed said. "Didn't see you there."

He glanced back at Jennifer Smith and her son, Saul. "That's a . . . pretty unique relationship they've got."

"They're very close," Trucker said. "The guidance says he was her father in a past life. Also, a prophet himself."

Ed stared at him. This was the same man who had pulled him out of the grasp of this very cult ten years ago? The same relentless detective who, on the HERA Network footage of the Convergence Conference, moved like a force of nature against the absurd?

That man was gone.

But Ed had to believe something still lived in him. Something buried deep that was just as innate, just as stubborn, as Jennifer's malicious manipulation. A sliver of resistance. A spark of freedom.

"That's interesting," Ed said, managing to keep the sarcasm out of his voice, but not the *seriously?* from his eyes. Then added, "Kinda reminds me of my mom."

Trucker looked at him, really looked at him. And for a moment, Ed thought he noticed a flicker behind the detective's eyes. Recognition, maybe. Or just the ghost of it. Ed couldn't tell. The stare lingered just long enough to make him wonder if the man remembered who he was, or if it was just a trick of hope.

Then Trucker turned and said, "Come with me. We have work to do."

21

THE GREENHOUSE

Inside the massive, modified glass-and-plastic structure was a sprawl of chaotic greenery. Vegetables, fruits, herbs, and flowers burst from every corner, growing in locations and directions that nature never intended. Some were thriving with unnatural vigor; others looked half-dead, wilted in place like they'd lost the will to participate in the agricultural anarchy.

Trucker held the door open and motioned for Ed to enter.

"Oh, my," Ed said, catching his first glimpse and a wave of humid heat from the jumbled jungle of vegetation. A pungent mix of wet decay, sour soil, and overripe fruit split on the vine surged into his nostrils.

A couple summers ago, Ed had gotten hooked on gardening after binging the first season of *Martha Gardens*. He imagined that if Ms. Stewart were to walk into this greenhouse, she'd quickly become a cast member of *Paramedics: Emergency Response*.

It was the kind of garden that could only be created by someone who desperately, and manically, wanted to grow their own food but had no interest in learning how. Plants and vegetables seemed to be arbitrarily shoved into whatever container happened to be available and could fit through the front door. Shoebox. Cracked antique bathtub. Repurposed rusty rain gutters. Fill them with dirt — or anything vaguely resembling soil — sprinkle in an overabundance of random seeds, and call it good.

It all reeked of sporadic care and misdirected effort.

And yet, a dozen Radiants and initiates moved through the mess with quiet, purposeful reverence. They watered things that didn't need water, misting already-mildewed leaves. One was whispering something to a coffee tin of suffering zucchini.

"The carrots came from here?" Ed asked, then immediately corrected himself, again. "The carrots came from here. Amazing. Delicious. The process looks very original. Bespoke." It surprised him how difficult it was to not ask questions. It would've been hard anywhere, but here? He questioned everything.

"They are good carrots," Trucker confirmed. "The tomatoes aren't bad either."

"Ya know," Ed said, embracing his best false positivity. "I'm not an expert by any means. And I'm *definitely* not questioning the process. At all. But this sure is something. Incredible."

Ed smiled a little too wide, feigning admiration. He had decided to gently plant a seed of his own. One of doubt. And hoped it would take root in Trucker's mind, "To think. Discovering a new way to garden after, what . . . thousands of years of agriculture. She cracked the code. It's amazing. Jennifer truly has a gift."

Trucker looked at him a bit sideways. Not quite defensive, not quite concerned or convinced, "She likes to play it by ear," he said slowly. "Unless the guidance suggests otherwise."

An initiate, carrying a mulch-filled sombrero sprouting arugula, collided with a Radiant. Both fell to the ground in a tangle of limbs and dirt. The initiate managed to hold the hat above his head, keeping the arugula intact.

"What are you doing?" the Radiant shouted.

"This needs much less light," the initiate said with confidence. "It has to be moved."

Another Radiant rushed over and helped them both to their feet. "What's going on?" she asked.

Ed and Trucker stood nearby as the group descended into a disorganized argument about light exposure, divine placement, and spiritual alignment. It became clear that Jennifer Smith had never given them defined instructions, only vague impressions of what she didn't want. Or wouldn't tolerate.

"They've got things under control here," Trucker said to Ed. "I've got another project you can help with."

And with that, he escorted Ed out of the greenhouse and into . . .

THE MAIN HOUSE

The back entrance of the greenhouse didn't make sense to Ed from the outside. It opened into a narrow hallway that looked . . . normal. Almost too normal. White walls. Soft lighting. Multiple doors lined up opposite one another, like a modest office suite or reasonably priced hotel trying very hard to be comforting.

The walls were decorated with black-and-white photos of Jennifer Smith, some posed, others candid. Several featured her son. A few included select members of *The Radiant Way*. Trucker appeared in a couple frames, as did a few other familiar faces Ed had encountered.

Between the photos were plaques and awards, recognition of Jennifer's online presence, digital reach, and massive following. One bore a platinum emblem: "1 Million Subscribers" with Jen's Sharpie'd signature underneath.

An overwhelming aroma of lavender and lemon oil hung heavy in the air. So strong that it had to be pumped in through the ventilation system. At first, Ed assumed it was meant to offset the odorous chaos of the greenhouse. But after a few steps down the hall, he started to wonder if it was masking something else entirely.

Trucker led Ed to an open room and said, "Stay here for a minute. Don't go anywhere."

Trucker stepped inside, and Ed stayed put, but inconspicuously peeked through the doorway.

Here it was: Jennifer Smith's global pulpit.

A production studio. A hub for her to reach out into the world and scoop up those looking for more. More meaning, more magic, more of whatever she was selling.

Expensive cameras were aimed at an ergonomic leather chair, which faced a large dry-erase board just out of view and being used as a towering cue card. A wireless microphone rested on the seat like it was waiting for the prophet to return. The whole setup was bathed in the glow of a professional lighting rig.

A young Radiant read from a sheet of paper and then wrote a title across the whiteboard: *Music and Menus Are Mystic*. He followed the topic's title with a partial script written underneath in neat, legible handwriting. The Radiant handed the paper to Trucker. The two exchanged a few words, and the Radiant began making edits, seemingly at Trucker's suggestion.

Ed shifted, casually, and caught a glimpse inside the room across the hall. The door was cracked just enough. He gently nudged it a little wider.

Inside, Radiants Noah and Levi sat in front of multiple laptops, each displaying live feeds from a smattering of cameras positioned around the compound. Ed spotted the view from the gate. Prospects were already waiting in the loose cobblestones hoping to become new initiates of Jen's *Radiant Way*.

Before he could take in more, Trucker placed a firm hand on his shoulder.

"Come with me," he said and took Ed to . . .

THE KITCHEN

"Ohhhggg," Ed let out an involuntary noise as Trucker led him into the open kitchen and dining room. Jennifer and the Radiants hadn't been cooking people, maybe. It was actually impossible to tell what was beneath the layers upon layers of filth. He now understood why gallons of lavender and lemon were being pumped through the vents.

If Martha Stewart had survived the cardiac arrest triggered by the greenhouse, she would've immediately called the United Nations from the kitchen to request a one-time use of napalm. Destroy it all. Start over.

Swarms of fruit flies waged turf wars between the rotting bananas, the piles of shriveled oranges, and the double sinks. Stinking sinks each filled with dishes crusted in spoiled food and half-submerged in a liquid that wasn't originally soup but had become one through sheer neglect. The unlucky flies that landed on one of the kitchen's rare open counter spaces found themselves in a life-or-death struggle with a sticky substance of unknown origin.

A leaning tower of unused kitchen gadgets slumped against the wall, crowned by a juicer sealed shut with a crust of hardened pulp.

Every inch of the room was so repulsive that Ed, suspecting he was about to be assigned cleanup duty, seriously considered calling off the whole rescue operation right then and there.

Good luck to ya, Trucker. Enjoy your life with crazy-pants cult leader Jen. I'm taking off, he nearly said out loud.

But Trucker didn't even give an order. He simply said, "Let me show you where the cleaning supplies are," and walked Ed to a large walk-in closet that was thankfully organized by someone who still clung to a faint desperate sense of order.

Inside were mops, buckets, brooms, and dustpans. All standard issue. But there was not a single commercially produced bottle of cleaner in sight. No bleach. No 409. Nothing with chemicals, warnings, or the promise of actual sanitation.

Instead, the shelves were stocked with spray bottles labeled *Lavender Purification Mist* and *Moonwater Solution.* Large clear jugs bore hand-scrawled labels like *Apple Cider Spirit Vinegar Cleanser,* as if vinegar and faith could lift the filth from the kitchen disaster zone.

Ed let out a low internal groan as he imagined himself scrubbing sticky cult muck with lemon-scented optimism for the next several hours.

Before he could process his impending fate, three Radiants shuffled past the closet, each struggling under the weight of overflowing laundry baskets stuffed with Jennifer Smith's clothing. They were mid-conversation, their tones somewhere between stressed-out roommates and temple servants terrified of offending their deity.

"I'm just sayin' . . . do you want another incident?" one Radiant asked with urgency.

"No," the second Radiant replied, "but what more do you want? I clean it out every day."

The third cut in with quiet exasperation. "Lint trap has to be sorted *twice* a day. Twice, at the very least. Everyone knows that."

"Hey!" Trucker barked, his voice sharp but familiar.

The trio froze, snapped to attention, and replied in unison, "Yes, Mister Trucker."

Without ceremony, Trucker peeled off his Hawaiian shirt and tossed it to them.

"Can you throw this in for me? Thanks."

"No problemo, Mister Trucker," one of them chirped with cult-trained cheer.

Ed looked over at the now shirtless former detective and tensed up, rigid. Trucker's wiry frame was marked by a six-inch surgical scar curling up the side of his abdomen.

There was no way to know what it was from, but that didn't stop Ed's brain from jumping to the most dramatic conclusion.

I knew it, he screamed internally. *That crazy B snagged one of his kidneys!*

Trucker handed Ed two jugs of homemade cleaner. Ed spun them around, held them up to the light, and started to ask, "What —" before stopping himself. He reframed.

"Say you were going to tackle . . ." Ed nodded toward the kitchen. " . . . that situation."

There was a pause, awkward and loaded, until Trucker broke it by modifying *The Radiant Way* rules for initiates. "If you have a question, ask it."

Ed let out a long exhale. "Phew. You have no idea how hard it is to not ask questions."

"Yeah, I do," Trucker said. "I'm giving you one. Make it a good one."

Ed held up the bottles. "Say you were given a daunting task. You really wanted to get it done. Do it right. But you weren't exactly sure where to start or how to proceed. Because it is just . . . messy. Unfamiliar. Maybe even a little overwhelming." He gave the bottles a small shake. "What would you do?"

Trucker didn't flinch. No visible emotional response. But Ed thought, just for a moment, he saw another flicker of something behind the man's eyes. Recognition, maybe. Or memory.

"Your honest take would be a big help," Ed said.

"Use the vinegar first," Trucker said abruptly. "And a lot of old-fashioned elbow grease. Then go over it with the lavender."

"Thanks," Ed said, genuinely. "I appreciate it. You're a lifesaver."

"You're welcome," Trucker replied. "You better get to it."

SEVERAL HOURS LATER

It was the most work Ed had done in literal years. Maybe ever. And he'd done it all on the least amount of sleep he'd had in just as long. Maybe ever.

He sat on the now-gleaming granite countertops — granite he hadn't even realized was granite until about an hour into scrubbing — and he imagined that if Martha Stewart walked in right now, she'd say, *"You did such an amazing job, I want to produce a show with you as host called 'Cult Kitchen Cleanup.'"* Naturally, he'd accept the offer. After thoroughly reviewing the contract and consulting the proper representation, of course.

His mind was fuzzy. He figured he was somewhere around his fifth or sixth wind, operating on a hallucinatory gear he didn't know he had — or existed. But despite the exhaustion, a strange sense of pride was flowing through him as Trucker walked in.

Ed swung his legs and spread his arms. "Huh, huh, check this place out, huh."

He hopped down and opened several cabinets in succession, showcasing every spotless corner. "Not too shabby, huh? That wasn't a question. It was a statement. *Not. Too. Shabby.*"

Trucker showed no reaction. "You can go to sleep now," he said.

"Hey," Ed replied, "Was wondering . . . see if I could ask —"

"No more questions," Trucker interrupted. "Go to bed."

On his way out of the kitchen, Ed, with a semi-deranged smile plastered across his tired face, placed a hand on Trucker's shoulder and said, "Good night."

In the dark of night, he stepped out of the main house, passed under the Gothic archway and over the Radiant motto: *Leave Resistance Behind. Let Radiance Flow.* He walked down the front steps and onto the flower-lined paver stone path that led toward the cargo-container barracks.

The sounds of the night, crickets chirping, owls hooting, and the mountains surrounding him on all sides, offered a soothing sort of comfort. Ed thought about how little Mother Nature cared whether Jennifer Smith existed or not. How small her manipulations and exploitations were in her eyes. How, to nature, she simply didn't matter.

He took a deep breath, exhaled slowly, and whispered, "Heavenly Father, please protect me."

Looking upward, he took in the beauty of the night sky, overwhelmingly alive with twinkling stars. One streaked across the top of the Wasatch Range. Then another.

He didn't make a wish. Not once. Not even two.

He continued walking toward his bed and once again patted his pocket, checking on his contraband, his possibly silly secret weapon. He wondered when the right moment would come to use it, or if it would work at all to jolt the detective's memory. He then softly said one last thing that he himself had memorized.

"I know. It's all wrong. By rights, we shouldn't even be here," Ed channeled the hobbit Samwise Gamgee. He recited aloud the speech Sam gave to Frodo as the shadow of Sauron's corruption loomed darkest. But he wasn't Gamgee. He was just Ed. And whether he realized it or not, he carried more courage than the fictional heroes from the films he loved. Not because he had to, but because he chose to.

He looked up at the stars and finished the line, "There's some good in this world. And it's worth fighting for."

22

IDA'S AIRBNB CABIN

"This was such a dumb idea. So, so, so dumb. I don't know what I was thinking," Ida said as she lay on the top bunk inside the tiny cabin, seven miles down a country road from her brother. Now known as Initiate Zeke of *The Radiant Way*.

"So dumb," she repeated, watching Ed's iPads running the last movie marathon he'd queued up: the *Rush Hour* series. Jackie Chan and Chris Tucker ran, jumped, and quipped in the background as she stared at the countdown timer on her phone.

33 hours, 17 minutes, 42 seconds. 41 . . . 40 . . . 39 . . .

When it hit zero, she was going into the compound to retrieve her brother. And Trucker, if Ed had managed to jump-start the former detective's critical thinking.

Ever since Ed had left, she'd been replaying their rushed, futile, and borderline unethical plan. She kept adding *borderline* to soften the blow. She knew it was a coping mechanism. Because the plan wasn't borderline anything. It was unethical to interfere in someone's life without a damn good reason.

What did she really know about Trucker's situation? Nothing, really.

She was operating on emotion when she came up with the plan to remove him from Jennifer Smith's group.

She had imagined what her own life might have looked like had she fallen for Jennifer's coercive game. And it was a nightmare. But what gave her the right to assume the same for Trucker?

Her moral relativism faded as she accepted that what was done was done. All she could do now was follow through. It helped that Chan and Tucker were doling out justice with high kicks and wisecracks against cartoonish villainy.

She knew life wasn't a movie. And wasn't as prone to the sway of cinematic storytelling as her brother. But sometimes, a reminder was necessary. Evil was evil. And sometimes, something had to be done about it.

33 hours, 16 minutes, 24 seconds. 23 . . . 22 . . . 21 . . .

23

EARLY THE NEXT MORNING

The sun had yet to rise, and in the darkness, a murder of crows roosted atop one of the trees near *The Radiant Way* compound. They were not pleased when a klaxon alarm shattered the stillness. Blaring repeated Ah-oo-gahs crashed through the forest and echoed off the hills. Moments later, security floodlights burst to life, bathing the entire compound in an unforgiving flood of bright intensity.

Much like the crows, Ed was not thrilled about the sudden wake-up call in his bunk inside the cargo-container barracks. But unlike the crows, he had no idea where he was or why. The alarm had jolted his body awake, but not his mind. He squinted against the overhead string lights, now cranked to eleven, and groaned.

Isaac and Ariel rushed past but paused just long enough to help him get his bearings. "Don't worry, Zeke, you're okay," Isaac said.

"We're all still safe inside Jen's radiant womb," Ariel added warmly.

They kept moving. Ed, still dazed, moaned, "Well, her womb is very loud . . . and very bright."

Shielding both his eyes and ears, Ed stumbled outside. Radiants had already gathered in circles, heads bowed, hands linked in prayer.

Gabriel took Ed gently by the arm. "Here. Follow me."

"What's happe —" Ed started to ask but stopped himself.

Gabriel didn't flinch at the partial question. "There's something wrong with Jen," he said and led Ed into one of the circles. They knelt with the others and joined hands.

The Radiants in Ed's prayer circle were in near-desperate states. Some wept. Some rocked back and forth. Some pleaded with Jesus to intervene, while others recited what sounded like well-rehearsed incantations. What was missing was any clear understanding of what actually happened, or why it required such forceful prayer.

Ed didn't know what was going on with Jen, but he couldn't help wondering, by some twist of cosmic irony, if his own prayers had been answered. He didn't wish ill on anyone, but a tiny slip and fall, a light bonk on the head that rearranged a few of her mental files? That wouldn't be the worst thing. Maybe it would knock out some of the manipulation and exploitation. Possibly even flip that long-lost empathy switch to the on position.

He glanced toward the main house. Trucker and Sam of Sams stood guard, flanked by Levi and Noah. Unlike the others, they weren't praying. In fact, they didn't seem emotional at all.

The klaxon had gone silent when Jennifer Smith stepped out from beneath the archway of the house, swallowed by a thick plume from her vape. The harsh floodlights filtered through the vapor, casting a ghostly aura around her.

Ed blinked through sleep-blurred eyes. Something was off about Jen's face. Something peculiar. But he couldn't quite make it out through the medicinal fog.

Trucker, Sam of Sams, Levi, and Noah remained at their posts behind her, still and watchful, as she moved to the edge of the front steps.

She took another drag from her vape pen and waited.

The Radiants broke from their prayer circles and began to drift toward her with quiet solemnity. Ed followed, swept along in the tide. It felt less like a gathering and more like a slow procession of the spiritually concerned and fearful. Not zombies in search of brains, but something arguably worse: A desperate horde, hungry for her words.

They slowly and carefully assembled as an audience before Jennifer Smith.

The floodlights clicked off, and the clouds around her began to dissipate. As her face came into view, some in the crowd covered their mouths in quiet shock. Others diverted their eyes.

"This is what can happen," Jen said, gesturing to her face.

It was burned red, streaked across the nose and cheeks. Her lips were swollen to the size of hot dogs.

"When I am taken for direct downloads . . . the human flesh is sensitive to their true glory. The angels. The divine."

She went on, asking if anyone had seen the activity in the sky during the night. She explained that the higher spirits were likely visible, even to mere mortal sight. That it was common for them to be mistaken for UFOs or other nightly anomalies.

Ed played along as best he could, but as soon as he saw her face, he knew exactly what had happened. He'd seen it before, on his own mother, the day after she went to the beach and forgot to put sunscreen on her face. Lip injections and other cosmetic work didn't love hours of direct sunlight. They cooked, producing a look not unlike the now bunless hot dogs on Jen's face.

This had nothing to do with random celestial phenomena. It was sunburn and swelling. But the misattribution would never register with the Radiants. Her words were precious. Her words were truth.

Jen preached to her congregation as the sun began to peek over the distant mountains. She told them how blessed they were that she was chosen. That she was willing to pay any price, even the price of scorched flesh and swollen lips, for the sake of their enlightenment.

Then, without warning, she veered into a lament about her biological family: a religiously abusive mother, an alcoholic father who neglected them for beer and prostitutes, whom she called *people pleasers*, and siblings who tormented her with their wickedness. That she had felt cursed her entire life by the evil of others, until the guidance.

There was no way for Ed to know whether any of it was true. Maybe she did come from a family like that. Maybe she did have bad luck with those in her life. But so had countless others, and most didn't use it to catapult themselves into the role of coercive prophet.

As expected, Jen shifted back to a reassuring tone. She told them she would be okay. That they were in the correct timeline. And that they would stay there, if they all stuck together and followed the guidance.

Her guidance.

Jennifer returned inside the house. The crowd dispersed. And Trucker descended the front steps, walking straight for Ed.

Ed wanted to scream, *"Trucker! They were just shooting stars! And she has a sunburn!"*

But he didn't.

He only hoped that somewhere, deep inside, Trucker could still see the truth.

"Are you ready to continue your initiation, Zeke?" Trucker asked.

"Yes, Mister Trucker. I am ready to continue," Ed replied.

And with that, Trucker led him into the main house.

24

RETURN TO THE MAIN HOUSE

Trucker took Ed down another oddly antiseptic hallway and opened a door. They stepped inside, and Ed found himself in what had maybe once been a large parlor room, now converted into a home medical spa.

It was another not-unfamiliar sight for Ed. There seemed to be many uncomfortable similarities between his own mother and the radiance-peddling con artist Jennifer Smith. One among those many: an aggressive refusal to gracefully accept the passage of time. Both had gone so far as to install rooms devoted to halting the unavoidable natural process of aging.

Some of the equipment he recognized. Quasi-legitimate devices that, when properly used, might offer genuine benefit. A red-light therapy bed. A cryotherapy chamber. An infrared sauna. All incredibly expensive.

But then there were the other machines. Ones that broadcasted their nonsense with flashing lights and futuristic labels. Fat-melting ultrasonic cavitation wands. Multiple skin-tightening devices using radio frequencies or argon gas. And one particularly absurd contraption that looked like a leftover prop from a canceled '90s sci-fi show, proudly labeled: *Energy Healing RIFE Machine.*

He was both grateful and disturbed that the similarities between his mother and Jennifer ended where they did. Because unlike his mother's pristine, peppermint-scented spa, this one looked like it had hosted a war between skincare and a gaggle of crud-covered orcs.

A thick film of grime coated nearly every surface. The vinyl on the therapy bed was split and discolored. Jars of creams and tinctures were left open, their contents hardened into crust. Towels — some clean, some questionably so — were tossed in chaotic mounds beneath a spiritual poster smeared with fingerprints. And in the corner under a flickering salt lamp was a juicing machine that looked like it gave up on life mid-cleanse.

But the worst of it was the stall at the far end. Its curtain, closed and stained with rings of brown, orange, and something vaguely green. It emitted a faint odor that suggested mildew, bodily fluids, and Ed did not discount the possibility of death.

"Jennifer was impressed with your work in the kitchen," Trucker said. "You know where the supply closet is."

He began to close the door behind him, but Ed stopped it with his foot.

"Hey," Ed said, pausing, searching for some magical phrase that might flip a switch in Trucker's mind. Something to snap him out of his current state and send them both walking out the front door forever. But nothing came.

Trucker looked down at Ed's blocking foot, "Yes?"

"Nothing," Ed said, hoping the desperate inflection in his voice would register. "Was just thinking, but I know I need to stop that. For the pure beauty of radiance."

"Okay," Trucker said, and closed the door.

As Ed got to work, he briefly questioned the logic of the cleaning aspect of this initiation process. But then it clicked. Anyone who made it this far, anyone already devoted enough to stand at the gate for hours in smiling obedience, they were already broken in. They were already indoctrinated. There was no need for a sales pitch. No final push. Just chores. Chores that served Jennifer's lifestyle, her ego, and whatever delusion she was feeding that day.

He made his way to the far end of the room and pulled back the stained shower curtain.

The floor of the stall was splattered in streaks and pools of something dark and crusted over. Along the edge sat several Mason jars, each half-filled with what looked like old, separated blood. They had been left there long enough to suggest they were not forgotten, but being saved.

Ed hadn't cursed in nearly two decades. The last time he vividly remembered, he had slammed his thumb in the door of his mom's Range Rover.

He would remember this time, too.

"What . . . in the fuck?"

Ed scrubbed, wiped, and scraped. And as the hours slipped by, so did the grime, the slime, and the calcified residue of whatever rituals Jen had carried out in her personal temple to eternal youth.

His limit had been reached long ago. He was done cleaning up after the manipulative monster. No more. He knew it was ill-advised to challenge Trucker's belief system directly — but what were the other options? None that didn't involve more slave labor. Days of it, even. And he was done picking up after the prophet.

Yet as he stood in the center of Jennifer's now spotless and absurd altar to impossible immortality, he was, against all reason, proud. He hated doing it, but it gave him a strange sense of accomplishment.

He was admiring his newfound janitorial skills when Trucker walked in. Ed threw an arm out toward the gleaming room and said, "Check it out, Mister Trucker! Look at this place."

He gestured toward the shower. "I left the . . . whatever that . . . science experiment is. I left it alone."

Trucker, once again, showed no emotion. But he did offer a flat, "Good job. Come with me. We're going to the kitchen."

Ed took the *good job* like a gold medal and followed, grateful for the kitchen detour. He assumed snacks, or some kind of treat, might be involved. He was famished. And if food was on the table, maybe a little conversation would be, too. Maybe, while they were enjoying something tasty, he could up the ante and try to wake the detective still sleeping somewhere inside the Radiant Mister Trucker.

25

RETURN TO THE KITCHEN

"What!?"

"How!?"

Ed fired off two simple questions, one after the other, and didn't care whether he got answers or ran out on a rail. He just wanted the truth, or at least something that passed for it in Radiantland.

Trucker didn't appear to be in a punitive mood. He ignored the questions entirely as they both stood in the center of what could only be described as culinary catastrophe. The kitchen wasn't as bad as when Ed had first cleaned it the day before. It was worse. Somehow. Utterly wrecked under an avalanche of chaos: overflowing sinks, new spills, sticky floors, a flour explosion, and at least one broken blender that hadn't been there before. For a brief moment, Ed genuinely considered timeline shifting as a viable explanation. Nothing else made sense.

"How is this even possible?" Ed asked, still trying to process it. "It hasn't even been . . . how many hours . . . I don't know how long."

"You know where the supply closet is," Trucker said. "I will get you something from the garden. Carrots?"

Ed stood in stunned silence. "Sure," he quietly let out because what else do you say when a woman like Jennifer Smith may or may not have just bent spacetime to ruin a kitchen?

Trucker left to claim the carrots, and even though Ed had previously declared he wouldn't clean or dust another inch for Jennifer Smith, he almost automatically slipped back into Zeke the Initiate. He noticed the shift, the automaton he had briefly become, but chalked it up to a compulsion to fix what the heathens had done to his impressive work. It wasn't an act of devotion. Not to Jennifer. At least he hoped she hadn't implanted some hypnotic trigger to turn him into another Radiant house elf.

As he began sorting through the mess, he made a decision. When Trucker returned with the carrots, Ed would break out the metaphorical mental stick and gently whap him in the noggin.

Trucker returned quickly, holding a biodegradable container of carrots labeled: *Zeke's Reward*. He handed them to Ed, and Ed, in turn, handed the former detective a thought.

"I love movies. And shows. So much streaming now. I might have a problem, honestly," Ed said, holding a carrot in one hand while casually wiping up a spill with the other. "Sometimes I go on binges. Comedies. British dramas. Documentaries. I got stuck in this phase where I was watching all of these exposés. One after the other. *Waco. Love Has Won: The Cult of Mother God. Wild Wild Country.*"

He looked Trucker dead in the eyes as he listed off every documentary on coercive control groups and cults that he could remember. From the well-known Jim Joneses and Mansons to the more recent Raniere and Daybells. "I thought those were super interesting."

Again, Ed thought he saw something flicker behind the former detective's dull eyes. A glimmer of recognition, buried just underneath a mountain of resignation.

"Haven't seen a movie in ten years," Trucker said. "None of those anyway. Jen has a strong Radiant principle that works. Only clean, guidance-approved entertainment. If one puts garbage in, it infects you. Then nothing but garbage comes out."

Ed looked around the wrecked kitchen.

"Well, it might be time to start putting some garbage in . . ." He paused, then forcibly delivered an unfunny nonpunchline with a horrendous fake laugh, ". . . into a trash can."

Trucker's expression didn't budge. "You better get to it."

And Ed did get to it.

While he cleaned, organized, and disinfected, the hours deteriorated. His thoughts wandered during the draining ordeal, but two ideas stuck with him. First: What if he were an actual Radiant? What kind of sequence of events would have to occur for someone to gleefully accept a life of endless servitude? Cleaning one room, only to be taken to the next, and then the next, forever. A closed loop of labor disguised as a path to enlightenment.

And second: his mom's maid, Miss Roberta, deserved a raise.

He was hard at work for the rest of the daylight hours. As the sun dipped behind the mountains, Trucker returned. He was carrying an empty industrial trash can.

Ed didn't make another big production about the quality of his cleaning. Not that he wasn't proud, but he had come to understand the point of it all. The labor wasn't solely or even primarily about cleanliness. It was about indoctrination. Repetition. Breaking in the new Radiant. And frankly, he was too tired and too hungry to care anymore.

"Hey, won't need that," Ed said, nodding toward the trash can Trucker had set down. "Been carrying stuff out in bags. I'm almost finished."

Trucker said nothing. He walked to the stainless-steel commercial double-door refrigerator, gripped both handles, and pulled it open.

What followed was an olfactory assault.

A head of rotting lettuce tumbled out and hit the floor with a wet *splat*. The stench that followed was instant and horrifying. A wave of spoiled produce, sour dairy, and fermented mystery fluids that had been marinating for who-knows-how-long. The loss of the lettuce triggered a minor avalanche: a half-collapsed container of something brown and leaking, an uncapped bottle of homemade almond milk that turned into yogurt, and what might've once been soup but now looked like biohazardous poison. More items followed, slopping down onto the floor in a grotesque cascade.

Ed staggered back, coughing and gagging, "Oh, come on."

He pressed the pit of his elbow against his mouth and nose, eyes locked on Trucker.

Through the crook of his sleeve, he managed to speak. "Mister Trucker. Trucker." He lowered his arm. This was it. This was his personal last straw. Was it the worst thing he'd ever seen? No. It was just a nasty refrigerator. But stacked on top of everything else, it was too much. His breaking point.

He was done pretending.

Still, he tried to stick to the guidance. The real guidance, Ida's educated, psychological strategy for breaking someone free from coercive control.

"Trucker. **Detective** Trucker," Ed said. "This is ridiculous." He gestured to the fridge. "There's nothing radiant about this. Look at it. This . . . this is mental illness. If you saw this in someone else's house. And that someone else . . ."

He rattled off a list. Bizarre behavior. Spiritual delusions. Manipulation. All of it was framed hypothetically, like it was coming from a neighbor and not Jennifer Smith.

Trucker cut him off, "Initiate Zeke."

Ed wasn't having it.

"I'm not Zeke. My name is Edward Young. You saved me ten years ago. Me and my sister, Ida. And now I'm here . . . I'm here to help you."

"I know who you are," Trucker said.

Ed had a tinge of shock, but was not completely, overly surprised. He knew he had seen some sort of strange flicker in the detective's eyes.

"You do?" he asked.

"I made a thousand copies of your face. Your mother's, too. I almost lost my mind trying to find you," Trucker paused. "Almost."

He thought about that *almost*. Arguably, it wasn't almost at all.

"You were the last case," Trucker said.

Ed let the weight of that sit in silence, and then asked, "You knew?"

"The second I saw you on the camera feed," Trucker answered. "I just didn't know why you were here."

"I'm here to get you out. Because the man who saved me and my sister would never willingly sign up for this."

"You don't know that man," Trucker said.

Ed didn't argue. Because Trucker wasn't wrong.

Then Trucker asked a familiar question, "Why do you care?"

256

Ed didn't have a speech. No rehearsed answer. Just the truth.

"Because you did."

Another silence settled over the two of them, broken first by the soft *ding-ding* of the refrigerator's door-ajar alarm. Then, by the one-and-only Jennifer Smith herself.

She walked in with her head buried in her phone, barely glancing up before wrinkling her nose. "Pee-yew. Shut that door. That's awful."

Trucker closed the stainless-steel doors without taking his eyes off Ed. The dings stopped.

Jen drifted through the kitchen, set her phone on the clean countertop, and began an impromptu inspection. She opened the cupboards, examined dish stacks, and ran her finger over clean glassware.

"Did you throw out Saul's favorite bendy straw yesterday? He couldn't find it anywhere and was in tears."

Ed wanted to point out how strange it was that a mother-proclaimed prophet, who had allegedly lived a million lives to become a teacher of light, would weep over the tragedy of a missing straw. Or that the real tragedy was a young boy being emotionally and psychologically abused by his delusional mother.

But instead, he said, "It's in the third drawer from the left." His eyes never left Trucker.

Jen opened the drawer, found the straw, and held it up like a prize. "The lost has been found. I am an excellent finder. He'll be so happy." She turned with a smile that didn't reach her own eyes, "Next time, make sure to put things where they belong."

She moved closer to Ed and Trucker, her body facing Ed though her words were aimed at Trucker. Her tone had taken on a light, almost flirty cadence.

"So, how's our newest member of *The Radiant Way*? I think he's special. Shows real promise."

"Me, too," Trucker said.

Jen asked Ed, "What do you think, Zeke?"

Ed was momentarily stunned. Trucker clearly remembered who he was, recognized him instantly. But Jennifer? Nothing. No sign of any recollection.

She had spent days with him a decade ago, grooming him, trying to shape his thinking, whispering her own manipulative scripture. And now she looked like he was just another smiling face in the crowd.

And then he realized that is exactly what he was.

One of hundreds, if not thousands, she had consciously or subconsciously targeted over the years, siphoning whatever she needed before moving on. She could be faking it, he supposed. Playing dumb. Keeping control by refusing to name things. But, and this felt most likely, she simply didn't care.

Whatever the reason, it didn't matter.

"I've found what I was looking for, here," Ed said, "and I look forward to seeing what the future holds."

"That's such a great attitude. Remember, the guidance is never wrong. It directs us."

She turned to Trucker. "Have you discussed the contract with him yet?"

"No, we haven't had the —"

Suddenly the klaxon alarm cut him off. A blaring Ah-oo-gah split the kitchen air. The lights snapped to full brightness, and from the window, Ed could see the floodlights outside had all been switched on.

Trucker moved like a well-trained dog, ready to respond, but Jen halted him with a sharp finger snap.

"You don't have to do everything! I am capable of taking care of things. I'm not an invalid. I swear you're ridiculous sometimes."

Then, in the very next breath, whether trying to placate or genuinely believing her own madness, her voice turned silken, "Stay here and help our little protégé with the fridge. You were always the best at that sort of thing. It is your expertise."

And with that, Jen hustled out the front of the main house.

26

FIFTEEN MINUTES EARLIER AT IDA'S CABIN

The *Rush Hour* movie marathon was still replaying on a loop from the top bunk as Ida paced back and forth across the tiny cabin. Her steps were short. Her patience was gone.

She glanced at her phone, gripped tightly in her hand.

8 hours, 42 minutes, 10 seconds. 9 . . . 8 . . . 7 . . .

At any point, she could've taken her pacing and overthinking outside for some fresh air and room to move with a view. But she didn't. Consciously or not, she was giving herself a short-term case of self-induced cabin fever. Winding herself up for what she was about to do. Even she wasn't sure if it was on purpose or just part of the process.

And what she was about to do, in a little under nine hours, would either take an already questionable, ethically dark gray, barely planned operation and make it catastrophically worse . . . or pull off a miracle. One that might save a stranger and get her brother out of there.

Either way, it was reckless. Top to bottom.

And it would officially end her brief Utah mountain vacation.

She looked at the timer again.

8 hours, 40 minutes, 32 seconds. 31 . . . 30 . . . 29 . . .

"Close enough," she said.

Then she darted out the cabin's front door, fired up the sensibly rented Nissan Sentra, and tore down the gravel country road toward *The Radiant Way* compound.

Hollywood stunt drivers would've been impressed with the efficiency and speed she took the turn up the private drive. She barreled toward the iron gate, foot on the gas, eyes locked forward. Then slammed the brakes and slid to a stop just inches from the barrier. A cloud of dust rose behind her.

Ida threw open the door, climbed onto the hood, and stood up on her tiptoes.

She scanned *The Radiant Way* grounds.

And then glanced over to the cobblestone patch and the men standing still like patient, glassy-eyed zombies, waiting to be chosen.

"Go home!" Ida yelled from the hood. "This lady doesn't need any more disciples!"

They didn't react. At all.

She looked back to the gate and nodded, "Okay, Jackie Chan. Let's do it."

She jumped, caught the top of the gate, and climbed, gripping hard, pulling herself over the top. Then dropped to the other side with a heavy thud.

A moment later, the klaxon alarm blared.

And the compound floodlights lit up the night.

Back in *The Radiant Way* kitchen, Jen had just left to investigate the disturbance, leaving Trucker and Ed to the cleaning of the rancid refrigerator. The fridge doors remained closed, and the two men stood in silence over a pile of rotten food.

"Those years ago. We all should have walked out of there together," Ed said. "But we didn't. And she got ya."

"You don't understand. She hasn't always been . . . like this. She really is a good person. I have seen it," Trucker said. "I admit, things have gotten out of control. But . . ." His words trailed off.

Ed wanted to give an Ida-style explanation. That the *good* Trucker saw was part of the system. It wasn't a baseline. It wasn't who she was. It was part of the pathology. Without the appearance of good, the manipulation wouldn't work at all. But Ed wasn't capable of packaging and presenting that kind of truth in any useful way. So instead, he said, "Maybe I'll just stay here with you. Call this place home. Until I'm no longer useful to Jen." Then he added, "And don't take this the wrong way — no judgment, no offense — but that would mean you failed your last case."

"Listen, Zeke . . . Ed," Trucker said. "I know how all of this looks. But it's not so simple. This is . . . this is a sort of family."

"It looks pretty simple to me," Ed replied. "One person abusing and taking advantage of everyone else . . . for whatever it is they want. Anything and everything." He shook his head. "These people aren't a family. Not by choice. They're a collection of her victims."

Trucker didn't respond.

"It's nobody's fault except one. Hers," Ed said. "People like her prey on the goodness of others. You weren't, and aren't, a dummy. You were lied to. Slowly cooked with lies, and your hope kept the burners going."

Still, Trucker said nothing.

"Just . . . for a minute. Not forever. Just one minute. Take a step back if you can, and try to see what's going on," Ed said. "How I, or anyone else, might see all of this. You know I am not evil. You know not everyone outside this place is evil."

At that moment, a Radiant ran through the kitchen, heading toward the greenhouse. As she passed, she called out, "Mister Trucker, some crazy woman jumped the gate! Screamin' and yellin' for her brother. Some guy named Ed."

The Radiant's words hung in the air with the spoiled stench. Ed barely breathed. His sister was here. His backup, his brain, his miracle was here. Somewhere out there with the fanatics under the floodlights she was confronting the monster. And whatever was about to happen out there, whatever clever plan Ida had up her sleeve, he had to make every second in here count. Because they were most likely the last seconds he had to turn Trucker toward the truth.

Near the front gate, Ida stood in the blinding security lights before Sam of Sams, Levi, and Noah. Their intimidation play had no effect on her. She only saw three men whom she would happily help if they ever found her office door.

Those men remained stoic and silent as Jennifer Smith walked before them.

Days and days of watching and studying the self-proclaimed prophet's videos, and now Ida was face-to-face with the delusional deity herself.

"Wow, Miss Jennifer Smith in the flesh," Ida said. "I'm truly blessed."

"You are trespassing," Sam of Sams growled.

Jennifer looked at him, and Ida witnessed her ability to command without a word as Sam of Sams took a step back.

"Why are you here?" Jennifer asked sweetly. "If you'd like to join, we have a process."

Ida laughed. A sharp involuntary sound that surprised even her. And then she had an epiphany. She hadn't realized it until now, but she'd been waiting for a moment like this her entire life. As a young girl, she had learned to silence herself. The religion she was born into taught obedience over voice, and when she finally walked away, her family and community sealed the exile. There had never been a moment, not one, when she felt she was free to truly speak her full mind without fear of consequence.

Until now.

"I know you. I see you. You're not a prophet. You're a parasite," Ida said.

Jen's pleasant demeanor didn't crack. If anything, her smile grew wider.

Still, Ida continued. "You wrap your disordered mind in spiritual language and call it love and enlightenment. But you don't empower people . . . you erase them. And replace them with a reflection of yourself."

Ida turned to the men, "She's not channeling truth. She's blasting her ego on a loudspeaker and saying it is godly." She took a breath. "She's built a theology that always validates her needs, not yours or anyone else's. That's not faith. That's pathology. There's no divine guidance. There's only a fragile false self and her need for you to worship it."

Ida wasn't done and turned to Jen. "You haven't built these people up. You broke them. You've done near irreparable harm. The dissociation in their eyes isn't enlightenment . . . it's trauma. You hijacked spiritual language to justify abuse. You're not misunderstood. You'll never be misunderstood. Because there will always be people like me who see right through you."

"You see nothing," Jen said. "Your eyes are not meant for the divine. These things are beyond your ability to understa —"

"Oh, I understand," Ida cut her off.

She continued her educated attack against Jennifer Smith's delusional, distorted belief system at the iron gate and hoped Ed was somewhere nearby working a miracle with Trucker's mind. Hoping that beyond all impossibilities her brother was able to kick-start the detective's innate critical thinking and dormant gut instincts.

Back in the kitchen, slipping on a patch of spilled fridge sludge, Ed was doing his best with what little he had. "There has to be a part of you still in there, Trucker," Ed said. "I feel it. I know there's something left of the detective."

"Edward," Trucker said. "I know you think that. But it's not true. A while ago . . . I don't even remember how long . . . I wanted to leave. But I just couldn't. It's impossible to explain. No one would understand. The door is right there, right? I see it. But I can't walk through it. I tried." He paused. "And what's on the other side anyway? More of the past? More of a life of failure?"

"Ida told me this would be nearly impossible," Ed said while rubbing his face. "Remember Ida? Yeah, she's only gotten smarter. She had a whole plan to help ya. She could see how dangerous this lady is. And we were willing to do anything to get you out. Just a couple of strangers. That care. Because you did." He paused. "I don't know what I could possibly do to convince you. Jennifer has had ten years to twist your mind. I don't even have ten minutes left. What can I do, Trucker? What would you do?"

Ed whispered softly, "Heavenly Father, help me," and was about to quote *The Lord of the Rings* when he saw it — Jennifer Smith's cellphone, sitting like a beacon of hope on the clean kitchen counter.

Ed bolted and grabbed it.

Trucker barked, "Stop! What are you doing?"

"Intel! Evidence!" Ed yelled back.

"You can't touch that," Trucker warned. "Radiant Fred once moved it a few feet to sit down. He was banished before he even knew what happened."

Ed tapped the phone and brought up the lockscreen. "So, she's gonna throw me out?" he asked, not waiting for an answer.

"It's an invasion of privacy," Trucker said, reciting the long-term programming Jennifer Smith had installed. "You say that you're not evil? That you're the good guy? This isn't what a good guy would do."

Ed raised his eyebrows. "What? *Puhhlease.* You want to know how many movie heroes break into the bad guy's phone or database or whatever? *All* of them. James Bond. Jason Bourne. The Mission Impossible guy. 21 Jumpstreet! 22! Every episode of every crime scene investigation show, ever. Modern Sherlock Holmes with the guy with the funny name. Batman! Want me to go on? It's literally all of them." He stopped, staring at the number pad. "You were a detective! How many times did you have to dig into something to discover the truth?"

Ed needed to break into Jen's phone, now. Something, somewhere inside might be something, anything, that could help him with the impossible task of reaching Trucker. He racked his brain, trying to recall everything he'd seen in the compound, in the videos, all of what Ida had drilled into him.

And then his sister's voice echoed in his mind: *None of this is about intelligence. These people are not smart.*

"What's a dumb passcode? Something an idiot would use," Ed said to himself. Then he remembered the passwords that he and his mother always used. Birthdays.

But what was Jennifer Smith's birthday? Ida had found it. The last video she watched was Jen losing it over a cake and candles. But what was it? What was the day?

"May," he whispered to himself. "I think it was May. The twentieth of May?"

May twentieth is her birthday, Ida's voice confirmed in his head.

"Pretty sure it is May twentieth," he said punching in the first four digits.

"But how old is she?" He didn't know. With the right light and makeup, she looked thirty-something. When her personality shone through, she looked like a corpse.

"She's forty-eight," Trucker said flatly.

Ed tried to do some quick simple math with his fingers but struggled.

"Nineteen seventy-seven," Trucker said.

Ed punched in two sevens, and the phone unlocked. "I need to change my passwords," he said and scrolled fast, looking for anything that could help Trucker find a way through that door that he thought was shut tight.

He opened her messages and found dozens upon dozens of conversations with men. Each thread followed the same script. Jennifer cast herself as the misunderstood victim, mistreated by people who "just didn't understand her situation." She poured on the charm, telling each man they had a rare connection, that she loved him, that they'd be together soon. One by one, they sent hundreds, sometimes thousands, of dollars. In return, she sent emoji kisses and promises of an idyllic future that would never come.

Ed held the phone out to Trucker.

Nothing. No reaction at all.

She had programmed him too well. Ed realized that Trucker probably already knew these messages existed. This wasn't beyond the realm of possibility. It was the realm he lived in.

Back at the iron gate, Ida was still at it. She was unleashing years of frustration and fury at a world where truth had been twisted on a minute-by-minute basis. Where the virtue of the good guys and truth itself were being destroyed by people like Jennifer Smith, all for personal gain.

She was condemning objectively evil behavior. The kind carried out by those who would strip-mine reality and the innocent good qualities of others just to feed their own ego, control, and wealth.

"You realize that *this*," she gestured at the compound, the men, Jen, and the small gathering of Radiants watching from a distance, "this whole scam will end. And it will end poorly. For everyone here. But especially you.

"There is no future where you achieve enlightenment and ride off into the sunset with everything you desire. And I don't say that because I *hope* you get what you deserve. I say it because every single con artist who's pulled the same unoriginal tired schtick has met the same brutal fate. Since the beginning of time. It is what it is."

Ida paused, then added one last question, "How does that make you feel?"

Jen smiled, outwardly unaffected, "Remember everything you just said. You can repeat it to the sheriffs when they arrive. Let's see what crimes they can uncover — besides the ones you're committing. On me."

Jennifer reached for her phone, then realized she'd left it in the kitchen.

"Don't let her leave," she said to Sam of Sams and started walking toward the main house.

"I'm not going anywhere without my brother," Ida said, "or anyone else who wants out of your nightmare."

Jen didn't respond. She just kept walking to get her phone.

Meanwhile, in the kitchen, Ed was scrolling through that very phone. Panic rising. There had to be something, he thought. Something damning to her divine delusion.

And then, buried among the messages to the men she'd seduced and drained, he found a curious contact:

Jesus Christ.

He opened the thread. And what he saw made even less sense.

Every sent message was the same as the one received.

"Remember you are my prophet."

>*"Remember you are my prophet."*

"Set up Isaac and Ariel."

>*"Set up Isaac and Ariel."*

"Have Trucker look after Zeke."

>*"Have Trucker look after Zeke."*

"Grow more cucumbers."

>*"Grow more cucumbers."*

"Throw out Roman."

>*"Throw out Roman."*

"You were taken for divine downloads last night."

>*"You were taken for divine downloads last night."*

Ed stared at the messages, then typed a new one:

"Hi, my name is Ed."

He hit send and it delivered instantly:

>*"Hi, my name is Ed."*

It appeared before him, on the same device.

Ed tried to understand what he was seeing. What was happening here. And then it hit him and his eyes widened. He was looking straight into the mind of madness. The contact *Jesus Christ* was her own phone number. She had edited the name. And was texting herself.

He held up the phone to Trucker. "Look! This is her guidance! These are the messages from the divine!"

Trucker stared at the screen.

"She's talking to herself!" Ed yelled.

And as that real revelation echoed in the room, Jennifer Smith sauntered into the kitchen. She moved slowly, gracefully even, like nothing was wrong, unbothered, and completely in control.

Then she saw it.

Her unlocked cellphone in the hands of an initiate.

And everything inside her stopped.

For a moment, the kitchen was silent. Even the funk in the air seemed to hesitate.

Her gaze locked onto Ed with the intensity of a predator identifying a threat. Her posture changed. Shoulders squared. Chin tight. Arms stiff at her side. The warmth on her face evaporated.

Something deep behind her eyes began to shift.

Her expression didn't immediately twist into rage. First, it hollowed. The muscles in her face froze, then twitched, like a mask slowly delaminating from her skull. Her breath shortened. Her lips trembled, not with fear, but with fury, trying to break through.

Her fists clenched. Her arms jerked like a puppet on a wire. Her entire frame seemed to buzz with voltage. Her voice exploded from her throat, low and unnatural.

"How dare you."

The pupils of her eyes expanded, swallowing the color entirely. What remained looked black, animal, alien, unknowable.

"How dare you touch what is mine."

Her voice warped, first gravel, then shrill, rising and falling like static through a broken speaker.

"How dare you assault me!"

"How dare you rape my divinity!

"This is rape!"

She was screaming now, screeching, a spiritual violation narrative twisting around her like a shield and sword of insanity.

Her arms flailed as she hurled accusations like spells. Each word hit like a blast of cultic theater, sanctified by madness.

Ed stood frozen.

Even Trucker blinked in disbelief. Then, almost instinctively, he snatched the phone from Ed and handed it to Jennifer.

She clutched it to her chest like a relic, gasping and glaring, spitting every breath like it was a curse.

Seething and trembling, she turned her back and began to dial.

"You'll explain it to the sheriffs," she hissed. "Let's see what they have to say about you and who I assume is your criminal sister."

Trucker and Jennifer escorted Ed out of the house, past rows of Radiants, all staring silently at Initiate Zeke. He was marched past the puffed-up and posturing trio of Sam of Sams, Levi, and Noah until he was finally reunited with his sister.

"Hey, Sis," Ed said, pulling Ida into a hug. "Everything going according to plan?"

"You should've seen me Jackie Chan it over that gate," Ida said.

"Huh?"

"Jackie Chan! Your stupid *Rush Hour* movies. I did a Jackie Chan right over the gate."

"Oh," Ed said. "We're on *The Lord of the Rings* now."

"Sorry," Ida said. "I can't keep up."

She looked at the detective that saved her all those years ago. "Hey. Good to see you. Been a long time."

"It has," Trucker said softly. "You two have grown up."

"What do you say we get out of here?" Ida asked him. "Go grab something to eat. Catch up. We never had a chance to really thank you. You can come right back."

Jennifer stepped forward.

"He doesn't want to go anywhere with you," she said, "He has found his purpose here. The divine."

"Come on," Ed sharply pleaded with Trucker. "Open your eyes, man. Whoever you thought this woman was, she's not that. She never was."

Ida glanced at Ed. "Has this been your approach?"

"No," Ed said. "But you spend hours . . . *and hours* . . . cleaning up this crazy lady's gross shit. It affects a guy . . . I guess."

"Swearing now, too?" Ida asked, not with judgment but curious about her brother's newly embraced expletive.

Jennifer watched Trucker closely and noticed what Ed had been seeing in the detective's eyes over the past two days. A flicker of confusion. Doubt. Something she couldn't fully control. And from within her, something rose. Something she had spent years keeping buried. Fear. Not fear of Ida or Ed. Not fear of the law. Fear of losing control.

She snapped her attention back to the siblings. "The sheriffs will be here any moment. But if you leave now, you can avoid the unpleasantness."

"Nah," Ed said without conferring with Ida. "We're not leaving without Trucker."

Ida tilted her head toward Ed. She wasn't a fan of surprises, but she trusted him.

"He doesn't want to be here," Ed said. "I know it."

"You know it enough to want to sit in a jail cell?" Ida asked.

Ed didn't flinch. "He's been in a cell for a decade."

The siblings stood their ground.

The iron gate creaked open just as three county sheriff's SUVs navigated around Ida's sensibly rented Nissan Sentra and pulled into the compound. Five deputies, a mix of armed and uniformed men and women stepped out of their small caravan and began walking toward the confrontation unfolding between Jennifer Smith and the Young siblings.

A tall, lanky deputy in a ball cap, who appeared to have some level of seniority over the others, stepped up to Jen. He tipped his hat. "What seems to be the issue, Miss Smith?"

Ida and Ed got a firsthand demonstration of Jennifer Smith's ability to flip the charm switch.

"Oh, Teddy. More of the same, unfortunately," Jen said sweetly.

In an instant, Jennifer became both a beautiful victim of circumstance and a powerfully independent leader.

"This woman jumped our fence. Trespassing," she said. "I don't think she has it all together. A few loose screws."

Ida stood tall, still proud of her gymnastical maneuver and unsurprised by Jen's ability to lie with such grace. But that didn't mean she wanted to go to jail.

Jen continued with Deputy Ted. "And her brother was a member who was caught rifling through things that do not belong to him. Their parents must be so proud."

Ida placed a gentle hand on Ed's back. She appreciated his new vocabulary, but this wasn't the time for any four-letter encores.

"How would you like us to proceed?" Deputy Ted asked Jen.

"Oh, I don't know," she said, leaning into the flirt. "This isn't the first time this has happened, you know? And it won't be the last. Crazies just seem to find me."

"We can take 'em in," Ted offered. "Make an example out of them. If that's what you'd like."

Trucker didn't mean to, but he gave Jen an involuntary glance. Unintentionally abrupt but not tipping his emotional hand or opinion because he didn't have either of his own. Not really. None that were against Jen's programming. But regardless, Jen could see a quiet unease softening his posture. A signal. A crack. And she couldn't let that form an internal rebellion.

Jennifer needed this to end. Now. Before the siblings said anything else. Before that flicker of revolt in Trucker's eyes turned into something she couldn't snuff out.

"I just don't want drama," Jen said with a tightened smile and a sigh. "If they're willing to leave me alone and not come back, I think that's enough. But do what you think is right."

"Sounds good," Ted said, tipping his cap once again.

"And before you fine officers leave," Jen added, "don't forget to grab some things from the garden. We have more than enough. Consider it thanks for keeping us safe."

Deputy Ted approached Ed and Ida. He adjusted his cap and belt, squared his shoulders, then jutted out his chin.

"You two should be thankful," Deputy Ted spoke as proxy and puppet. "Miss Smith is generous enough to let you go. But I warn you — if you come back, you'll be arrested and charged to the fullest extent of the law."

Ed looked to Ida, then to Trucker, who still stood silently beside the self-proclaimed prophet. Radiants drifted closer to the sheriffs, guiding them gently, like acolytes ushering pilgrims to a temple of greenery.

This wasn't justice, Ed thought. And it wasn't the ending he had seen hundreds of times in his favorite movies. The cavalry did indeed come. Ida arrived. But the villain did not fall to her knees in defeat, and the good guy didn't snap out of the sinister spell.

It was just this. Quiet. And wrong.

"Let's just go," Ida said, her voice soft with finality.

"No. This isn't how it is supposed to end," Ed said, shaking his head. "There has to be something we can do."

"There isn't," Ida replied. "We tried. That's all we could do."

They turned and began walking toward their rental car.

But after a few steps, Ed stopped. Something inside him resisted this ending. He was pausing this, right here. He wasn't about to let the credits roll.

He looked back at Trucker, at Jen, at the sheriffs, at the hive of Radiants. He reached into his pocket and felt the contraband he had smuggled in days ago. It felt ridiculous, far more silly than any actual sort of secret weapon. But it was all he had left.

There would never be another moment, and he prayed that this would do something, anything, against the delusion, the corruption, the control.

What he really needed was an act of God.

But this would have to do.

"Detective!" he yelled.

Trucker stopped. He turned toward the man who said he cared. The missing man from his last case ever.

"Something to remember us by . . ." Ed yelled.

Ed pulled out a small, battered cardboard box. The corners were soft. The silver foil on the lid was barely legible but still read:

The Aura Authority.

The silly secret weapon. A reminder of Trucker's past life. His past self. One of small heroism, of kindness, of truth. And now Ed was offering it back, not as a gift of gratitude, but as a symbol of reality and connection.

He underhanded the box through the air, past the deputies whose hands hovered instinctively over their service weapons.

Trucker stepped forward and caught it, eyes locked with Ed.

"A gift," Ed said.

Ida raised her voice just enough to carry. "Thank you," she said. "For giving me a future."

The compound buzzed behind them as the Young siblings walked past the open iron gate, climbed into their sensibly rented Nissan Sentra, and drove it slowly to the end of *The Radiant Way's* private drive.

27

EXIT THROUGH THE GREENHOUSE

Trucker felt utterly alone as he stood near the greenhouse, surrounded by Radiants and sheriff's deputies. They shuffled around him, here and there, carrying box after box, a moving line stretching between the greenhouse and the SUVs. Jen's syrupy voice floated through the night. She issued sweet commands between the chirping crickets and the harsh hum of the floodlights. Trucker had witnessed this kind of performance before. Too many times. He had become numb to it. Numb to everything.

But it wasn't just numbness. It was worse. He didn't know how to measure it, and maybe there wasn't a way, but he felt dead. Not tired. Not depressed. But dead. Technically alive, but hollow.

That emptiness had stalked him for a few years now. Alone in the group. Still capable of feeling, yet cut off and numb. Alive, but dead.

A deputy passed with a sealed box. Jen stopped him with an effortless smile, placing her hand on his arm.

"Let me help you," she offered and turned to a cluster of idle Radiants. "Gabriel. Isaac. All of you. Please assist our guests. Let's show them our eternal gratitude."

The Radiants obeyed and moved into action. One taking the deputy's box and the others falling into step, joining the human chain bound for the SUVs.

Trucker had stopped paying attention to the choreographed coercion around him and instead focused on the small cardboard jewelry box in his hands. Ed's gift. He recognized it. His own gift, returned to him after all this time. He traced the worn foil lettering of *The Aura Authority*, then lifted the lid.

Inside, nestled in a small tuft of aged cotton, sat the mood rings. Their bands were black, but deep within that darkness shimmered a spectrum of color waiting to swirl to the surface.

He knew they were not magical. He knew what they were and where they came from. But holding the gift sparked something undeniable inside of him.

A catalyst. Magical or not, the effect was real. His chest jolted. His heart hiccupped, then beat harder and faster. War drums thundered in rhythm with his pulse. Drums of rebellion. Of awakening.

Every part of him that had been covertly and overtly silenced and suppressed over these past years began to rise. His intuition. His self-esteem. His loyalty to truth. His courage to name right and wrong. And more, much more than he even realized he had inside himself. They lit torches, pounded the drums, and marched forward, led by his authentic self. Together they declared:

Enough is enough.

But another force surged back. Jennifer's indoctrination. Years of deception, manipulation, and delusion, enforced by fear, guilt, and shame.

The battle raged within him. At first it seemed beyond his control, as if everything was already written and inevitable. But the truth was the opposite. What surged inside him was not futility, but freedom; his self-determination breaking through at last, his autonomy rising to its full voice. And that voice, his authentic self, shouted through the darkness: *You can choose at any moment. Your life belongs to you.*

Jennifer continued to direct the traffic of Radiants and deputies as she sidled up next to Trucker. She let out a sigh. "Phew, has been quite the night. Always something, huh."

"Mm hm. Quite the night," Trucker agreed, even as the war inside him grew louder and his authentic self rallied more strength to make a defiant charge of truth against the deranged prophet's programming.

Jen placed a hand on his shoulder. "No one gets me like you do. No one has ever understood me the way you do. I know I don't say it enough, but I appreciate you so much. You have no idea."

Trucker didn't respond, but his authentic self roared: *How many times have we heard this? Her words are empty without effort or action. This is not love. This is not care. Only control.*

"You're so good with me and with everyone. I don't know what I'd do without you. My rock," Jen went on. "The guidance always shows us the right path, and thankfully we have listened."

His authentic self yelled again: *This is more of the same. It is all meaningless nonsense, and it will never end.*

Trucker raised a mood ring and held it up to the harsh floodlights. Beneath the black band, he could see the colors shimmering, waiting to break through.

Jen smiled sweetly at the crowd of Radiants and deputies, then glanced at the ring in his hand. "Can you believe those people? The nerve of them, trying to ruin our home with their . . . their evil."

Trucker stayed silent. His authentic self whispered: *That isn't true. We know the truth. We've only been afraid to name it.*

Jen's voice hardened. "Actually, I can believe it. Because they're all the same. I'm cursed to be attacked."

Ed was right, Trucker's authentic self said. *She isn't who we thought she was. She never was. We don't have to be afraid to accept that. We just have to make a choice. Stay here in a place where the truth is not only forbidden but treated as a threat. Stay here and nod along and remain alone, numb, and dead.*

Or embrace the truth and what the unknown future holds. It is a risk. It may be awful, and we may be alone. Or maybe it will be amazing. But regardless, it will be ours. And we will be free.

There was, in the end, only one choice.

Trucker slipped the ring on his finger. It barely fit, but it stayed. And the black band shifted from green to yellow to orange to red. The rainbow of colors alive and swirling.

"They're both criminals," Jen suddenly snapped. "That woman and her brother." She somehow became angrier and unhinged with each word. "The both of them are rapists. Him — digging through my phone. Her — invading our sanctuary. They basically raped me. Rapists."

The drums of the internal battle raging inside of Trucker pounded louder and louder. His heart raced. His authentic self let out a blood-curdling war cry.

And then everything fell silent.

"They aren't what you say," Trucker said softly. Then louder. "Those two are not what you say they are."

Jen stopped cold. "Excuse me?"

They faced each other. Trucker looked into Jennifer's eyes, and all he could see was darkness. All he could see was what had been hidden under her mask. And he was not afraid. He was ready to embrace the truth. His heart stopped racing. The drums were gone. And his authentic self could now speak through his own voice. No longer silenced and suppressed.

"They are not what you say they are. Nothing is what you say it is. And I am done with all of it. This is done."

And with that, he began his walk toward the iron gate, making his exit and leaving Jennifer Smith and *The Radiant Way* behind.

With each step he felt a little lighter. A little more like himself. As he passed Radiants and deputies, a few gave him puzzled looks and asked questions in low, hesitant voices.

"Mister Trucker, what's going on?"

"Where ya goin', Mister Trucker?"

He might have liked to stop. To explain. To offer them something honest on his way out. But that wasn't an option. Not with Jennifer Smith's voice rising behind him, shrill and frantic. She was shouting about exile, betrayal, evil, and something about a fatal mistake. Or maybe it was about Trucker being a divine failure. He couldn't quite make it out, but it didn't matter. He no longer cared. It was no longer his job. And he realized that it never should have been.

But the real reason he did not stop was that along with Jennifer's insane screeching, he could see Sam of Sams, Levi, and Noah. And he knew what they were capable of. Any pause in his exit would be against his own best interests.

So, he walked on.

He let go of the goodbyes he wished he could give.

And he stepped, finally, into a fearful kind of freedom.

28

OUTSIDE

At the end of the long gravel drive of *The Radiant Way*, Ed and Ida sat in their sensibly rented Nissan Sentra. Before them, the red and blue strobes of the sheriff's SUVs' emergency lights pulsed against the night sky. Radiants moved in lines, ferrying boxes into the deputies' vehicles. And on the cobblestone patch near the open iron gate, two hopeful initiates remained rooted in place, unshaken by the chaos, staring at the entrance as if it were their only passage to something sacred.

"I can't say this enough. You really should have seen me Jackie Chan it over that gate," Ida said, still proud. "And then I let that crazy monster have it. Felt good."

"I'm sorry I missed it," Ed said, then added, "You know we are not leaving without Trucker."

"I know," Ida replied. "We aren't."

They sat in silence for a moment.

"Okay, Galadriel," Ed said. "Then what do we do?"

"Galadriel?" Ida asked, not keeping up.

"Cate Blanchett. Smart elf-lady from *The Lord of* —"

"Oh, I don't know what we're going to do," she interrupted, "but we can't sit here much longer unless we want to be cellmates."

They both stared at the scene unfolding before them. One group under Jen's control bribing another group also under her control.

The siblings' options fell somewhere between limited and nonexistent.

"We'll go back to the cabin. Regroup," Ida said, shifting the Sentra into drive. "Maybe something will come to us. You can watch movies, get ideas."

The car barely rolled forward when Ed grabbed the wheel. "Stop!"

From behind the iron gate, a figure stepped into the light.

Trucker emerged from the shadows, framed by the harsh floodlights and the pulsing strobes. His silhouette stretched long across the gravel drive, each step deliberate, each one shredding the weight of the compound behind him.

"The rings worked," Ed exhaled. "An act of God."

Halfway down the drive, Trucker slowed. He lifted his head and found the headlights of the siblings' sensibly rented Nissan Sentra. For a moment he stood still, and the chaos behind him seemed to fall away. His eyes caught Ed's, then Ida's. No words shouted. No gestures. Just a flicker of a silent agreement.

Only then did he move again, closing the last stretch of gravel until he reached the car. He opened the back door, slid inside, and let it shut with a muted thud.

No one spoke. Ida pressed the gas, and the car carried the three of them away from *The Radiant Way*, its headlights cutting a clean path through the darkness.

29

ONE WEEK LATER

It was two in the afternoon, late August, when the California sun broke through the diner's window and struck the etched, beveled logo that read *Grandma Mary's*. The light bent and split, scattering a spectrum of rainbow colors across a table loaded with pancakes, cinnamon rolls, pastries, and every other sweet carb the kitchen could cater for Ed, Ida, and Trucker.

The three sat safely tucked into a cushioned booth, working through what amounted to a second breakfast.

"You can talk if you want to," Ida said, slicing into a stack of fluffy, butter-soaked pancakes. "Or not. You can do whatever you'd like. Whenever you'd like."

"Oh, it's been great," Ed said. "He's got his own spot in the guest house. Mom and Chuck love him. It's like I got a big older brother. New uncle, whatever. But he's pretty much been sleepin' 'round the clock."

"I was talking to Trucker," Ida said, chewing her bite.

"Things are fine," Trucker said, unraveling a cinnamon roll on his plate. He glanced out the window at the Los Angeles traffic cruising past. He toyed with his food. The siblings, by contrast, worked

286

through their plates in an easy silence, broken only by the clatter of cutlery and the hum of voices around the diner.

Ed was about to break the booth's silence, mouth half-full of pastry, when Trucker beat him to it.

"I feel dumb," Trucker said.

He pulled the cinnamon roll apart, searching for words. "It's . . . hard to explain. I feel dumb. But more . . . more than that. There's this ball . . . or knot . . . of emotions . . . or whatever. Feelings. A mess of them that don't belong together but won't come apart either. Anger, at her, the whole . . . situation. Anger at myself." He peeled off a piece of the roll. "Sadness. A deep . . . ache . . . for a person and future that apparently never even existed. Then, there's shame and guilt. For falling for it, for staying when I could easily see what was happening. For every choice I made that kept me there and kept me hoping I could eventually get things back on track."

He let the words hang, then exhaled. "There's more, much more, but most of all . . . I feel dumb. It's just confusing. All of it." Trucker bit into the piece of cinnamon roll, chewed, and said, "Sorry. You two don't need to listen to this nonsense."

"You don't need to explain anything and have nothing to apologize for," Ida said. "It's not your fault."

Ed swallowed a mouthful of pastry. "Did you just *Good Will Hunting* him? How many years did you sit in a classroom? All those years in school and you go straight for the Robin Williams line? *It's not your fault?* R.I.P."

Ida rolled her eyes at Ed, "It's true, no matter who says it. Nobody signs up for a cult. Nobody chooses to be abused. And you may feel dumb, but you're not. You're human."

She leaned back and gestured with her fork toward the other diners. "Every person in here. No matter their background, education, income . . . doesn't matter. Me, Eddie, you, the saint who made these pancakes. All of us are susceptible."

She took another bite, then added, "Your best traits were used against you. Your loyalty. Your empathy. Your trust. All used by someone who, at the end of it, is just a liar. A skilled liar. A talented manipulator. But that doesn't make her smart and you dumb."

Ed set down his fork and leaned forward. "I had to imagine her as the most evil thing I could think of. Something obviously villainous, just to shut down whatever spell, whatever voodoo she has going on. It was unbelievable. But the truth is that she is worse than the most comically evil thing I could think of. At least with Sauron or Voldemort or the Joker . . . you can see those guys comin'. The obviously evil are easy to spot and avoid." He paused. "But the true evil? The real evil. It walks in wearing a smile. It's in a package you welcome into your life."

"It's so strange," Trucker said.

He unraveled another cinnamon roll without looking at it. "I gave her ten minutes. Then another ten. And another. It seemed good in the beginning. It felt good. She made me feel . . . whole. And the minutes kept piling up. By the time she was calling herself a prophet — by the time things got so weird . . . so wrong — those ten minutes had turned into years. And I couldn't find the exit, no matter how hard I tried."

"You were caught in a charismatic and very disordered person's trap," Ida said gently. "You don't have to figure it all out. Not now, not ever, if you don't want to." She broke off a piece of almond danish, licked her fingers, and went on, "All you have to think about is you. What do *you* want to do? How do *you* want to live? That's all that matters."

"I don't know," Trucker admitted, staring out the window. "Feels like I'm right back where I started. Worse, even. Ten years gone."

"I'm not going to pretend it'll be easy," Ida said, "but you can rebuild. You can recover. You can do whatever you want. It's your choice now. No one else's. And if you ever want to unpack what happened, or need someone to talk to, my door's open. Or we'll find you someone else. Whatever you want to do."

"You know what I want to do?" Trucker asked. "I want to finally live the dream she only pretended to offer. Truth. Purpose. Helping others. She sold it as a lie. None of it was real. But it could be." Trucker paused and the siblings did not interrupt while he tried to organize his thoughts into what he desired. "That's what I want. To find some kind of good. Some kind of truth. Not just for me, but for anyone that needs it. That's what I wanted from the start. That's what I still want. To make all of that real."

He smiled at the siblings. Hopeful.

Ed fake-coughed and clinked his fork against his plate. "Ahem. I hear words like *rebuild, recover, help,* and *purpose.* And I'd like to put a little something on the table. Not that we have room." He stacked two plates and laid his phone on the now-empty spot. With a tap, the app for Trucker's investigation services appeared. "This baby's been up and running for the last ten years. An autopay glitch? Or maybe, dare I say, an act of God? We don't know. But it has been on and collecting cases for a decade. Mom alone had been referring people left and right saying *he's the best.* Obviously, she had no idea he had been busy being some crazy cult lady's sidekick." He grinned, holding the screen up to Ida. "Ten years' worth of cases."

"That's not a horrible . . ." Trucker started, but his voice trailed off. He looked back out the window and froze. Sam of Sams, Noah, and Levi stood across the street, watching him. His heart skipped and his palms went clammy. Traffic passed, a pair of buses rumbled by, and when the view cleared, the trio from *The Radiant Way* were gone.

Ed kept going, oblivious. "I'm telling you, it's a great idea! Me and Truck Truck solving mysteries, righting wrongs. That's a TV show I'd binge if I've ever heard one."

"It's not the worst idea," Ida said, "but it's whatever Trucker wants. My only advice . . . start small. Simple."

Trucker turned from the window. "I'll think it over. But yeah. Not a bad idea, Eddie."

Ed beamed, carved off a bite of french toast, and dipped into a pool of berry sauce. He was just about to raise it to his mouth when the diner door banged open.

A young woman in a dirty white dress stumbled inside, eyes wild. "Please, someone help! My husband . . . my poor husband . . . he's lost his shadow!"

Ed lifted his french-toasted fork. "Our first case!"

TRUCKER, ED, AND IDA

WILL RETURN.